I0638579

BILLIONAIRE'S CURVY FAKE FIANCÉE

AN ENEMIES TO LOVERS SLOW BURN ROMANCE

ANNIE PAIGE

Sunflower Horizon
PUBLISHERS

CONTENTS

1

THE PERFECT OPPORTUNITY
ELLIE

THE BAKERY WAS BUSTLING with our after-lunch regulars and my hands were going on autopilot, piping, mixing, getting everything ready. Just like every other day I spend in my bakery, time just flew by.

I always felt such a rush when the bakery got super busy which was happening more frequently now. I'm a bit of a workaholic and built this bakery from the ground up, figuratively speaking. I reveled in the influx of work, the demand for my pastries, and the unbelievably busy days and nights.

It's when our chocolate chip cookies and caramel donuts are flying off the shelves, when I have to make batch after batch of red velvet cupcakes, when I'm so tired at the end of the day that all I can do is order takeout and sleep, that's when I know I made it.

And it hasn't been easy. It took a lot of risks, a lot of guts, and a lot of early mornings and late nights. I've always loved cooking in general and baking in particular, so much so that I set out to make my 'hobby' into my job. I worked for a restaurant for a very long time and I'd loved it, but it turned out to be a dead-end. I then, rather stubbornly, decided to start my own bakery. The process was long and difficult but I managed to pull through.

And here I am, Eleanor Rodriguez, 26 years old, the sole owner of Ellie's Sweet Haven. I still feel giddy when I think about it. I mean, how many 26-year-olds can say they own their own popular bakery in LA?

Smiling to myself, I remembered the first few days. It was a time when every minute that passed without a customer filled me with anxious dread and every customer that did come in gave me fresh hope and enthusiasm. Those first few weeks were a real rollercoaster ride. I was just a tightly balled-up bundle of nerves back then.

Now I have experience, confidence, a good number of regulars, and hardworking people on my staff. It seems almost impossible to think I've come this far and landed in this place.

I was still reminiscing when Kate abruptly opened the door to the kitchen, arms crossed over her chocolate-stained, pink apron. Kate Jones has been working at the bakery as an assistant pastry chef for almost half a year. She didn't have any formal training when I met her but she was a very talented baker and had years of experience in running a bakery. I would teach her the finer points of baking and she helped me run the place. We were a good match.

"Do you realize what time it is?" she asked, pointing at her watch. She was trying to look stern, but it was hard to take her seriously—she had the friendliest face that never held a sour expression. She was a joy to work with. Kate was 26 years old, like me, but she was a little taller and lankier, with a shock of red hair that was all natural.

I looked up at the wall clock and realized it was already 4:00 pm. "Oh no, shit I'm gonna be late," I said, quickly running my batter-splattered hands under the kitchen tap. "I have to go, like now."

"Yeah, you do. You've been talking about Aaron's party for a week now and how you have to leave early today," Kate said, giving me a knowing look. "You gotta get your butt out of here. I can't believe you'd forget."

"I didn't forget, Kate, I just..."

"Lost track of time," she said, finishing my sentence for me. "You always lose track of time when you're in here. But today should not be one of those days."

Aaron was my brother and one of the most important people in my life. We're having a send-off party for him. He's going to Singapore on a project for the tech company he works for which is owned by his best friend, Conrad Young, a douchebag who also happens to be a very successful billionaire. It's a good thing Conrad is out of town so he probably won't be at the party. Conrad and I do not get along. Aaron is a Technical Development Director at Conrad's company, YoungTech. He's heading to Singapore tomorrow night to talk to clients so the company can branch out in Asia.

With our parents away, I had to step up in planning and hosting the party. It sucks that my brother is going away, but he's been really excited and I know this is the right step for his career, so I have to show my support. That's what a sister is for after all.

I smiled at her as I took off my apron and started getting ready to go home. "The cupcakes are almost done, the cake orders for tomorrow are in the refrigerator. The muffin and cupcake batter are ready, you just have to bake them before you leave," I said, running a checklist through my head as I gathered my things. "Oh and don't forget, the cake for Aaron's party has to be delivered at..."

"At 9 o'clock sharp. I know Ellie," Kate said, taking my hand. "Don't worry about it. Glam yourself up and go to that party. You deserve a night out, especially tonight."

Kate was a godsend. The bakery is only a year old but, after just a few weeks after opening, word got out and orders started flooding in. I suddenly found myself with more work than I could handle. I'm a hard worker but the influx of orders was overwhelming and I desperately needed extra hands.

I'd gone through a difficult hiring process for an assistant pastry chef, and went through some bad fits before I finally landed Kate. She was hard-working, competent, and totally reliable. She's been with the bakery for over 5 months now, and the change has been drastic.

With Kate around, I finally had enough time to experiment with different flavors and even created our signature strawberry macaron cupcakes, one of our most popular items right now. Kate was always early, always reliable, and she really seems to love the bakery as much as I do.

"What would I do without you?" I said to her, squeezing her hand.

"Well you do have me, so make the best of it and get out of here. I promise you, the bakery will still be here when you get back tomorrow. And anyway, you've paid off the insurance so it should be all good," she said jokingly.

I widened my eyes as if I was shocked, "Don't even joke about that! This bakery is my life!"

I took a second to look around the bakery, customers looking through our displays, the beautifully polished wooden counters, the rustic decor, and the delicious smells wafting through the place. "Oh I almost forgot, the delivery for the new display cases is for tonight, so make sure to check the tracking number..." I stopped. Kate just looked at me, almost impatiently.

"Go." She practically shoved me out the door.

I hailed a cab, got in, and immediately called Sarah. In my short 26 years on earth, Sarah is definitely one of the constants in my life. I'd known her since we were in high school. I was the chubby, awkward teen, as most people are at that stage, but Sarah, she was something else.

She'd been a long-legged, blonde bombshell since I met her. She was with the popular crowd and I definitely wasn't. Before Sarah and I became friends, I was mostly invisible, even bullied a little for being chubby.

She was the cheerleader and I was the nerdy bookworm and I never thought becoming friends with her would even be a possibility. During our senior year, though, we shared a biology class and got paired up. I found out she was struggling with schoolwork so I helped her out with it. We started hanging out more and really started to like each other. She introduced me to her friends and we became close. We've been best friends ever since.

I could hear the phone ring on the other line. She finally answered. "Hey, Ell, are you getting ready for the party?"

"I'm on my way home, I need your help picking out my dress. Tyler's gonna be there..."

Tyler was Aaron's co-worker and had the body of a Greek god. He was a dashing man with dreamy hazel eyes. I always felt butterflies when I saw him and he was always so charming. He could probably charm the pants off a nun if he wanted to.

I never thought a guy like him would have any interest in someone like me, but he's been giving off some hints lately. He'd always turn on the charm around me and even asked for my number. We haven't gone on a date yet but he'd text me a lot. He'd become our official third wheel when we went out for dinner. He would pay for the dinner and we'd have a lovely time. I'm actually glad that Sarah and

Tyler appear to get along so well, since it makes the prospect of having a boyfriend and a best friend seem so harmonious if it ever happens.

"Oh, your hunky dreamboat?" Sarah knew all about my crush on Tyler, and she'd been teasing me ever since. "Well, you're in luck because I am on my way over right now. I'm bringing my dress and makeup. I don't like the ones you have."

I laughed. Sarah was always a bit blunt, but I liked that about her. Although she can be a bit brutal sometimes, that was just how she was. "Well, I don't have thousands of dollars to splurge on designer makeup," I replied. "I have a business to run, remember?"

"Of course, you're a successful business owner. You know, given your successful career, you should be more willing to splurge on yourself every once in a while."

"The bakery has been running for less than a year. Beauty isn't really one of my top priorities right now."

"Which is why you still don't have a boyfriend. And that's why I'm bringing my makeup over. You won't get you-know-who's attention if we don't glam you up. I'll see you in fifteen minutes."

THE CAB STOPPED in front of our quaint two-story, cottage-style family home. It was a really lovely house with white paneling, wide windows with flowers underneath, and a pretty tile roof.

We grew up right here in Silver Lake and this house held many precious memories for me. It was a nice neighborhood but a lot of the people I knew growing up had moved on and there were always people moving in it seemed. My father, who is now retired, insisted that we live at home for as long as Aaron and I didn't have our own families yet.

You might think it was a bit weird for grown adults to still live at home, but it was just natural for us. We are a very close-knit family but we also respect boundaries, so that was never a problem. Plus, starting a business was risky and knowing I'd have a roof over my head no matter what was very comforting.

With our parents finally fulfilling their dream vacation of backpacking through Europe, it was just the two of us for now. And, after tomorrow, it was gonna be just me for a while.

I go through the backdoor and put my things on the kitchen table. We had a beautiful kitchen: it was nothing fancy, we had the basics and a lot of counter space. This is where my love for cooking started. My mom and I would make cookies, then cupcakes, then we started trying out fancier recipes. I just never stopped.

I could see Aaron with his back to me in the kitchen doorway that led to the living room. He didn't notice me coming in and I could see that he was talking on the phone.

"Yeah, yeah, no, it's perfect timing. I can't wait to finally see you again..." he was saying.

"I'm home," I said softly. He turned and looked surprised to see me there suddenly. He gave me a little wave and quickly walked upstairs to finish his phone call. I decided to take a quick shower before Sarah arrived, wondering who Aaron was talking to and why he looked a bit guilty.

After my shower I started picking out my nicer dresses from my closet to wear to the party. I generally don't like dresses that are too body hugging or tight. They accentuate my hips and breasts too much and I always feel awkward. Sarah always teased me for being too 'conservative' about my outfits.

"You know what Ellie, if you have it, flaunt it. Do you realize how many women spend hundreds of thousands of dollars just to have your figure?" she'd say when we went out shopping, shaking her head at my choices. "Show a little cleavage, let your boobs breathe. I wish I had your figure."

"Yeah right," I said in disbelief. Sarah couldn't possibly want a figure like mine. I had to choose clothes that "fit right", that complimented my body, clothes that were stretchy enough to hold my curves but loose enough to be comfortable. Sarah had a slender figure without an ounce of fat. She was the type who could wear a sackcloth and make it look high fashion.

I've always been self-conscious about my body. My breasts started growing out when I was 11, before any of my classmates, and I was labeled as a freak. By the time I was 18, I had C-cups. The boys teased me and the girls hated me. I was also kinda chubby in high-school and kids could be cruel.

In fact, Conrad, my brother's best friend and his current boss, was one of my bullies. He always brushed it off as a joke, and even Aaron thought it was harmless, but it definitely added to my insecurities.

Now, as a grown woman, I've learned to appreciate my curves. I just don't like calling attention to them. I've had guys talk to me and be so obviously distracted by my breasts, or I've been cat-called on the street for having a "juicy ass", all which led to me choosing to wear loose dresses or baggy shirts.

I picked out a few floral dresses and a long, flowy dress made of cream chiffon from my closet. I was standing in front of the mirror holding up the cream dress and a little black dress with rose prints on it when Sarah arrived.

"Hey, Aaron let me in," she said, breezing through my room and setting her things down. "Now," she said, turning to me and taking a seat on the bed, "are those your only choices?"

I looked at myself in the mirror. The black dress had a simple sweetheart neckline, and off shoulder sleeves. It was a cute dress and I looked pretty in it, but it wasn't a show stopper. The chiffon, on the other hand, was asymmetrical at the top and flowed down to the floor with thigh-high slits. It showed off my figure but not too much and kept it well covered.

"You've worn those before," Sarah commented, looking over the other dresses on the bed. "Why isn't the chrome dress even in consideration? You've never had a chance to wear it. This would be the perfect opportunity to try it out."

The chrome dress was a super-tight, stretchy dress that had a scoop neck and was a shiny, metallic silver with hints of blue. Sarah convinced me to get it when we were out shopping on Rodeo drive. It was one of the edgier, sexier items we had found. I had to admit it was a beautiful dress and I looked hot with it on. But hot isn't really what I was going for at my brother's going away party.

"Oh come on, just try it on," she said, getting up and looking through the dresses in my closet. "Here it is. Seriously, it'll look great. You'll stand out in that dress." She picked out the chrome dress from my closet and handed it to me.

I tried it on and I had to admit, I looked really good. The shiny silver-blue color looked great against my tan, my ample curves were in full display, and the short dress made my legs look long and shapely.

But the cleavage, the hips...it hugged my body in the places I was most self-conscious. Don't get me wrong, I'm very fit: I eat healthy and workout 3 times a week; I have a flat stomach and love cropped tops...but this was a bit much.

"You look fucking gorgeous," Sarah said, smiling. I think

I blushed. Sarah was a tall, platinum blonde stunner. She could be a model if she chose. In fact, she did some modeling in college and was living it up while I was sweating it out in culinary school. She was now working for a PR firm and was dabbling at being an influencer.

She stood next to me in her sparkling, floor length, backless red gown. She was beautiful in a way that I knew I never would be. She had fine features, pouty lips, and legs for days. I felt plain in comparison, but I suppose anyone would, standing next to Sarah.

"That dress is a head turner," she said, trying to reassure me. She must have noticed my indecision.

Heads will turn, but maybe not for me, I thought ruefully. But, I didn't want to be a downer so I tried to snap out of it. "You're the head turner. You're beautiful. The only head I wanna turn is Tyler's."

I saw Sarah smile a little to herself, as if remembering an inside joke. "You don't have to worry about Tyler. All eyes will be on you tonight."

Somehow, I found that hard to believe.

There was a light tap on the door. "Aaron? Come in, we're decent," Sarah called out laughing. Aaron popped his head through the door and was visibly surprised.

"Woah, did I just walk in on a photo shoot, you guys look great!"

"When did we ever disappoint?" Sarah laughed, teasing. I loved Sarah's breezy confidence, it was so effortless. I wished I was more like her sometimes.

"Ellie," Aaron said, turning to me. He seemed a bit serious. "You are my sister, and you know, you're the only family I have right now and it's so important to me that I have your support for my career."

"Yes... So..." I said doubtfully. I probably wasn't going to like where this was going. Aaron always spoke this way when he was giving out bad news. You studied so hard and passed your exams like a champ, but... You did everything you could about the situation, but...

"And you realize that you have to go to this party no matter what, alright?"

"Get to the point Aaron," I snapped, getting worried.

"Conrad's back, he's coming to the party later." I groaned, which Aaron proceeded to ignore. "He's my boss and my best friend, which just shows how important and strong our friendship is. I haven't seen him in forever and I really miss him. You're my only sister and I love you."

I was stunned. I was relieved when I found out that Conrad would not be at the party, and now that he was going, I could feel the anxiety building up again. And Aaron could see it in my face.

"I know you two never got along, but he's a good guy and he's been so busy," he said, coming to give me a hug. "Please, please don't let it ruin the night."

And how could I do that to my brother? He was making major leaps in his career, how could I ruin that for him?

"Okay," I sighed, "I'll be fine. He's your friend and it's his company, of course he's gonna be there. Your party is gonna be great," I said sincerely, returning the hug.

The minute Aaron left the room, I felt my anxiety boiling over. "I can't wear this with Conrad at the party! I can't! I have to change," I said, almost running to my closet before Sarah grabbed me.

"So what if Conrad is going? Look at yourself," she said, pulling me toward the mirror. "You look amazing. What better way to get revenge than a glow up?"

Well, she had a point.

"And don't forget," she added, "who do you really want to impress at that party?"

I sighed again. Sarah could tell I was giving in. Her face

broke out into a beautiful smile. "Great! It's settled, the chrome dress and some hot stilettos," she said triumphantly. "And now, for makeup!"

2

A LITTLE, BIG LIE

CONRAD

"YEAH, I promise I'll be there. Of course. Yes, I know It's been a while. Thanks man, I'll see you later. Bye."

I hung up the phone and looked around. The long hallway was empty and had that antiseptic smell hospitals tended to have. There was a quiet buzz throughout the place. The nurses walked silently and spoke in whispers, but there was always urgency in how they moved, like suppressed energy. It seemed unnatural to me.

I never liked hospitals—I guess nobody does unless you work in one. They always meant an end to me, a goodbye. Sometimes they weren't even that. Sometimes, you didn't even get to say goodbye.

I walked back into William's spacious VIP room. I told the doctors to spare no expense to make my grandfather as comfortable as possible. His bed faced large bay windows that opened up to a beautiful view of Malibu beach. There was a small sitting room, spacious counters, and a little bed to rest in for his watcher. All the medical equipment looked shiny and new. We had access to the best doctors and nursing staff.

What else could I do other than that?

I was greeted by the humming and beeping of hospital equipment, all connected to William's frail body. He looked nothing like the big, robust grandfather I'd grown up with. His thick gray hair had thinned and lay lank on his head, shimmering in sweat. He looked pale now and it was a stark contrast to his healthy tan from just a few months ago, when he had still gone out golfing several times a week with his buddies.

After losing my parents, William became my father, mentor, even my therapist at times. He had cared for me, provided for me, and became everything I needed. He'd always supported my career and my choices, even when they occasionally back-fired.

The hard truth hit me again, looking at my only family left in the world, so small and fragile in the big hospital bed.

We had rushed William to the hospital after he'd suddenly collapsed at breakfast. It was harrowing. He hadn't regained consciousness until several hours later in the hospital. The doctors put him through a barrage of tests but they couldn't find anything really wrong with him. It had been two weeks and there still wasn't a definitive diagnosis. I had called specialists and gotten the best doctors, but not one of them could tell me anything.

Finally, Dr. Monroe, his primary care physician, had come in for a visit earlier and he'd taken me aside. He was a taciturn individual who liked to talk through the nurses. It was a surprise when he asked to speak to me personally.

"The truth is, Mr. Young," he'd said, looking grim. "It could just be his age. He's 89 and he's lived a good life. It may be time to prepare yourself for any eventuality."

I was dumbfounded. I could only stare at him. "I'm really sorry. We will do the best we can for your grandfather, but it may be that his body is just...giving up."

"Well, can't you do anything? He was fine a few weeks

ago. Expense is not an issue. You have to do everything you can. We can get more specialists, order more tests. Tell me you can make him better or else we're going to find some place else!"

The doctor looked a bit uncomfortable with my outburst. "We are doing everything we can and I assure you this hospital has the latest technology and your grandfather is receiving the best care available. But there are many cases like this once a patient has reached a certain age. We can't find a specific cause for his loss of consciousness. All of his organs and systems are working well enough and yet the patient remains weak. The best thing we can do is keep him comfortable and not let him worry or get stressed unnecessarily."

I cursed. I had spent the last two years brooding away in Europe, Asia, then finally South America, moving from place to place every few weeks. I'd go to a new city, see everything there was to see, and move on. I wasn't out there to change my life, or find new beginnings; it was just something to do, somewhere to be instead of being here. I had waited till I was good and ready to come home, brushing off William and Aaron when they begged me to return.

I'd call every few months to check in and no one ever said anything about William's health. And now that I was finally back, this doctor was telling me William didn't have much time left? The implications nearly would have made me laugh if they weren't so soul crushingly devastating. I knew only one thing: I couldn't lose William, it was inconceivable. William had to pull through, even if I had to drag him.

I went closer to the hospital bed. I didn't want to leave for the party, but William had insisted. He went on and on about Aaron being a good friend and how it was my responsibility as the CEO of YoungTech, my cybersecurity company, to be there.

"You expect Aaron to bring YoungTech to a whole new market and be away from his family and friends, the least you can do is be there for his send-off. It reflects how committed you are to your company's growth and to your friendship. You can't skip that."

William was right of course. He tended to be in situations like these.

Aaron was my best friend since high school. I was a loner even then but Aaron's friendship helped me open up and remember to have fun again. For a teenager, losing your parents can change your whole world, but having a fun, easy-going friendship helped get me through the darkest times.

I was always welcomed at Aaron's family home and William encouraged me to go visit all the time. I think he knew I was missing something in that big mansion with him. I started hanging out at Aaron's house more and more. I ended up spending most of my day and having most of my meals with them. It allowed me to feel like I was part of a family again.

I did owe it to Aaron and I had agreed to go to the party, on the condition that I would be contacted right away if anything changed. William had seemed pleased when I relented.

Of course I wanted to see my best friend again, but going to a party seemed wrong with William here in the hospital. But, as William pointed out, there was very little chance that his condition would change while I was gone. On the other hand, Aaron would be leaving in the morning and I wouldn't see him again for a while after.

I held his frail hands, once so strong, and remembered all the times he had been there for me. Unlike the past few days, his sleep seemed more peaceful now. "I'll be back as soon as I can," I whispered in his ear, knowing he would hear none of it.

I left the room and stopped by the nurse's station. "If anything happens, you have my number. I need you to contact me right away if anything changes at all."

The nurse gave me an understanding smile. "Of course sir, I'll call you if anything changes with his condition."

I got into my car and headed for the venue in Hollywood. The last couple of weeks had been hard and it didn't help that all William could think about even in his condition was my personal life. When William realized that a diagnosis was not forthcoming he had asked the nurse to leave the room and told me that we needed to talk privately.

"You know for a fact that I love you Conrad. You have made me unfailingly proud and grateful to God that I got to raise you. You've made something of yourself that is all your own effort and I know you can take care of yourself. You have more than enough," he'd said, holding my hand at his bedside.

"But no man is an island, I always say," he continued, "You're grandmother, though taken sooner than I wished, brought me joy and love. She gave me a family, she gave me a home. Though it hurt to lose her, every moment I spent with her was a precious gift."

I knew where this conversation was going and, though it had been a touchy subject before, I knew I had to hear him out.

"Your father was the light of our lives and after losing him and your mother too, the pain was almost unbearable. But then I had you, and I knew you needed me. I've done the best I could for you. Everything you are, everything you've achieved, I hold in their honor."

I could tell he was struggling to find words, but he went on.

"You've always been fiercely independent. Maybe it's because of what happened to your parents. But independence and achievement can be very lonely. I can't leave this world thinking of you living alone in that massive, empty mansion. I just can't."

"You better stick around then," I said jokingly, but William didn't think it was very funny.

"Conrad, what is it all for? All your money, your properties, this abundance that you have, if you have no one to share it with? A man lives fully when he provides for his loved ones, when he has people to share his success with!"

I could see he was getting agitated and decided to hold off on the jokes. I nodded and squeezed his hand.

"When you left and stayed away I thought, 'He must be getting on and meeting people'. I was sure you'd find someone and hoped you'd bring her home to introduce to me, but here you are, as closed-off as you've ever been. Sometimes it makes me think, if only I hadn't allowed Jessica into your life. I always had a bad feeling about her. If only I had warned you, if only I'd paid more attention..."

"Jessica was no one's fault," I said, "You can't blame yourself for that. Jessica is Jessica. And I just happen to be me. It was my decision, not yours." Yes, Jessica. The beautiful ice queen, brittle, cold, and painful to the touch. I never let anyone get too close, but I let my guard down with Jessica. It turns out that even beautiful, exciting women could be heartless too. I hated that this past relationship was affecting William almost as much as me.

I can't fathom how I could possibly do it and I regretted it the moment it came out of my mouth, but he looked so worried that I found myself lying to the only person who actually truly knows me. I wanted him to stop worrying, I wanted to get Jessica's shadow out of our lives.

"The truth is I do have someone. We've been dating and it's getting pretty serious. I've been holding off on introducing you because I didn't want to get your hopes up until I was sure, especially after what happened with Jessica."

I could see him raise his eyebrows in surprise, then a soft smile which encouraged me to carry on with this outrageous lie. "We've been together for a while now, almost a year actually. I'm planning to propose to her soon and bring her out here to see you. I'm pretty sure you'll love her, she's nothing like Jessica."

William seemed at a loss for words. "And you didn't think to tell me until now? Why did you keep this from me for so long?" William looked animated now and was even struggling to get up. I was glad to see him with energy again.

"I...I didn't want to scare her away. She's very independent and, like I said, I wanted to make sure she's the right one," I said, trying to steady him as he sat up on his bed. I laid another pillow behind him.

"So tell me all about her, who is she?" he asked, obviously excited.

I was floundering. "I...I'll introduce you soon and she can tell you all about herself...when I bring her here to meet you." If I actually find her, that is.

"But how did you meet her, what is she like?" he asked again, looking very excited and pleased. I felt myself burrowing deeper into the little hole I'd dug up with that first lie.

"Oh you'll get to know her soon and we'll both tell you our story. You have to focus on getting better so we can do that, okay?"

"Well, if you want me to be there for your wedding,

you'd better be proposing soon. I'm not sure how much time I have left you know."

My throat was dry and I couldn't look him in the eye. I don't remember much else about our conversation after that but the urgency of finding a suitable 'fiancée' weighed me down like a ton of bricks.

I'd been driving for a while now and found myself pulling up to the venue that was reserved for the night. It's been two years since I've socialized with people from my past and I'm not sure if I'm ready. Going to a big party isn't exactly the best way to dip your toes into the water after a two-year hiatus, but William is right. Aaron has been my closest, most dependable friend, and I have to do this for him. I took a big breath to settle my nerves and stepped out of the car. I handed my keys over to the valet and got into the elevator.

"Hey, hold the door please!" I heard someone shout and I quickly held the button down to keep the doors open. A man quickly stepped in and thanked me. He was tall and wearing an expensive looking gray suit. I was just a little taller than him at 6 feet 2 inches. He was well dressed and I could see him looking me over on the reflective elevator walls.

He cleared his throat and held out a hand to me. "Hey, I'm Tyler Perkins. Are you here for Aaron's party?"

"Yes, I am actually," I said. He smiled and nodded.

"I thought so. I work under Aaron's department at YoungTech. I've been a systems developer there for 2 years now. He's a really nice guy but he's a workaholic, you know? How do you know him?"

I decided to omit some details and simply said, "I knew him from school."

"Really?" he said eagerly. "Then you must know Conrad Young. He and Aaron went to school together too, he owns

YoungTech. I've never seen him. He hasn't come to work in all the time I've been working there. A bit eccentric from what I could gather."

"I suppose I've heard of him," I replied. Before the man could say more, the elevator doors opened. I had no time or patience for pleasantries with someone I hardly knew.

Without saying another word, I stepped out. The restaurant was pretty crowded by then and I couldn't see a familiar face, though most of them probably worked for me.

As I searched the crowd I noticed someone familiar. Aaron's little sister Ellie was going around the place talking to people, playing the perfect hostess. And she looked stunning. She was wearing a silver-metallic dress that complimented her complexion and her curves beautifully. She looked especially good in her dress, but it wasn't her usual look and it made me realize how much things may have changed during my absence.

This was the first time I'd seen her in two years and I realized that I missed our little back and forth every time we spoke. I was fond of Ellie, but the only way that ever manifested was through teasing.

We basically grew up together and I spent a lot of time in their family home. She was like a little sister to me, and as is typical with teenagers, our relationship mostly consisted of jokes and constant bickering. She was a little chubby in high-school and as most boys do, I used to tease her relentlessly by calling her pet-names. They always rubbed her the wrong way and we would have little fights about it, but it was all in good fun. My favorite pet-name for her had always been Ellie-belly, and it always sent her into a rage.

The truth is I always found Ellie to be a breath of fresh air. She wasn't like most girls I knew. She worked hard and wasn't obsessed with looks as most people are. She was so unassuming that I'm sure she didn't realize how every man she passed turned their heads and followed her form going through the room.

Damn, she looked sexy in that dress. I had to fight the urge to go straight to her. There would be time for that later. I had to find Aaron first and congratulate him. It had been a long time since we got together. It was bitter-sweet to see him again only to say goodbye almost immediately. I walked around a little, picking up a glass of champagne from a passing waiter.

I finally spotted him talking with some old college buddies. Finally, people I knew. I quickly walked over to them.

Aaron was talking animatedly to Brad Shaw, his old college roommate. I could see his face light up the second he set his eyes on me.

"Conrad!" he exclaimed, catching me in a big bear hug. "Damn it man, it's been two years!"

"It's been a while," I said, returning his hug.

"God, I'm so glad to see you. Where've you been? Damn it, we missed you. the company's been running on autopilot since you left," he said, taking a step back and looking me over with a big smile on his face. "I'm glad you decided to come."

"I had to, this is a big deal. This is our dream, remember? YoungTech wouldn't be a reality if it weren't for you. I'm glad you're on my team," I said.

"I've always been on your team," he said, smiling. There was so much being left unsaid. He knew about Jessica, he probably had an idea why I had decided to stay away, but he never intruded or pressured me. We'd get in touch once in a while; he'd ask how I was and if I wanted to talk or meet-up, but he never pushed me. It showed how well he actually knew me.

Aaron seemed to suddenly remember the guy he was

talking to and turned to introduce us, even though I did vaguely remember Brad from college.

"Oh you know Brad, he's a doctor at Cedars-Sinai. He'a got a baby on the way, can you believe it..." We talked about the past, the present, the changes in our lives. Or at least, they talked and I mostly listened. My story wasn't exactly a story for the boys, and I was never one to share much, even to people I was close with. William's health was a personal matter and I didn't think they'd be interested in that.

More introductions were made as I stood there. Aaron seemed to be making up for lost time and trying to get me to meet as many people as possible, from old school friends I had lost track of to tech experts and managers in the company. It was a lot of small-talk and it was draining.

I found myself zoning out and scanning the crowd, hoping to catch another glimpse of Ellie. I was already running scenarios through my head about our next exchange. I realized I was counting down the minutes until I could finally talk to Ellie-belly.

3

FRIENDS AND BULLIES

ELLIE

I BUSIED myself greeting important guests and chatting up old friends, going from table to table to make sure everyone had drinks and were comfortable. I wasn't a natural hostess. Being outgoing was hard work for me, but after a few glasses of champagne it got easier. At least being a natural people-pleaser made me a great host, or so that's what Sarah often said.

The fact that everyone complimented me on my dress helped out a lot with my confidence. I had to admit, Sarah was right about the outfit: heads did turn. Aaron's cowork-ers, who were mostly polite when we met before, were defi-nitely staring now. Some of them even started getting flirty. Unfortunately, none of the guys who'd asked me out was Tyler. In fact, I hadn't had the chance to speak to him all night.

On the bright side, this was also true of Conrad which was a fact that gave me great relief. I was dreading meeting Conrad in this dress. I could only cringe at the thought of what might happen and what he might say.

Despite all the attention, I still wished I was wearing a different dress. The super-tight dress restricted some movement and made me painfully aware of every curve on my body. I didn't enjoy all this attention on what were, in my opinion, the wrong aspects of my body. And I was sure that in this dress, no one was thinking about my personality.

I did want to catch Tyler's attention, but what if Conrad spotted me? The jokes and name-calling still left a sour taste in my mouth. I remember prom night when I was a senior and getting ready. I thought I looked absolutely beautiful in the dress Sarah and I had picked. It was a tight-fitting pale blue, strapless dress. But when Conrad saw me he started laughing and called me Ellie-phant. I was so embarrassed I ran out of the room crying. I almost didn't go to prom and I only went after I changed into a different dress that didn't show as much skin.

Thinking of him laughing now when he sees me makes me shiver. But there was nothing I could do about it. Despite my protests, Sarah would not let me bring a back-up dress. She knew well enough how I'd probably lose my nerve halfway through the party and change into something more conservative. Wishing I had on a different dress wasn't gonna help change the situation, especially when I had hosting duties to attend to.

I walked around the room, talking to seated guests and greeting newcomers. I could see Aaron laughing and talking with some of his college friends. Their little huddle was getting bigger and I could see that he was really enjoying himself.

I still felt a sliver of annoyance, remembering that he hadn't told me Conrad was coming until the last possible moment. He knew how much I disliked being around Conrad. I mean I'd complained about it enough, but he never took it seriously. The last thing I wanted was to feel like I was in high school again while wearing this outrageous dress.

Sarah was intrigued at my reaction after hearing Conrad was coming. She said I was being ridiculous when I panicked and started taking off the dress. She had to physically restrain me from removing it.

She hadn't mentioned it again as we did our makeup. I opted for a simple smokey eye and a nude lipstick. Sarah wore gold eyeshadow and red lipstick. We had changed the subject by then and started talking about Tyler.

"Do you think he'll finally ask me out? He asked for my number a long time ago but he's never asked me out on a date," I asked, looking at myself. I had light brown eyes that were almost hazel, a fine nose, and heart-shaped lips. My chestnut brown hair was pulled back with a few wavy wisps framing my face.

"Maybe he's just waiting for the right time? Anyway, if he sees you in this dress, he'd be crazy not to," Sarah said as she was applying mascara. "You just have to be cool and confident, guys love that."

Sarah always gave me advice on men because, between the two of us, she had a lot more experience and I trusted her. If Sarah ever set her eyes on a guy, she was sure to have him in her back pocket by the end of the day. I, on the other hand, had very little experience. Or no experience at all, really. She had teased me about it constantly, encouraging me to at least try being more flirtatious and outgoing.

It had never been a priority before. I was busy with school, then culinary school, then work. I hardly had time for myself. I went on a few dates now and then, but I always held off on doing 'it' until it was serious. Call me old fashioned, but I didn't want to have sex with someone I hardly knew.

Then came Daniel. He was everything I wanted. Or at least I thought he was. He was sweet, sensitive, and he made me feel so special. When I told him I wasn't ready to go all the way he didn't pressure me or guilt me into it, even though we'd been dating for a few months. When I was finally ready, I decided to surprise him. I went to his apartment out of the blue, wearing sexy lingerie I'd just bought. It was gonna be a big romantic night, one that we would look back on with fondness. At least that was the plan.

When I got to his apartment a woman answered the door. She was wearing an oversized T-shirt, no bra, and her hair was disheveled. I thought, foolishly, that she might be his roommate. When I asked for Daniel, she called him, referring to him as 'babe'. The guilt in his face when he saw me was enough evidence. Apparently I was unreasonable to think that we would be exclusive after refusing his advances for so long.

It took me a long time to recover. Daniel was my first real relationship and I really thought we were going somewhere. It turns out he couldn't even wait for me for a few months. I was devastated. Then it felt like a relationship was just too much heartbreak for nothing. I held off on dating for a while after that.

Later on, it just sort of slipped my mind. The only time it would come up was with Sarah, but I never took it seriously. I guess I hadn't yet met a guy that really intrigued me. Until I met Tyler that is. I wanted Tyler, I dreamed of Tyler. He made me feel giddy and breathless. I wanted nothing more than to have those hazel eyes locked into mine and feel his hands on my skin. I wanted to know how he kissed and what he liked. I wanted him to...that's enough of that. Dreaming about it wouldn't help.

When we were done with our makeup, we accessorized with a few pieces of jewelry and headed out. It was almost half past 7 in the evening when we finally got in the cab.

I guess the conversation about Conrad must've been

weighing on Sarah's mind. She'd looked at me slyly and decided to speak up on the cab ride over.

"What's with you and Conrad? You seem close," she said, giving me side-eye. "I remember he used to be at your house all the time. Have you guys been in touch all these years?" she asked, knowing full well how much I hated Conrad's guts. Maybe it was because Conrad was always popular at school despite being a loner or how successful he'd gotten, but Sarah was always asking about him. Whenever she'd come to visit she'd ask if he'd be there. When I told Sarah he wasn't coming to the party, she seemed very disappointed, and I knew she was probably excited to know he was coming after all.

"You know we aren't, okay? He came to our house but we never spent time together. And I haven't seen him in, like, two years. Why would we stay in touch? We weren't exactly friends growing up," I said, a bit irritated. Now that Sarah reminded me, I was suddenly preoccupied with the thought of Conrad seeing me in this dress and teasing me about it.

"I don't know, you seemed pretty close. I can't help thinking there must be something more to it. You have such strong feelings..." I couldn't let her finish her thought.

"The only feeling we have between us is pure, unbridled hate!" I blurted out. "He has never done anything other than tease me all these years, remember? He was one of my worst bullies. He's done nothing but make me feel bad about my weight and my figure. How could you even suggest that I have feelings of any kind other than complete, utter disgust and revulsion at the thought of seeing him there tonight?"

Okay, so maybe I was exaggerating a little. But I was getting very anxious. It was just a bit too much. The hope of seeing Tyler and finally getting him to see me in *that* way, saying goodbye to my brother, having to play hostess, and the prospect of seeing Conrad made me prone to melodramatic outbursts. I was hot and cold at the same time, and I felt like I was going to burst the dress wide open. The shape and fabric of the dress didn't allow for a bra so we'd used a lot of tape. Sarah had assured me over and over that it would hold and that I was 'secure', though that was hardly how I felt at all.

"Oh come on, calm down. You can't still be self-conscious about your figure. You've lost a lot of weight. You look sexier now than you did two years ago. I mean look at yourself, you are not that chubby teenage girl anymore. You look so sexy in that, if Conrad finds a way to make fun of you now, he's out of his mind."

If only I could believe her. Sarah had always been lucky in the looks department. She couldn't possibly know what it felt like to be so insecure.

"Drink, ma'am?"

I nearly flinched, jolted out of my memory of earlier in the night. It was a good-looking waiter carrying shots on a tray. I smiled at him and quickly took one. I could sense his eyes on me. He gave me a look that was dripping with innuendo. I had to get out of there. I placed the glass back on the tray and quickly walked off.

I scanned the place, looking for Sarah. At social functions like this, she was always my security blanket. She was a little hard to miss in red, and she was easily one of the tallest women here, but she was nowhere in sight. I figured she must be talking to "the right people". She had been so excited to go to the party, saying it was the best place to further her career and client base. I was sort of hoping Sarah would be there to be supportive, but she was also always practical. I didn't mind and I knew Sarah's presence would make the party a lot more interesting for a lot of people.

Though I couldn't seem to find Sarah, I spotted Tyler

making rounds as well. That was when I decided it was time to finally do it and get it over with: I had to go over and try to charm Tyler, although I had no way of knowing how that was gonna go.

"You have to take risks if you want something. You can't expect him to just land on your lap, you know," Sarah had said, and she was right. That's what this dress was all about after all. I just wished there was another way to meet someone, a more genuine way. But I guessed looking really good at this party was going to open up the way to genuinely getting to know Tyler better.

Just as I was about to head in his direction, another waiter with a tray of shots was passing by. I decided to take a couple of shots to calm my nerves and recharge my social batteries. I had to seem cool in front of Tyler, even though the truth was my heartbeat was racing and butterflies were working up a tornado in my stomach.

I headed to where Tyler had been and couldn't find him. He was not where I'd first seen him and the direction he was headed to then looked like a dead-end. I noticed the door to the balcony and decided to try my luck there. The venue had a beautiful view of the Strip, but hardly anybody had ventured out onto the balcony. By this time the party was in full swing and everyone was more concerned about socializing and drinking than the view.

I opened the door and stepped into the chill night air. With the door closed behind me, the balcony was very quiet. I headed to the far end of the balcony.

I saw Tyler immediately, looking tall and dashing in his expensive gray suit. There was a woman's slender silhouette standing beside him, and my heart sank. A setting like this was more than romantic, and I could imagine people coming over here for some alone time, away from the party.

"Ellie's playing the perfect hostess, isn't she?" the woman

said. I knew immediately that it was Sarah and felt relieved. I was about to call out to them when I noticed how closely they were standing together, with Tyler's hand stroking Sarah's bare back. This would have been understandable inside, with the music blaring so loud that you had to lean in to hear what was being said, but out here it was quiet. I could practically hear myself breathing heavily.

No one would stand that close unless...I tried to brush the idea off. Sarah wouldn't do that. I mean it was obvious that any guy would go for her instead of me, but she knew I liked Tyler and she'd been so supportive. I had to give her the benefit of the doubt.

I tried to get as close as possible without being noticed, which was at least easy because it was darker out here. They both had their backs to me and were oblivious to my presence.

I hid behind a large plant a few feet from them. From here I could hear every word being said.

"Have you talked to Ellie at all?" Tyler asked.

"I haven't. I'm waiting for the right time, it's a very sensitive subject," Sarah replied.

"I know it is but I can't keep doing this. I can't really keep avoiding her for long and Aaron's my boss. I don't want to make it more complicated than it is, and the longer it keeps up, the messier it's gonna get," Tyler said. I could see him move closer to Sarah, as if to whisper in her ear. "If you can't bring yourself to tell her, I can talk to her. I'll let her down easy..."

"I have it under control Tyler," Sarah snapped, and then I heard her sigh. "I don't want you talking to her, it'll just hurt her feelings. She's very sensitive. And anyway, she's my best friend, it should come from me. I'll talk to her...when I find the right time."

I felt my blood run cold. I was mortified. My face was hot

and I felt nauseous. I had to get out of there. They were talking about me behind my back and the implications left me winded. I staggered to the balcony door and went straight back to the party.

There were no explanations needed; it was very clear what was happening. Tyler was not interested in me, he never had been. He knew I was interested in him and it was quite clear that he did not feel the same.

All I felt now was foolish and silly, cursing myself for choosing this dress and thinking it would make a difference. I wasn't anything like Sarah. How could I think that I could seduce a man, no matter how much I planned it?

But how could Sarah not tell me? She knew from the beginning how much I liked him, she let me hope, and even 'helped' me think up ways to approach Tyler. She teased me and encouraged me. She made me buy this dress and wear it tonight to get Tyler's attention when she knew full well he was not interested in me. It seemed apparent that they were closer friends than I thought. Why couldn't she just tell me the truth?

All the while, here I was, the little fool who hoped he'd give me the time of day and confided in Sarah about those hopes. I really wanted to give Sarah the benefit of the doubt. After all, she always had men falling at her feet. It was normal for her. But a nagging feeling still crept up and I kept asking these uncomfortable questions, and I didn't know what the answer was. I didn't want to think about it.

It was too much to go through sober. I headed straight to the bar, fighting back tears that I didn't know were already flowing. I wiped my face and ordered a couple of shots of whiskey.

I had downed my second shot when I felt my phone vibrating inside my purse. I pulled it out and saw that it was

Kate, probably calling about the cake. I realized it was a quarter past 9 o'clock.

"Hey Ellie, I'm here. There's so many people, I can't find you or Aaron. Where are you?" I could hear the music in the background, so she must already be in the room.

"I'm at the bar, you can just give the cake to the organizers. Ask a waiter or something, I don't know," I said, feeling the effects of the alcohol already. Kate must have sensed something in my voice because she was immediately worried.

"Ellie, what's wrong? Are you okay?"

"I'm fine, I'm having a good time. I'm drinking. This is a party and I'm having fun." I could tell my words were getting slurred, but I was already signaling to the bartender for a few more shots.

"Okay, I'll find the organizers. Where are you exactly?"

"I'm at the bar, I already told you. Just hand off the cake to a waiter or something. They'll know what to do," I said, not really caring anymore at this point.

"What's happened? Wait for me there okay?"

"I'll see ya later, Kate," I said, slurping another shot down my throat.

"Wait..." before she could say more I'd hung up the phone and was taking my fourth and fifth shot in quick succession. I ordered more from the bartender, who was shaking his head by this time.

"You sure you gonna take more, doll-face? Those hit pretty hard, you know," he said, a bemused smile on his lips as he started preparing my drink.

"Keep 'em coming," I said, leaning against the bar now. "I need it." I was shouting over the bar by then.

That's when I saw Sarah and Tyler emerge from the balcony. I could see they were still very close together and quickly separated only as they entered the door. They gave each other lingering looks as they headed in different directions. I gritted my teeth and threw my head back to force the next shot down my throat.

That was when three things happened in such quick succession that I ended up reeling:

First, my head hit a hard chest and all I could think was, *Oops, I hit someone.*

Then two hands popped out on both sides of me and rested firmly on the bar, trapping me in place. I couldn't move.

Then, a voice whispered, "I think you've had enough, Ellie-belly. Long time no see."

Only one person ever called me that. I could feel the blood running cold in my body. I was screaming in my head. This was the worst timing. I was drunk, heartbroken, and here was Conrad, whispering utter bullshit in my ear.

4

AN ILL-TIMED ENGAGEMENT

CONRAD

THE NIGHT WAS DRAGGING ALONG. To be honest, Aaron's optimism and positivity was starting to brush off on me. By this time, he'd introduced me to most of the people, from other department directors to old college friends. More and more people were coming over to greet me.

I suppose I was becoming a bit of an attraction. Everyone I already knew wanted to know what I'd been up to in the last two years since I'd gone AWOL. The ones who didn't wanted to finally meet the owner and CEO of Young-Tech and see for themselves if he really was as eccentric as they had all heard.

No one really said as much, but I could tell I was a bit of a curiosity to them. The only thing that made it bearable was seeing Aaron look so happy. It had been over an hour now though, and I was getting impatient.

By the tenth or so exclamation of "It's such an honor to finally meet you," I had decided to make a graceful exit. I pulled my phone out and pretended I was getting a call.

"I'm sorry," I said, as I stepped back holding up my phone and nodding to the people in front of me. "I really need to get this." I could see Aaron cock a brow at me. He could tell I was faking a call. The others just nodded politely.

I placed the phone to my ear as I turned around and walked away. When I was out of view, I put my phone back into my pocket and headed for the bar. I decided to get a few shots. The night was still young and I needed to recharge.

At that moment, I noticed Ellie heading to the bar from the balcony. She looked stunning, but her expression seemed a bit off. I wondered what could have happened. I saw her taking shots one after the other. I never had any idea Ellie liked to drink. In fact, she was never one to go to parties. I guess things must have really changed while I was away.

I started plotting out the best ways to approach her. Should I act mysterious, just tap her shoulder and surprise her? Should I play it cool and act like I had just then noticed her? I wonder how she'd react to finally seeing me. Knowing Ellie, I'm sure she'd have a stinging comeback and the verbal repartee was going to be invigorating. I was starting to get excited by the prospect of talking to her again.

I could see Ellie talking on the phone. When the conversation was over, she quickly ordered more shots. This was going to be interesting. She was starting to lean against the table and even from the other side of the bar I could hear her shouting and slurring some of her words.

What's going on Ellie? I thought to myself, as I slowly made my way toward her. As I approached her, I was hit by sudden inspiration, and I knew exactly what to do.

I was standing right behind her now, and I could see she had another set of shots placed in front of her. I waited a little for her to finish her drinks. I wanted to catch her off-guard, which would immediately give me the upper hand.

As I placed both hands over the counter, effectively trapping her in position, and leaned in to whisper in her ear, she knocked her head back to down another shot. Her head hit my chest and my lips brushed her ears as I whispered, "I think you've had enough, Ellie-belly. Long time no see."

It was immediately clear to me that she was drunk. She seemed very unsteady and her head rested on my chest a few seconds too long for her to be sober. And as I breathed so close to her, I caught a whiff of her intoxicating scent. It was a mix of her subtle perfume, sweat, and alcohol. It hit me with a force I didn't expect and I was a bit dazed.

Catching her off-guard was the right choice. I had enough time to get myself under control as she tried to regain her composure. I felt her freeze in her chair when I whispered in her ear, and now she was slowly turning to face me.

By the time she had turned, I already had my winning smile plastered on my face. I could see various emotions running across her face as she looked at me. First was disbelief, followed by fear, then confusion. As she took a long, steadying breath, her face finally settled into an expression of simmering rage. I couldn't help laughing.

She was still my little Ellie-belly, but not quite. I finally got a good look at her and she had changed. The last two years had been good to her. Her face wasn't round anymore; it had a lot more definition. She'd lost all her baby fat. She wasn't chubby anymore, she was just downright sexy, with curves in all the right places.

I couldn't help thinking that she must be very popular with the guys. She'd been perpetually single in the past but I could see how that would have changed by now. I wondered if she finally had someone in her life.

"Conrad Young," she said, managing to make every syllable drip with resentment. I could see fire and murder in her eyes as she looked at me.

I laughed a little. I was almost sure she wasn't in a relationship. It would be impossible for her to love anybody else when she clearly hated me with such a passion. I almost felt flattered.

"How have you been, Ellie?" I asked, expecting some colorful words to come out of her mouth. Instead, she just sighed and leaned back in her chair. I could sense she was feeling dejected.

"So glad you asked. I've been great," she said, not really looking at me now. "I'm in this beautiful dress that's pinching me in, I've made a total fool of myself, and nothing has gone according to plan. And the best thing about it? Here you are!" she said, laying her hand on my chest.

That reply got me curious and I was just about to ask when we were interrupted. It was a woman around Ellie's age. She had firmly wedged herself next to the bar and had grabbed Ellie's hand.

"Ellie, are you alright?" she asked loudly, obviously concerned. She had to lean in and almost shout to be heard over the music. I noticed how she was glaring at me, a dozen scenarios probably playing in her head.

"Hi Kate!" Ellie cried out, giving the woman a hug, oblivious to the woman's aggressive energy, which was mostly directed at me. "Conrad, this is Kate Jones. She's so great and works so hard. I wanna give her a promotion but then she'd be replacing me so..."

Ellie then proceeded to turn to me and laid both her hands on my chest, unmindful of our position or how it looked. Or how it affected me.

"Kate, this is Conrad Young. Billionaire, CEO, all-around asshole. He's a dear family friend. He's the other brother I wish I never had," Ellie said, laughing, then laying her head on my shoulder. I felt my body go stiff. I could feel her breasts pressing against my chest and her scent was overpowering.

I could see the woman's expression turn from suspicious aggression to relief. She finally smiled at me. "Hi, I'm Ellie's assistant pastry chef. I came to deliver a cake, which reminds me," she then turned to Ellie and whispered in her ear. I could make out none of it and simply assumed it was about work.

"Thanks so much, Kate, you're such a trooper," Ellie told her. She was leaning against the bar this time and patting Kate on the shoulder.

"Call me if you need anything okay," Kate said to her before turning to me. "Hi, I'm the assistant pastry chef at Ellie's bakery. I've heard about you. It's great to finally put a face to the name." We shook hands. "I'll be going now, please keep an eye on her. She's not really a drinker."

"Don't worry, I will," I said and watched her leave, painfully aware of Ellie's presence. I steadied her with one hand as I took a seat beside her.

"So, your own bakery huh? That's a big deal. You've really grown up, Ellie-belly."

"I hate that name and don't you play all impressed Mr. Tech-Company Billionaire. You have like a hundred people working for you. I have four employees at my bakery, and one of them is me."

I actually employed around 250 people, but I didn't think I should correct her right then.

"Still, you used to be a pastry chef, right? Going from that to owning your own business is a big leap," I said, genuinely interested in the turns she'd taken with her career.

"I wasn't going to keep working at that hotel. The hours were horrible, the pay was abysmal, and the chef was a jerk. They were never going to let me be in charge anyway, it was a dead-end," she said dismissively.

"Leaving a job to start your own business still takes a lot of courage, you must be proud."

"You know what, Conrad? I am. I had to build my company from the ground up, I didn't have a big trust fund to fall back on or giant loans from my grandaddy to get my business off the ground," she said resentfully. I honestly felt attacked and I could feel myself bristling for a comeback when Ellie suddenly called out to Aaron.

Aaron had wandered over to us as if he was looking for someone.

"Aaron, Aaron, over here! Look who I found!"

Aaron came over to us, looking a bit concerned with the state of his sister. I started to feel inexplicably guilty. "Hey, Ell. Conrad, I was wondering where you'd gone," he said, giving me a questioning look and then turning to his sister. He finally seemed to notice how wasted she was. "You've been going at it, huh?"

"Lighten up, Aaron, this is a party and I absolutely had to be here for you. I'm having fun!" I could sense some irony in Ellie's tone.

Aaron turned to me and said, "Hey, man, I know you came here for a party, but can you do me a huge favor and just please take her home. I don't know what happened, but she doesn't usually drink this much."

"Hey I can't go home yet, you haven't even made your speech!" Ellie protested before I could agree.

Aaron laid a hand on her shoulder. "Okay, I'll do my speech right now so you can get some rest, okay? Then Conrad's gonna take you home. Deal?" Aaron looked at me then and I nodded.

"Fine, fine. But first, your speech," she said, hugging her brother in a drunk embrace.

Aaron patted her back and pulled Ellie's arms off of him.

He headed toward the center where I assumed the orga-nizers would be.

I called the bartender and asked him for a glass of water. Ellie had her head in her hands and looked like she was done. The bartender then handed me the water and I tapped her on the shoulder, holding the glass up to her face.

"Here, drink up," I said, putting the glass to her lips. She raised her head and took a sip. She looked at me with a puzzled expression, taking the glass from my hands.

"Why are you being so nice to me?" she asked suspi-ciously.

"What are you talking about?" I replied, "I've always been nice to you." My answer caught her by surprise and she almost spit the water back into the glass. It was appar-ently funny to her and she couldn't hold back her laughter. She was snickering and holding her sides.

"Are you being serious right now? You've been every-thing *but* nice to me all this time," she was still smiling when she said it, but I could feel the anger bubbling in her voice. "Those stupid, fucking names you kept calling me, your constant, never-ending fat shaming, and I'm not even fat but you still somehow have a way of making me so insecure about my weight. You ruined my prom night, remember?" she was still laughing, but I realized how she was hurting. I did remember that night. She had gone back to her room in tears. I had half-heartedly apologized to her and her mother convinced her to still go to prom but I remembered that she had changed her dress. I stopped calling her Ellie-phant after that and had settled for the milder Ellie-belly.

"And you know what I've always loved most about you, Conrad? The way you'd look at me all smug and proud of yourself, like you're better than everyone else because you're a billionaire. Well, guess what, I'm not an insecure teenager anymore and you were NEVER nice to me. We can't just pretend that it was all in good fun."

I could feel the fiery energy of her hatred toward me slowly dissipating. She just seemed sad now. "I could never tell where I stood with you. You were my brother's friend and my parents loved you, but I couldn't feel safe with you always chipping away at my self-esteem. Even now I still can't take a compliment. I don't know if someone really likes me or is just messing with me. And even when they do like me, I can't believe them."

I was speechless. I was scrambling for something to say, something to make the hurt in her eyes go away, something that would make her forgive me. Before I could get a word out, she had finished drinking her water and moved away. I turned to follow her but the music suddenly stopped. I could see Aaron in the middle of the stage holding a microphone. He was probably about to make his speech.

"Hey everybody, sorry to cut in on the fun but I just need to say a few words to everyone who came," he said, holding a glass of champagne in his hand. "I am so thankful for all the love and support that you've shown tonight, and throughout my career if I'll be honest. It was a long, hard road, but working with people you love and care for always makes it easier." There was applause and glasses clinked, toasting Aaron's successes.

"I want to thank the great people I've had the pleasure of working with for the past five years I've been in the company. I've had the privilege to work with the most talented, hard-working people in the industry. To my amazing team at YoungTech, we really put in the hours and we're reaping the rewards, guys. I appreciate all the work you've put in. I would not be here without you." There was a brief pause that was followed by more applause.

"YoungTech started out as a dream and has grown into

one of the leading companies in cybersecurity right now. I am so grateful and excited to watch this company grow even more in Singapore, and I will do everything I can to make sure this trip ends in unprecedented success. You have my word." More applause and cheers followed as Aaron paused again. He was a great public speaker, which is one of the reasons why he was chosen to lead the Singapore team.

"YoungTech gave me the opportunity to work on something I truly love and it changed my life, it changed my family's life and opened up a lot of doors for me. I'd especially like to thank my friend, my brother, Conrad Young, who's somewhere in the room. I know Conrad doesn't really like the spotlight so I won't take too long thanking him," he paused to some mild laughs.

"Conrad Young is the driving force behind YoungTech. Without his skill, his brains, and his sheer will, none of this would even exist. And I'm proud to be able to call him my best friend and brother." He was walking around, probably scanning the room for my face. I had moved out of his line of sight so he just went on.

"I want to thank everyone again for all the support. The night is still young, let's enjoy ourselves and I'll be back before you know it. Let's party!" This was followed by loud cheers and more applause which only died down once the music started up again.

I could see Aaron step down from the stage as Ellie quickly caught him in a big hug. She was laughing and excitedly talking to Aaron. Aaron started to say something to her and she was visibly deflated. Aaron gave her another hug and Ellie started heading back to the bar, looking very unsure of herself.

I walked over to her and laid a hand on her shoulder. She looked up and when she saw it was me, she gave a rueful smile.

"Aaron thinks you should take me home," she said sadly. I felt sorry for her but I could also understand Aaron's way of thinking. This might be a party, but it was still a work party and he'd always been very protective of Ellie. One of the reasons Ellie didn't get asked out much in high school was because Aaron tended to cast an intimidating shadow on any kid who seemed remotely interested in Ellie.

"Yeah, I'll take you home, Ellie-b..." I stopped myself as she gave me another murderous glance. "I'll take you home, Ellie," I said, offering her my arm. She sighed and let me lead her down the elevator. She was still very unsteady on her feet and she grabbed onto my arm.

I helped her into the car and by the time I got in the driver's seat, she was already dozing. It was a short drive to their house on Silver Lake. I nudged her shoulder to wake her up but she only muttered in her sleep.

This was the only time tonight that I'd seen Ellie so serene. Damn, she was beautiful. She had an exotic look and lips begging to be kissed. *Woah, where is this coming from? She's Aaron's sister.* She was my Ellie-belly.

But as I looked at her I realized that she wasn't, not really. She'd grown up, she owned her own business. There was more to her than I thought. I nudged her again and called out her name, but she didn't seem like she was waking up anytime soon. I finally decided to pick her up and carry her into the house, her intoxicating scent filling my senses once more.

5

THE AFTERMATH
ELLIE

HE WAS WALKING TOWARD ME, half-naked, shimmering in the soft glow of the dim lights in my room. Without a word, he grabbed me and pulled me to him. He looked me in the eye before coming down for a kiss that touched my soul. I could feel his tongue exploring my mouth, his strong hand supporting me, wrapping me in a tight embrace. I kissed him back, opening my mouth wider to let his tongue deeper into my mouth.

His hands started exploring my body. I was still wearing the chrome dress and he could feel every bump and curve of my body through the thin material. His hand reached my breasts and he rubbed his thumb against an erect nipple. I moaned.

"Tyler," I whispered, "finally."

He pushed me back down on the bed and looked me over. I waited for him to kiss me again, but he took a bit too long. I opened my eyes and could see him looking at me critically.

He stepped back from me and said, "Not really my type though."

I got up and saw him walking away, hand-in-hand with a tall, beautiful blonde in a sparkling red dress.

~

I WOKE up with a raging headache. My body felt stiff, my throat was dry as a desert, and I felt like my head was disconnected from the rest of me. I had to squint and rub my eyes before I could see clearly. I realized I was on my own bed. The covers were strewn on the floor. My room was a mess and some dresses were still on the bed.

My heart was still racing from a dream that I could hardly remember, but it disturbed me. I tried to get my bearings, not really remembering what had happened the night before.

Then I saw that I was still wearing the chrome dress and still had my heels on. I must have been wasted last night. I groaned internally for a few minutes before pulling myself together.

I decided to go to the bathroom and freshen up. I could hardly remember anything about last night, and I couldn't remember the last time I had a hangover like this, but it did not feel good. I got the water going and stepped in, feeling relief as the hot water touched my skin. What had happened last night? Why had I had so much to drink?

Then it hit me like a baseball bat to the face: Tyler and Sarah, talking on the balcony. About me. Their words flooded my mind and I suddenly felt nauseous again. I couldn't believe it. How could Sarah keep this from me? She was my best friend, one of the few people I truly trusted. *Now I remember why I started drinking.*

I could only hope that I hadn't done anything scandalous or caused a scene. All I could remember was sitting by the bar and drinking, and a faint memory of seeing Kate last night. I finished my shower and dried myself with my fluffy blue towel. I put on an oversized shirt and a pair of worn cutoffs. I had to talk to Aaron and find out what exactly happened last night.

As I was walking down the stairs I could hear Aaron's voice. He was talking to someone. I thought he might have been talking on the phone when I heard a familiar laugh. I knew that laugh; that laugh filled me with dread when I was younger, and here he was in my kitchen once again. And here *I* was, with a blinding hangover.

Another memory hit me like a sledgehammer and I stopped in my tracks. A shot, then a whisper, Conrad's voice asking how I was, and, oh my God... I remembered my angry rant. I had poured my rage on him. I couldn't exactly remember what I said, but I knew I said more than enough. I remembered the faint satisfaction I'd felt when I left him standing there in shock. This day could not get any worse.

I debated whether I should just go back into my room and never come out, just live the rest of my days as a hermit in the figurative woods. But that was impossible, even if it was just for the day. Aaron was leaving later and I won't be seeing him for a while. There was no definite schedule of when he'd be back, but I assumed it would take a while, a month at least.

I had to take him to the airport and give him a proper goodbye. I'd have to face Conrad too, eventually. I couldn't keep putting it off. I decided to just rip the bandaid right off and be done with it.

I sheepishly walked into the kitchen feeling super awkward. Aaron and Conrad were obviously laughing about something and they both grew quiet when I walked in and sat on a chair by the kitchen island.

"Good morning, Ellie. Nice to see you up and about,"

Aaron said as he was stirring something up in a bowl by the counter. Conrad was grinning like the Cheshire cat at me.

"There's our Ellie-belly," he said, beaming. The nerve of this man. It was almost impressive how thick skinned he was. He was too comfortable for my liking.

I let out a groan that could have been a growl, but I had no energy for anger at this point. Aaron just laughed and handed me a cup of brownish goo.

"What is this?" I asked, grimacing at the look of it. There were little flecks of red and black and it smelled slimy.

"It's Aaron's tried and tested hangover cure. I wouldn't want you suffering all day because of some poor decisions you made last night. Go on, it's not as bad as it looks," Aaron said in encouragement. I thought of all the times Aaron had woken up with a headache and thought he probably had a lot of experience. I decided to trust him.

I pinched my nose and took a deep breath before gulping down the contents of the cup, trying not to let any of it linger too long on my tongue. I couldn't tell what it was but I'm pretty sure raw eggs were the main ingredient. It was spicy with a hint of sweetness, but also oily and kind of gross. I nearly gagged.

Aaron and Conrad laughed and one of them handed me a glass of water. "Oh God, that was definitely worse than it looked," I said, retching a little. Trying to keep the concoction from coming right back out was hard work. I was actually sweating.

"It's fine," Aaron said. "Don't be such a baby. You'll be feeling better in a minute."

I turned to Conrad, still wearing that annoying self-satisfied smile on his face. "I haven't seen you in this kitchen for more than two years. What are you doing here so early, anyway?" I asked Conrad, making my annoyance at his presence obvious, still feeling queasy.

"Come on Ellie, don't you remember?" he asked, trying to act serious—but I could see a hint of glee behind his eyes. "You practically begged me to stay the night."

I froze and my eyes nearly popped out of their sockets. I could vaguely remember a car ride. What had happened? Did I shamelessly throw myself on Conrad in a fit of drunken lust? Did something happen between us last night? Then I saw him holding back his laughter and I realized how preposterous that was. Seeing the mischief in Conrad's eyes made me sure. I knew it didn't happen.

"You're making that up, there's no way I would do something like that," I said, vehemently defending my honor. "And if I did, you're the last person I'd do that with!" Conrad just laughed.

"I'm joking Ellie. It was all PG. I really get you worked up, don't I?" he said with a self-satisfied smile. "The truth is I came here early so I could give Aaron a ride to the airport. I figured we could catch up a bit more and it's the least I could do. It is technically my fault he has to go to Singapore, you know."

"Come on man, it's not your fault, it's my job, and I want to go," Aaron said. "I haven't really had the chance to travel much and this is a great opportunity to see Asia. And the best part is, I'm gonna get paid while I'm doing it."

"That reminds me, make sure to get a few days off and see Sentosa Island. It's beautiful and the weather's great this time of year..." Conrad's attention suddenly drifted away from the conversation as he pulled out his phone. It was vibrating.

He looked at the screen and I immediately noticed a change in his mood. He'd suddenly stiffened and looked troubled. "I'm sorry guys, I really need to take this," he said as he abruptly left the room.

I could see Aaron looking after Conrad worriedly.

"Just my two cents," I said, looking Aaron dead in the face, "It is his fault you're leaving. I don't care how grateful you are to him."

Aaron just ignored me, still looking a bit worried. He was making breakfast on the stove. It's weird that even though I'm the chef in the family, it was always Aaron making our meals. He said that making food was work for me, just like programming was for him. He figured I'd want to do anything but cook when I got home, so he took on the cooking duties. Aside from a few mishaps in the beginning, Aaron was a pretty good cook and he'd been getting better. I did the cooking when we had any get-togethers with friends and family but Aaron cooked our daily meals and it actually made us closer.

I remember when the bakery had just opened and I always had to leave super early and come home late. He'd usually have a little lunch packed for me in the fridge with a note that said, *You're gonna WIN today*, or, *They're gonna love the cakes* just like mom used to. I was starting to realize that cooking was Aaron's love language.

"Hey Ellie?" he said after some silence, "I need a really big favor from you..." he paused for dramatic effect.

"What is it?" I demanded. I could tell this was another one of his 'and-but' conversations. I also knew he was expecting me to say no.

"I'd really appreciate it if you could look after Conrad while I'm gone."

I laughed, thinking he was joking. When he refused to join in my mirth I realized he meant it. My mouth was open in shock.

"You can't possibly be serious."

Aaron turned off the stove and walked around the kitchen island to where I was, taking my hand in his.

"Please, Ellie, he's my best friend and I won't be here for

him," Aaron came closer and dropped his voice. "His grandfather is sick, he needs someone right now."

I was surprised at Aaron's request. I knew Conrad had lost his parents at a young age and that his grandfather was basically his whole family. Mom and Dad had always said that we were supposed to be his family, but why was I suddenly given the task to "look after him", as if I was even remotely capable of doing that?

"Are you crazy? You could hardly call us close and you know we don't like each other. How the hell do you think I can possibly look after him? He's 4 years older than me and I'm busy with the bakery. He can take care of himself nicely. Come on, be realistic Aaron."

Aaron tightened his grip on my hand, looking me dead in the eyes with a puppy dog look that stopped being cute like fifteen years ago. "Ellie, he has no other family. I know you guys don't get along but Mom and Dad always considered him a son, and he's my brother in every sense of the word except by blood. We're the only family he has, and you're the only one who'll be here to actually, physically, be able to help him out if anything happens. Please Ellie, for me?"

"I hate it when you pull the family card on me," I mutter under my breath. I finally relented, knowing he would accept nothing less.

"I want you to know you're being really unfair and I'm only doing this because I'm an amazing sister," I could see him starting to smile. "Fine, I don't know how you think I'm going to do it, but I'll try."

"That's our Ellie. That's all I'm asking from you, to try," Aaron said, giving me a big bear hug. I hugged him back, knowing how much I was going to miss him.

Conrad stepped back into the room as we let each other

go. He looked a bit awkward, probably feeling like he'd intruded on a private moment.

Aaron had gone back to the stove and I decided to get some plates from the cupboard. Aaron had prepared a veritable feast: He laid out fried eggs, sausages, ham, pancakes, and even some vegetable fritters I had made and kept in the fridge.

"Wow, you really outdid yourself," I said, complimenting the chef. Aaron smiled and handed me a glass of orange juice.

"Yes, frying is definitely something I mastered," he said with a laugh. He always thought I was being sarcastic when I complimented him on cooking. "Well, I figured this was the last breakfast I was going to make for you for a while, and considering the state you were in last night, I thought you'd appreciate a big breakfast."

I ate the food with gusto. I only now remembered that I had had nothing to eat for dinner at the party and the last meal I had eaten was a couple of tacos for lunch yesterday from a nearby Mexican place at the bakery.

I was almost done with my meal when Aaron got up and said he was going to his room to freshen up and get his bags. When he left the kitchen, Conrad and I were left in uncomfortable silence. I decided to clear the table and clean up a little. I had to put a lot of the breakfast into the refrigerator because Aaron had decided to cook for a family of six.

As I was loading up the dishwasher, I decided to ask Conrad the question that had been nagging at me this whole time:

"Hey, um, what happened last night?"

He looked puzzled and asked me what I meant.

"Well, I mean, did I do anything stupid or embarrassing? I was pretty hammered and I've never been that drunk before... I just hope I didn't embarrass Aaron or anything."

He looked me dead in the eye and it made me feel uncomfortable and a little giddy. I squirmed. He seemed to snap out of it and said, "You never do or say anything stupid Ellie, and you could never embarrass Aaron."

The sincerity in his voice made me feel warm inside. I almost couldn't believe it. Was Conrad Young finally, genuinely, being nice to me? I was speechless. I was about to clarify that what I meant was if I'd done or said anything while I was stupid drunk, but Aaron came in before I could say anything more.

"Okay, guys. I'm ready to go."

Aaron only had one medium-sized luggage and a carry-on bag. Most of the clothes and personal items he needed had been shipped ahead so he could travel light, all courtesy of his Asian hosts. Apparently, arrangements had been made for him to stay at a four-star hotel for the entirety of his time in Singapore.

I locked up the house as Conrad loaded up Aaron's things into his Bentley. I didn't have the chance to see the car last night, but it was really impressive. It immediately reminded me that Conrad was a billionaire and lived in a different world. Sometimes I would genuinely forget, only thinking of him as my brother's annoying friend instead.

Aaron got into the passenger side and Conrad held the door open for me as I got into the backseat. When we were all settled in, Conrad started the car and we headed to the airport.

I was absentmindedly looking at the LA scenery as we drove. I looked up and could clearly see Conrad looking at me through the rearview mirror. I mouthed the word 'what', acting all annoyed at him. He just smiled and looked away.

As we drove on, Aaron and Conrad started talking about business. I think they were discussing strategies on how to close the deal or something, I wasn't really sure. I was no longer paying attention.

Then a tall, sparkling building caught my eye. It was the venue for last night. It was a beautiful building, and one of the reasons I had convinced Aaron to book it was because of the view. But instead of getting a memorable view of the strip, all I got was betrayal when I went out onto that balcony, a view I hoped I would one day forget.

Suddenly another memory came back. Me, hanging onto Conrad's arm as he led me into his car. Then I remembered being gently carried and laid into bed. I felt my body grow cold at the recollection. *Please let it be Aaron who carried me to bed, please...*

I looked up at the rearview mirror again and could see Conrad staring at me. The nerve of this person. I definitely held his stare but he wouldn't let up. I was getting a little hot and was thankful when Aaron unknowingly interrupted our little staring match with a well-timed question. I zoned them out and tried to relax, looking out the windows and willing myself not to look at that rearview mirror again.

After a few more minutes we finally started pulling up to the airport. We walked Aaron as far as we could. We exchanged hugs and finally, it was time to say goodbye. Aaron's plane was boarding.

"Please don't forget, you promised to try Ellie," he quietly whispered in my ear. I just nodded.

"Hey," I ventured, "thanks for taking me home last night." I still had my fingers crossed, willing it to be true. He pulled his head back and looked at me funny.

"What? I didn't take you home last night," my heart was already sinking when I heard this, but he went on. "I was the guest of honor, I couldn't leave the party early. I asked Conrad to take you. He even waited up for me before he left. You were zonked out last night."

I just managed to smile nonchalantly, as if it didn't matter. Why did everything have to happen the way it did? First, Tyler and Sarah, and now this? Was I going to lose every ounce of dignity I still had left?

Aaron had gone on and was heading to his gate. For a moment I thought about how alone I suddenly was. Aaron was leaving, Mom and Dad were on their own exciting little adventure, and Sarah was...not who I thought she was. I didn't have anyone else.

Conrad cleared his throat and I felt my annoyance bubbling up to the surface. I turned toward him, ready for a fight, but instead I was greeted by a look of genuine concern.

"You're really gonna miss him, aren't you, Ell?" he said, looking at me kindly. He looked just as sad as I felt and I realized what it must be like for him, feeling alone, on the brink of losing his grandfather. I suddenly felt for Conrad in a way I never thought I would. I felt sorry for him.

I decided to ignore the question. I didn't want us to dwell on...feelings.

"Come on," I said, walking past him. "I really need coffee right now." I slid into the front passenger seat and waited for Conrad to get in. I don't know what came over me that suddenly gave me all this confidence, but I thought I'd run with it. Maybe it was the realization that Conrad was just human after all.

"I know a great café not too far from here."

Conrad let out a soft laugh and started the car. We drove back to Hollywood in silence.

6

CONFESSIONS
ELLIE

THE OLD CAFÉ was tucked away in a little street off Downtown Los Angeles. It was a hidden gem I'd found years ago. The place had great coffee, authentic Italian sandwiches and pastries, all with great prices, and was open 24/7. For a young chef struggling to make ends meet and working impossible hours, it was a haven.

Since then, I'd always made time to come to Paolo's, or find an excuse to be downtown at least once a week. Joey, our server, often made the coffee for us at the bakery. I appreciate Joey's efforts but his coffee just couldn't compare to Paolo's. I also loved the ambience of the place. It was very comfortable, nothing like the high-end, almost uninviting, new-age restaurants and cafés that riddles Los Angeles.

We drove in silence after I gave Conrad the directions. The nagging questions about last night's events still haunted me so I thought this was a good time to get a straight answer to my question from earlier.

"Can you please just tell me what exactly happened last night? Please? I don't want to have to find out through gossip," I said, all seriousness. Conrad just laughed.

"Nothing important. You're still the sweet and proper

Ellie-belly we love..." he said, smiling in a way that said something did happen. I was getting annoyed again. In my current state I just couldn't deal with all the teasing. Conrad always had that effect on me. I would forget everything that I'd built and all I'd be was the awkward teenager who fell for all his teasing.

"I told you not to call me that," I said, my anger simmering again. Why couldn't I have a normal conversation with this person? "Why can't you just get that through your head? I've grown up, Conrad."

"Now what I want to know is how you got your own bakery. That sounds interesting. Our Ellie-belly, a business owner," he said, smiling that self-satisfied smile again. All I wanted to do at that moment was wipe that stupid smile off his face.

However, I did promise Aaron I would try, and I wanted to give it my best effort. I clenched my fists and I was trying —so so hard!—to control my temper.

"It's fine," I managed to say, gritting my teeth. It took all of my will power to stay civil at this point.

"Oh come on, it's fine! Tell me, why'd you leave your job? I thought you always wanted to work at a four-star hotel," he continued, totally oblivious to how upset I was becoming.

I took a deep-breath. "Just because, okay?" I snapped. I couldn't help it, the continued name calling was too much. I had practically poured my heart out to him last night, told him about how his words affected me, and it had all just fallen on deaf ears.

Conrad let out a breath, obviously annoyed. *Good! He should feel some of what I'm feeling.*

"Why are you being so difficult? I just want to have a conversation with you!" he said, raising his voice. I had to laugh.

"I'm being difficult? I just asked you, in all seriousness,

that I need to know what happened last night and you completely blew me off. Now, that's being difficult."

"Nothing happened, okay? How many times do I have to tell you that?" he said, giving me a wicked side eye in the process. "If you don't recall, I already answered your question half a dozen times, you just won't fucking believe me."

"I don't know, you're just being so weird about it," I replied, refusing to look him in the eye.

"What are you talking about? How am I being weird?"

"You're being nice... I don't know. It's suspicious. Like you did something bad and now you have to make up for it," I said honestly. I could see him shaking his head and taking a deep breath.

"Look, my grandfather's in the hospital right now, I don't know if he'll pull through. My best friend in the world is on that airplane heading halfway across the globe and who knows how long he'll be out there?" he said, clearly upset. "The only person who I can remotely consider family is my best friend's sister who hates my guts for no fucking reason even though I'm going out of my way to be nice to her. She's so suspicious of me that everything I do has to have some dark meaning behind it. My whole world is falling apart in front of me. I feel like I'm losing everyone I care for. I don't know about you Ellie but I just want to put the past behind us. I'm tired of bickering and fighting over nothing. Can't we at least be friends?"

I'd heard enough. "No reason? Do you think I don't trust your motives for no reason? I thought I explained it to you last night?" I said, willing the hurt out of my voice. "It may have been nothing to you, but it was something to me. Do you know how hard it is to not feel safe in your own home, to be teased and bullied in the one place you thought was safe? You don't remember any of this Conrad because apparently it was 'nothing', but I used to run to my room whenever I heard your voice in our doorway. I used to change my clothes when you visited because I was afraid you'd find something to tease me about. I was so insecure, I'd be afraid to go to the kitchen because you were there, let alone eat in front of you. Ellie-phant, Ellie-belly? Those words followed me around until I was an adult. Your ten minutes of niceness won't erase those years of meanness. It won't make us friends. Friends trust each other and feel safe with each other. I don't, not with you, and I don't plan on being friends, ever."

I felt a pang of guilt, remembering what Aaron had asked of me, but the feeling of sympathy I'd just had for Conrad was a faint memory. All that was running in my head was how pig-headed, insensitive, and cruel he could be. How could he possibly relate to someone like me? He was a blessed billionaire who grew up with a trust fund and had women falling at his feet. How could I possibly look after him? It was impossible.

Conrad clenched his jaw and pulled up to the café. He took a deep breath before saying, "Fine. That's your decision, but as for me, I'll try to be your friend Ellie and maybe one day, we can put this behind us."

I groaned in frustration and got out of the car, not bothering to see if he was following behind me. I walked toward the café in a huff. I opened the door and walked straight in, not pausing to look around. I was in such a state that I almost bumped into someone.

The guy was surprised and had to steady himself. I was just about to apologize when I looked up. It was Tyler, wearing a rumpled sweater and shorts. We just looked at each other and I immediately saw he was holding a woman's hand. He noticed that I was looking and quickly let go of the hand, but there was no question who he was with.

She had had her head turned away from the door and

hadn't noticed me, but she turned when she felt Aaron let go of her hand. Sarah froze when she saw me. Her hair was a bit disheveled and she wore no makeup. I was almost sure they must have spent the night together. She was looking intently at my face. I don't know what my expression was, but I was all kinds of hurt on the inside.

"Ellie, it's not what you think. Please let me explain," she said, grabbing my hand. My body had grown limp and cold, and although all I wanted was to push her away from me, I let her pull me aside.

"I'll...go and get us some coffee," Tyler said sheepishly, walking to the counter to order.

I couldn't believe it. Sarah brought Tyler here, to my special place. I was the one who had introduced her to Paolo's Cafe, it was *our* thing. We'd have brunch or breakfast here once a week, our special meeting place and my little haven. But now, I wouldn't be able to think of Paolo's without remembering that this was where I bumped into them, my best friend and her lover, the man I had just dreamt about the night before.

"Ellie, please. I've been meaning to tell you, really I have. It just got complicated, then the longer I put it off, the harder it was to tell you. You have to understand I've been so worried and anxious about this. I hope you can find it in your heart to forgive me."

"Explain it to me Sarah. Explain the complication, I can't seem to grasp it," I said, finally finding the energy to pull my hand away from her grasp.

"I just didn't know how to tell you. I was waiting for the right time," she said. "I knew how much you liked him and I was really all for it. Really, I genuinely wanted you to be happy. When we first went out without you, I was set on making him see what a great girl you are. But he...he confessed that he liked me and that he wasn't interested in you. I tried to stop him but he was very persistent and I found myself falling for him too," she said, looking at me pityingly. *Poor Ellie, the guy she likes doesn't like her back.*

"I tried to fight it. It felt like I was betraying you, even though you weren't really with Tyler yet and it made me feel super guilty. But all those things you said about him, the way you'd moon over him and how you kept saying he was such a great guy, it made me realize he really was a catch. I couldn't help it, Ellie, even though I fought it. I fell in love."

Wow, it didn't take her long to paint herself as a victim of fate and good looks, while making it seem like her falling for Tyler was somehow my fault too.

"How long?" I asked. "How long have you been together?"

"It's just over a month now. We've been going out for a while and I did try to put it off, but it was just too much, I couldn't possibly deny my feelings for him," she said quietly. It was almost surreal. I'd been telling her about my crush on Tyler for the past year and she'd encouraged me. She was my confidante. And all this time they were going on secret dates and probably talking about me. *Poor Ellie, how do we tell her?*

"Well, I hope you're happy," was all I could manage to say. Sarah was completely oblivious to the sarcasm and hurt in my voice. She smiled and looked absolutely relieved.

"We are Ellie, I'm so glad you approve! I knew this wouldn't come between us! Don't worry Ell, I'm sure you'll find someone as great as Tyler who'll make you just as happy as he makes me."

The smug, condescending smile on her face made me want to punch her. For the second time today, I was sorely tempted to wipe the smile off someone's face, and it was still early. I hated how she was trying to sympathize with me, how she could even pretend we were still on the same side. A wave of vindictiveness washed over me.

"Actually," I found myself saying, "I do have someone in my life, and he makes me so happy. I've never felt this way before, I'm actually glad you're with Tyler. This makes the whole situation so much easier to explain."

I could see her smile fade, just a little. "You were right you know," I said, "heads did turn. Men were looking at me last night in ways I thought they never would. I actually have to thank you, you gave me such good advice. You helped me find the man of my dreams."

Sarah was looking at me as if I was crazy. She let out a laugh. "Oh come on, you wore that dress to impress Tyler. You've been crushing on him for months. Who else could there be?" I noticed how quickly she went from sympathetic and wishing me happiness to wanting to pull me back down a peg and put me down.

"No, like you said, all eyes were on me, especially his."

As if on cue, Conrad popped his head through the door and called to me. "Ellie? Is everything alright?"

For once, Conrad had the perfect timing. I turned to Sarah and could see her jaw drop in shock. Her head turned from me to him and back again. She looked me up and down and said, "You've got to be kidding me. You can't be serious."

At that moment, I realized that Sarah was not who I thought she was. And I could sort of tell what she was thinking. She can't believe that I would land someone as hot and successful as Conrad, she couldn't believe he'd prefer me over her.

"So you don't believe me? Hey Conrad, come here," I called. Conrad came over obediently. He could probably tell something was up. When he was close enough, I grabbed his hand and hooked an arm around his. Conrad, without missing a beat, placed a hand over my arm.

"Isn't it funny?" I said, feigning mirth, "Sarah doesn't believe we're dating. I told her about how you finally confessed last night and she just keeps calling me a liar." I had to hand it to Conrad, there was not an ounce of surprise, cluelessness, or question in his eyes. I guess he must really be a good liar.

He just cocked his eyebrows at Sarah. "Is that so? Well I suppose it is understandable, given how we've been like cats and dogs before. But to set the record straight, it is true you know. Last night, she finally gave me a chance."

"And wasn't it the dress that finally pushed you to ask me out?" I added. I just wanted to rub Sarah's face in the possibility that the awful thing she did to me actually resulted in something good. Conrad was stroking my arm by now, and it took every ounce of self-control to not freak out about that, to ignore the little flashes of heat I felt from his touch. I never noticed it before, but Conrad had very manly hands.

"Well, yes. When I saw Ellie looking so good last night, I just couldn't pass up the opportunity anymore. I knew I had to grab my chance before someone else snatched her up. She's a great girl, I know that better than anyone," he replied, holding me a little closer. He then proceeded to hook an arm around my waist, a fact that I couldn't protest or forgive right away. My own little charade was being used against me, but I couldn't be anything but thankful to Conrad. On the bright side, I could see the color drain away from Sarah's face.

Conrad and I play acted being in love a little, looking at each other and smiling. It took Sarah awhile to recover. She looked surprised and almost annoyed. She finally cleared her throat and spoke up.

"I don't know what to say. Congratulations, I guess?" she said, smiling like her life depended on it.

"Thank you so much, Sarah. I'm so glad you approve," I said, reaching out and squeezing her shoulder. The vindictive side of me was taking over, and given I didn't want to break down in front of her, I reveled in it. I couldn't let myself think about how she'd hurt me or question our entire friendship right now. All I could do in this moment was keep it up and carry on.

"I guess I'll see you in the car, Ell. Don't take too long," Conrad said, booping my nose in a romantic way. It was almost funny, we were ready to tear each other apart just a minute ago.

"I'll be right there babe," I called after him as he headed out. Sarah was still quite shocked. "I have to admit, I wasn't expecting this. You'd think someone like Conrad would have models and celebrities on his radar and you did say you hated his guts," Sarah said, bemused. She made me feel ridiculous. I knew there was truth to her words, but I just pressed on.

"Well, you can't really hate someone so much without loving them first, I guess. We just never admitted it to each other," I said, looking her in the eye. I couldn't really put a finger on it, but it seemed like Sarah was disappointed that I had somehow won. I liked the feeling.

It wasn't long before Tyler came over, carrying the coffee they'd ordered. He was looking a little guilty but relieved. He was probably expecting a cat fight over him. He smiled at me with the same sympathetic, pitying look Sarah had used earlier.

"You're never gonna believe this but Ellie's dating Conrad," Sarah said.

Tyler's eyes widened. "You're dating Conrad Young? *The*

Conrad Young?" he asked eagerly, like a dog who had caught the smell of a bone.

"Is he here? Where is he?" Tyler went on, looking around and scanning the café for a trace of Conrad. "Ellie, you have to introduce me, please."

"I'm sorry Tyler," I said, "but we're in a bit of a hurry." I coolly took a cup of coffee from his hand and took a sip, winking at Sarah as I did it.

"I really do have to go, you know, Conrad has plans for us today," I said, breezing through the lies like a champ. "This one's on you right? Thanks." I said, indicating the coffee. Sarah just cocked an eyebrow at me, unable to say a word.

"Can't I at least walk you to your car, Ellie?" Tyler said, sounding a bit desperate. I could feel Sarah bristle up. She nudged Tyler roughly. I only smiled.

"That won't be necessary Tyler. But thanks anyway."

I walked as gracefully as I could toward the car and I managed really well. Conrad was already in the passenger seat.

The minute the car door closed though, it finally hit me. I was lying about dating my brother's best friend because the guy I liked was more interested in my best friend. How pathetic could I get?

7

PROPOSALS

ELLIE

I SAT in silence for a while with my face buried in my hands. I couldn't speak. All the confidence and rage I felt inside the coffee shop gave way to sadness and loneliness. I felt like I was alone in the world.

I felt Conrad start the car and pull out of the parking lot. After around five minutes he finally cleared his throat. "Should I take you home?" he asked.

I thought of the house, empty. I couldn't bear it. I just shook my head, not knowing what to say, not knowing where to go.

"Bakery then?" he asked again. I felt a flood of relief when he said that. Yes, the bakery still existed. My whole life's work was waiting for me with the sweet smells, hot bread, and the comforting warmth of the oven. I wiped my eyes and nodded, not looking at Conrad at all.

A month...they've been going out for a month. My best friend, the one person who stayed with me through high school and college, up until I had my own business. The person I trusted with all my secrets, who I thought would always be my friend. She'd played me for a fool.

I couldn't be angry at Tyler. He had nothing to do with

me. He was being nice to me because he liked Sarah. Sarah, on the other hand, always knew. It had been almost a year since I thought I'd fallen for Tyler. I had told her everything, I had told her my innermost feelings.

How could she do this? How could I even consider her my friend anymore? How could she be secretly dating him for a month and still let me hope, help me pick out a dress, and even give me advice on how to seduce the man she was dating already? Why would she do that?

And she was so casual about it. If she was really my friend, she would have been upfront and honest. She said she was sorry, but it didn't feel sincere. She seemed sorry that I got hurt, that she got caught, but it seemed to me like she didn't think she'd done anything wrong.

If she'd told me right away, I would have been hurt but I could have gotten through it. Finding out this way was different. It hurt so much worse.

I thought back to them on the balcony, talking intimately. Apparently they were much more intimate than I first suspected. It wasn't Sarah trying to spare me from the pain of getting rejected, it was both of them talking about how to tell me they were together.

How could I have been so blind? I wanted so much to see Sarah in the best light, I had fooled myself into thinking she was still looking out for me, that they were just friends. I couldn't fathom the fact that my best friend could actually date the guy I liked behind my back. But I couldn't turn a blind eye anymore when the truth was staring me in the face.

And what did it all say about me? What kind of person was I? Just a naive, silly fool who couldn't see people's intentions, who couldn't sense the hidden meaning in things.

"I'm so stupid," I exclaimed, unable to keep it inside me anymore. I was crying by then.

"You're not stupid, Ellie. You just trusted the wrong people," Conrad said quietly.

I wiped the tears from my eyes and realized we were outside of the bakery. It was still early but there were people going in and out of the bakery in a steady stream. I didn't even notice that we'd stopped.

"We're here," I said, not knowing what else to say.

"Actually we've been here for five minutes."

"I'm sorry, I didn't even notice. I'll get going. Thanks for driving me," I said, gathering my things. As I started to get out of the car, Conrad stopped me.

"Ellie, before you go, can we talk?" he asked, seeming hesitant. I settled back into the seat and waited, clueless as to what he could possibly want to talk about. He looked a bit uncomfortable as he struggled to find words.

"Ellie, I know this isn't the best time for you and you're probably processing a lot. I just want you to know I'm here if you need someone to talk to. And for the record, I never liked Sarah..."

"Let's just not talk about Sarah, please. Just say what you have to say."

He fiddled with the seat belt and wouldn't look me in the eye. "I need to ask you for a favor."

I waited a beat but he didn't go on. I was growing impatient but I was worried about what kind of favor he meant. "Just...please tell me what it is you want."

He coughed and began to fidget in his chair. When he finally spoke it was almost in a whisper. "It's not something I want but more something I need. I...I need a fiancée."

I was speechless. I almost couldn't believe my ears. "What?" was all I could say, dumbfounded. "And you...you need me to find you a fiancée or something? I didn't think you'd have trouble finding one for yourself."

Conrad let out a long sigh and it seemed to give him

some courage. "I don't mean find me an actual fiancée, I need someone to be my fiancée temporarily. What you did in the café earlier, it gave me an idea. You see, I happened to walk into a sticky situation with my grandfather. I kind of told him that I have a girl I've been dating for a year and that I'm going to propose to her. Now, I need to find a girl to present to him, and who better to play my fiancée than you?"

I was so surprised my mouth fell open. "Me? You're fiancée?"

He turned to me, eager to convince me. "A fake fiancée, to be specific. Who else can I ask? And you would do it perfectly, Ellie! We've known each other since we were kids and my grandfather already likes you. Nobody is sure how long William's got, it was a spur of the moment lie, and I can't disappoint him."

"You're serious? You're really serious," I was almost ready to laugh. It was such a surreal situation: Conrad and I trying to convince everyone we were in love?

"I need this, Ellie. It's William's dying wish. He just wants to see me happy with someone in my life, someone he can trust. I want to give him some peace, even just for the time he has left."

I could sense his earnestness and I remembered Aaron's request. "If I go along with this, then what's in it for me?" I asked cautiously. I had a feeling that this was going to unleash a whole new can of worms.

"Well, you'll get a fake boyfriend. You'll help me keep up the lie with William, and I'll help you keep up the lie with Sarah and Tyler. It's a win-win."

I laughed. "No, that was a mistake. I never should have said that. I'm gonna have to come clean eventually," I replied. "I don't need a fake boyfriend."

He scoffed, "Are you sure about that? Do you really think

that Sarah's gonna let you off the hook if you admit you lied to her?"

"What are you talking about?" I asked, incredulous. "Why don't you just mind your own business? I know Sarah, I can handle her."

"Yeah right, don't act all tough all of a sudden Ellie, I see you when you're with her," he said, curling his lip as he spoke. "You follow her around like she's some kind of god. You're like her little groupie and I know you probably put her high up on a pedestal but I hate to break it to you Ellie, your precious Sarah isn't all that great. And if you're even considering going and taking her back as your friend then you're crazy."

"I don't know what you're talking about!" I gritted my teeth as I hissed this out. It was hard for me to hear that Conrad saw me that way when I was with Sarah.

"Come on, Ellie. She went behind your back and dated the guy you liked... Tyler, was that his name? That's not something a real friend would do. Don't let her get away with this one."

"What do you mean with this one? How many times do you think Sarah's gone behind my back like this?" I couldn't believe what I was hearing.

Conrad sighed. "What I meant was that she treats you like she knows she can get away with anything, that you would do anything just to be friends with her. She's always treated you like a doormat and you laugh it off and let her. It's like she's doing you a favor by being your friend. That's not real friendship."

The weight of his words cut deep, I couldn't help but start to realize that he might be right after all. Then another realization made me freeze: "How did you know that I liked Tyler?"

Conrad looked away and seemed a little guilty. "Conrad," I warned, his name coming out like a growl in my throat.

"Okay," he finally said, "It was on the car ride home. You fell asleep the second I put you on the passenger seat. Then you started talking about him...how he seemed to like you, flirted with you, taking you and Sarah out. You were almost sure that he liked you but you found out last night that he didn't."

I was sure I had turned beet red. I couldn't believe that I had been sleep talking last night and told Conrad my sob story. *He must think I'm so pathetic.*

"You probably don't want to hear it, but the truth is," he said, not noticing how embarrassed I already was. If he did he wouldn't have said what he said next. "The truth is I think he just used you to get to Sarah."

The moment he said it, I knew it was true. Tyler would only ever show up if Sarah was there, he only ever complimented me when she was around, or took us out to dinner if he knew Sarah was going to be there too. All the little hints I thought he was giving me, all the charm, that was just a smokescreen. And I was too naive to realize what was happening right under my nose. Before I knew it, I was crying again.

I could feel Conrad shift in his seat; then his hand was on my back, trying to console me. "It happens sometimes you know," he said, "You trust people who don't deserve to be trusted. We all do it. It's going to be okay, Ellie."

I pushed his hand away, trying to collect myself. I took a deep breath, wiping the tears away. "I'm fine, I am," I mumbled, talking more to myself than to him. He handed me his handkerchief. I fixed myself up as best I could, looking at my reflection through the rearview mirror.

"Thanks for the ride, now I really have to go to work. Kate must be swamped right now," I said as I opened the car door. I was just about to get out when Conrad shot an arm out and held my arm before I could go. He was looking at me earnestly. "Think about it Ellie," he said before he let me go. I just nodded and headed out.

The walk to the bakery seemed longer than it was. I was trying to shake off all the hurt before I walked in. I didn't want my personal problems affecting my work. I steeled myself and smiled as brightly as I could before walking in.

The place was busy. There were several people lined up at the register and a few more sitting around in our seating area, waiting for their number to be called. "Good morning!" I said as brightly as I could, trying not to make eye contact with Kate and our servers at the register as I hurriedly headed to the kitchen.

"Everything okay?" I heard Kate say as I passed her.

"Of course!" I said, not slowing down and closing the door behind me.

The kitchen brought me some comfort. Here I knew who I was, I was in my element. Dead love lives and false friends didn't have a place in my kitchen. I quickly washed up, put on my apron, and got to work.

I thought I'd done a good job hiding the drama when I walked in, but apparently it wasn't enough. It wasn't long before Kate walked into the kitchen under some pretense of checking on the pastry batter. She actually went over and looked into the refrigerator before coming over to my work station.

I tried to act normal and just kept working, putting cookie dough onto a baking sheet. I could feel Kate's eyes on me. "You okay?" she asked quietly.

"Of course," I said, trying to sound as upbeat as I could. "Why wouldn't I be?"

"Oh no reason, you just seem distracted," she said, still trying to get me to look at her.

"Why would you say that?" I asked, trying to sound care-free, intent on my work.

"Well, because you're supposed to be working on the seasonal menu right now, remember? We've been talking about it for weeks."

She was right, I'd completely forgotten. We had to come up with a fun and creative menu for the holidays ahead, Halloween especially. Today was supposed to be the day I would start thinking it up.

"You're right. It slipped my mind, you know, with Aaron and everything," I said, taking off my gloves and apron. "I'll be in my office. Let me know if you need any help."

Kate didn't reply, she just looked at me quietly as I left the kitchen and went straight to my office.

I loved my office. It was a small space but I managed to make it comfortable and warm. There was a small desk with the drawers filled with paperwork. The invoices from our suppliers were all stacked neatly, held down by a crystal paperweight. There were notebooks to one side: one was filled with recipe's we were using, the other was an idea notebook where Kate and I would play around with different ingredients or themes for the café.

I had an old leather desk chair that I got on auction. It was a warm tan and was so comfortable. It paired nicely with my oak desk. There was another chair next to the desk for when someone came to talk business. Beside this was my favorite part of the office, a large pullout couch and a coffee table. The couch was my first purchase when I was still a struggling hotel cook. It was cream colored and had several blankets and pillows over it. It was cozy looking. You wouldn't even think you were in an office just looking at the couch.

I went to my desk and pulled out the ideas notebook, picked up a pen, and tried to get to work. I don't know how long I'd been staring at that blank piece of paper when I heard a light knock on the door.

"Come in," I said, straightening up in my chair. It was Kate.

"How's it going?" she asked as she walked in.

"It's going..." Before I could finish the sentence, Kate was looking over my shoulder at the blank piece of paper in front of me.

"Are you sure you're alright?" Kate asked again. I could sense the concern in her tone.

"I..." I gulped. "I don't know," I said honestly.

"I'm ready to listen if you need it. Why don't you tell me what happened?" Kate was the first person who had asked so sincerely. I realized how much I trusted her and how much I had to talk to someone about everything that had happened to me. I decided to tell her everything.

"I'd liked Tyler for so long, last night was going to be the night I told him how I felt and Sarah knew all about it. I dressed up, I wasn't myself. All I wanted was to impress him, get him to like me. I actually thought I had a chance. Then I saw them, Sarah and Tyler. They were hanging out on the balcony talking about me, about how Tyler wasn't interested and how Sarah was gonna be the one to break it to me, I felt so humiliated," the tears were welling up in my eyes by then and Kate had sat down on the chair in front of my desk. She reached out a hand and held mine in hers.

"Then this morning, I walked in on them at a café downtown. They've been going out for a month! My best friend and Tyler Perkins!" I could hear Kate hiss as I said that, but she didn't interrupt me. "It was a stupid thing to do and I don't know how to get out of it, but I lied to them. I told them I was dating Conrad, that we were in love. Thankfully, Conrad went along with it. We fooled them.

"And just now, before Conrad dropped me off, he told

me he needed a favor. He told me he needed someone to pretend to be his fiancée in front of his grandfather and he asked if I would do it. He said he'd help me keep up the lie with Sarah if I'd help convince his grandfather who might just be dying. And it all sounds so crazy and I don't know what to do!"

I had buried my head in my hands again, confused and distressed. Kate just stroked my hand.

"Do you want my advice?" Kate asked. I nodded, saying, "Yes, please. I need someone else's thoughts on this because it all seems so impossible to me."

"I think that Sarah is an asshole for doing that and you should reconsider your continued relationship with her. I also think that what Conrad is offering doesn't sound too bad, although it is a bit crazy. People pretend to be in love everyday, at least this way you won't be hurting anybody and you can put an old man's mind at ease," she said. I was a bit surprised that Kate thought it made sense. It made me think that the situation might not be as hopeless as I thought it was.

"I also think you're going to make better decisions if you sleep on it, fix yourself up, get some food into your system. You haven't eaten since you got here."

"Oh, I forgot," I said. No wonder I was feeling woozy.

"I'll order you some food so you can clear your head. It won't hurt to consider his offer, Ell," Kate said, stepping out.

Our talk made me feel better. I didn't feel so alone or hopeless anymore. I decided to take a nap as I waited for the food Kate promised.

～

THE HOUSE WAS UNUSUALLY QUIET. Even though I was used to a quiet home, there were always other noises as Aaron went around the house. I was intent on my night-time routine, applying some cream to my face, when my phone suddenly beeped. I jumped at the noise.

I wiped my hands on a wash towel and picked up my phone. It was a text from Sarah. I read the text. It was a long one:

> Hey, watsup? I had no idea bout u and Conrad. I can hardly beliv it! I ges everything turnd out 4 the best. Tyler and I were thinkin it wud be a fun idea to go on a doble d8 w/ u guys. Lets catch up n have dinner! Im so glad my bestie has sum1! Txt me soon Ell, luv ya!

I had no idea how to respond. At first I started to say that it was all a mistake, that I had lied, that Conrad and I were not together.

But then I remembered her pitying look at the café this morning. I re-read the text and finally saw how fake and superficial it was. If this was Sarah's game, I might as well play it and see where it went. I couldn't just admit defeat now.

I replied:

> Sure, wuld love to go on a doble d8 with you and Tyler. Will tell Conrad about it and set it up. See U soon.

After I sent the message, the next thing I did was dial Conrad's number. He answered on the first ring, without even a hello.

"I'm on my way over, Ell."

8

TERMS AND CONDITIONS (AND THE FINE PRINT)

CONRAD

AFTER I DROPPED Ellie off at the bakery, I spent the rest of the day trying to get my head clear. I thought it was time I took care of business and got back to being productive. I drove to the YoungTech offices in LA. We had a few locations in California, including one in Silicon Valley but it had all started here in LA.

I checked on the place and talked with some of my directors. Most of them were hired as the company grew but some, like Aaron, were people I'd known since school. One of them was Jordan Hartford. He was a year younger than Aaron and me, but he was a good businessman with a good head on his shoulders. He and Aaron had basically been running YoungTech while I was gone.

He took me on a short tour of the changes in the office layout and introduced me to some more key people. We then went to lunch and talked about business some more. Even though I'd been on my 2 year hiatus, I still stayed in constant contact with Jordan, and Aaron and I still had a good handle on how things were running—but I had to admit it felt good to see the place again. It was a substantial business, something I'd really *made*.

I'd known Jordan for almost as long as I knew Aaron, but my friendship with Jordan revolved around business ideas and marketing plans. It was more of an intellectual connection based on shared interests rather than anything personal or even fun. Jordan was a bit of a stick in the mud, but he was very reliable.

Throughout all this, scenes from last night and this morning kept creeping back to the forefront of my mind. Ellie, always Ellie, the answer to my problems. I would never have considered it if she hadn't put the idea in my mind. *Who else could play the perfect fiancée?* She was beautiful, smart, independent, and best of all, William already knew her and liked her.

Plus, Ellie was definitely an attractive girl and I had to admit I was curious to know more about her. I was also very curious to know what it would be like to actually be with her, even if it was just temporary. As Jordan droned on and on about analytics and software, my mind wandered and constantly found its way back to Ellie.

It was nearly sunset when I left the office. I'd called the hospital ahead of time to see if there were any updates on William's condition and they had said he was fine. I informed them that I was on my way. William had called me early in the morning and I'd almost panicked. I thought something bad had happened, but it turned out that he just wanted to check on me.

"Did you enjoy yourself Conrad?" he'd asked. I could sense he was a bit breathless as he spoke. "Was it a fun night?"

"Yes, grandfather, it was fun. I got to hang out with Aaron and met some of the new people who work at Young-Tech. I also caught up with some old school friends."

"Ah that's good. You need friends," he'd said, then he coughed. I was worried.

"Are you sure you're alright?" I asked him. "I'll be right there after we drop Aaron off at the airport."

"No, no," he protested. "This is nothing, just a catch in my throat. I just need some rest. Enjoy your day. And say hello to your fiancée for me."

My heart sank a little as I recalled the conversation from earlier. It was harder and harder to find a way out of the situation. But what had happened with Ellie, though I know it was devastating for her, was a blessing for me. It was an easy and simple way out of a very complicated situation.

I was already headed to Malibu when my phone rang. I was surprised it was Ellie.

"Hey," I answered. "I'm on my way over." There was some confused silence on the other end making me think it might have been an accidental butt-dial situation. I was about to say something when she finally replied.

"What makes you think that I need you to come over?"

"I just know that you'd never call me unless it was an emergency or if you butt-dialed me, and since I can now safely assume that this call was intentional, I'd rather talk about important matters in person."

I could hear her laughing through the phone. I was impressed that she was still so light-hearted even after everything that'd happened. "Alright Conrad, I'll wait for you I guess," she said before she hung up. I immediately called the hospital and told the nurse in charge that I might be arriving later than expected. They informed me that this was fine.

And just because I couldn't resist, I told the nurse to tell my grandfather that I was out with my fiancée, if he asked that is. At least he wouldn't worry so much, and he'd probably even be happy to hear that.

I ended the call and took a turn, heading back to Ellie's home.

I WATCHED Ellie pacing nervously in the kitchen as I sat sipping a late night coffee. Other than the compulsory greetings, she hadn't said a word. I waited for her to say something—it was her decision after all.

She seemed to be gathering her courage and finally took a seat in front of me. Her eyes were still a bit puffy from earlier but it was her lips that seemed to draw my eyes. She had such luscious lips and seeing her with no makeup made her lips look so much softer.

"I just want to make one thing clear," she said. "You are the last person on my list of possible fake boyfriends. Actually, scratch that, you're not on the list at all. Don't let it get to your head." She was biting her fingernails by then and driving me to distraction. I decided to look away and politely waited for her to go on.

"You just happened to be in the wrong place at the wrong time when all the shit hit the fan," she continued. "Sarah knows the both of us and what was said was said, which means I can't exactly ask someone else to be my fake boyfriend."

I laughed at this. She said it like it was a death sentence. "I have to admit, Ellie, this situation is far from ideal. You're not really my first choice to be a fake fiancée either, but here we are."

She seemed to take this well. I think if I'd said something less casual, or actually said what I felt, she would have run for the woods.

"Okay. But before we do any of this we have to set some ground rules, okay?" she said. "This can get very complicated and we need to have clear agreements on what is and what isn't expected."

I had to hand it to her, she was thinking like a real businesswoman. I just nodded. "What do you have in mind?"

"Well, first of all, if we agree to create this fake relationship then both parties have to get something from the arrangement somehow. It has to be a mutually beneficial relationship. If one party finds that the fake relationship is no longer beneficial to them, they have a right to end things immediately. Is this agreed?"

I paused and thought. Ellie was really treating this like a business venture and I didn't know if I was comfortable with that. I felt like I had more on the line.

"What exactly do you mean by benefits?" I asked.

"Well, for example, our situation right now. You need a fake fiancée and I need a fake boyfriend, so pretending to be in a fake relationship is something that could benefit both of us. But what if a time comes when I don't need a fake boyfriend anymore but you still want to keep up the charade? Then I should have the right to say no."

She had a point. A fake boyfriend was much easier to ditch than a fake fiancée, and ultimately I'd have a lot more to answer for. I almost didn't dare, but I had to ask her.

"What if...I paid you for your services as a fake fiancée? Wouldn't that count as a benefit for you?"

I could see the color drain from her face and then slowly turn red. I knew she would misunderstand. Before I could explain what I meant she exploded.

"What do you take me for Conrad Young? Do you really think I would stoop so low and sell my...my services just like that?"

I got up and took a step back, wary of her anger. "Ellie, please calm down, I didn't mean it in any inappropriate way. I understand your point. For now, this fake relationship is going to benefit both of us but when the time comes that I still need a fake fiancée and you don't, then I think I should compensate you for your time."

I could see her starting to calm herself so I went on. "You're a business owner, can't you consider it like a side hustle? Plus you'd be helping out a friend."

I was actually quite surprised that she didn't immediately speak up and say we weren't friends, not ever. "I know it probably comes from good intentions Conrad but that is one of the stupidest, most insensitive things you've said to me today. I refuse to be paid for any of this."

"I understand, but if you change your mind in the future, I want you to know I'm keeping the offer on the table." I could see her roll her eyes and I had to smile. She stepped out of the kitchen and I could hear her rummaging around in the next room. She came back out with a small notebook and pen.

"I think it would be a good idea to write this down, just so we can make sure we're on the same page and no one gets confused about this in the future." She set the little notebook in front of me and sat on a chair next to mine. I caught her scent again. No perfume this time, but still intoxicating.

She scribbled down rule number one and I insisted on adding the clause that if, and only if, she agreed, I would compensate her for any time she spent pretending to be my fake fiancée.

"Okay, moving on," she said. "Rule number two is, Aaron cannot know about any of this." I was a bit surprised. The first person I thought of telling was Aaron. I thought we'd have a good laugh about it.

"Why do you think that?" I asked.

"Are you kidding? Aaron would freak out. He's always been a protective brother and he thinks it's his duty to fight for my honor or something. That's why I never dared tell him about Tyler," she said. "I know you guys are friends, and that's actually just gonna make it worse. Anyway, I'm not comfortable thinking of you talking about me with my own brother, okay? And even less comfortable talking to him about my relationships, even the fake ones. If we can keep him out of it, which is pretty easy since he's not even in the country, then we should."

I nodded. "Aaron already knows about my past relationships and...you're right it would be too weird seeing as you're his sister. I agree with that rule."

She wrote down rule number two. "Okay next," she cleared her throat before she continued. "No kissing or PDA."

The thought of kissing her suddenly made my heart race but I didn't let it show. "That's not possible," was all I could say. She looked at me questioningly so I went on.

"We're pretending to be a couple in the throes of passionate love, no one would believe us if we didn't at least kiss or hold hands," I said. "Of course holding hands won't be a problem, it's basically a long handshake, but I promise we'll only kiss when absolutely necessary."

She let out a sigh. "Fine, you do have a point, but only when *absolutely* necessary, okay?" Then we got into a 15 minute discussion about what "absolutely necessary" meant. She stipulated that it meant: being toasted for our engagement, when William specifically asked for us to kiss, or if Sarah and Tyler started questioning the fake relationship. I tried to convince her that the rules should be a bit more general and flexible but she wouldn't listen.

"Okay, rule number four, no sex. We can talk about it like we do it, or pretend that we've had it but absolutely no sex," she said solemnly. I didn't answer and just slowly shook my head.

I could see her cheeks starting to turn deep red. "Conrad! You can't possibly think..." I laughed before she could finish. I loved how innocent Ellie sometimes seemed. She was really a breath of fresh air.

"I'm just joking. No sex. Do you have anything else in mind?"

She looked a bit unsure before she finally spoke up. "No pet names, no comments about my weight, no jokes about my body."

I could tell it was hard for her to say all that. I remembered her words, from last night and this morning. I had no idea my adolescent teasing had such a devastating effect on her self-esteem. I made no jokes this time.

"No pet names, no comments, and no jokes." She seemed taken aback by my simple and sincere answer. "Good," she said. "That's it I guess."

She started capping the pen but I stopped her. "I do have one rule Ellie, just one." She uncapped the pen and waited. "No personal histories," I said. Playing lovers could lead to awkward questions and I didn't want to have to explain later on.

She looked like she was about to say something but I stopped her. "No personal histories," I reiterated. She seemed satisfied with that and simply wrote it down. Then I could see her drawing two lines on the paper. "Your name and signature," she said, indicating one of the lines. I smiled and signed my name and handed it back to her. I watched her sign and write her name down on the other line. She then ripped out the page and neatly folded it.

"I'm going to keep this safe and we'll go through it whenever we have disagreements, okay?" She then extended her hand toward me and said, "Looking forward to our partnership, Mr. Young."

I shook her hand firmly. "To our partnership, Miss Rodriguez."

I don't know why I did it but I found myself holding her

hand just a little too long. When she started pulling her hand away, our eyes met and held for a little while. I suddenly realized what I was doing and let her go. She seemed a bit uncomfortable but she appeared to just shake it off.

I could sense that no matter how detailed our 'contract' was, things would never be the same for me and Ellie.

"To business, then," she said, pulling her phone out from her pocket. She handed it to me. "It's a text from Sarah," she said.

I read the text and was immediately angry. Of all the callous assholes in the world, why did Ellie have to be friends with the biggest one? When you hurt someone whom you consider a friend, even if there was no malicious intent, you would at least be a little ashamed and be sensitive to that friend's feelings, no?

Sarah was just going on as if she'd done nothing wrong, as if she hadn't just done a number on her own best friend. I gripped the phone a bit hard and I knew that if Sarah was standing in front of me right now, I would probably throw the phone at her face or at least shout at her.

I controlled my anger and handed the phone back to Ellie. "This sounds about right. You can tell Sarah that I'll take care of the details," I said, making sure my voice didn't give away the annoyance and protectiveness I felt.

"And also," I added, as if as an afterthought. "You'll be meeting my grandfather tomorrow." I was expecting her to protest but she just nodded. I continued. "I'll pick you up at the bakery around 10?"

"Sure." I don't know what happened to Ellie but she seemed more demure. She yawned. I could clearly see the outlines of her body as she stretched. I couldn't help wondering how she felt under that shirt.

"I think it's time to turn in, Conrad. Thanks for coming

right away," she said, smiling almost to herself. Meanwhile, I was fighting all sorts of urges. She walked me to the door and we said another awkward goodbye.

Under different circumstances that would have been the perfect time to lean in for a kiss, but I wasn't crazy enough for that. Not yet anyway.

$$\sim$$

SHE WAS SITTING across from him, caramel skin glowing. Long, reddish brown hair framed her face and covered her breasts. Her legs were crossed but it was evident she was wearing nothing. Her supple lips were half parted and her eyes beckoning. He couldn't stop himself.

He pushed the clutter off the table and climbed over it, locking his lips to hers and breathing in her intoxicating scent. She opened her lips to him and he groaned, all the pent up, stifled emotions he'd felt for her suddenly gushing out.

That kiss sent him to another dimension. He was surrounded by her, her softness, the wet warmth of her mouth, her scent. His senses went into overdrive. His hands started to explore her body, her soft, voluptuous breasts, her silky skin. He reached down and touched her thigh, seeking that throbbing, wet sex that he could only dream of.

Before he knew it, she was gone. He opened his eyes and she was standing before him, fully clothed in a big T-shirt and cutoffs looking accusingly at him. She was unfolding a small piece of paper she had taken from her pocket.

"That's why we had to write this down," she said, looking very annoyed. "It is stipulated in the agreement that no physical manifestations of your feeling for me are permissible beyond kissing and holding hands. You have violated the said agreement Mr. Young and now you must suffer the repercussions," she said in an overly business-like tone.

The scene changed before his eyes and he felt himself being held down with straps. His clothes, or whatever it was he had been wearing before, were replaced by leather briefs that only made his erection painfully obvious.

He looked up to see her suddenly clad all in leather, too. She wore a black leather corset and her breasts looked like they were about to overflow from them. Beneath this she wore a black thong and thigh high boots, and she held a whip.

"You've been a bad boy, Conrad," she said, walking sensually toward him. He watched her lick the handle of the whip and he groaned. This was when he noticed he was gagged. He started to panic, but it was not fear, or at least not entirely. The tight leather briefs constricted his throbbing member and he was begging for release, but she just chuckled.

He was splayed out in some sort of contraption and he couldn't move. He was painfully aware that every inch of his body was open to her, vulnerable. She cracked the whip as she came closer and he flinched. She touched the whip to his face and slowly dragged the handle down to his neck, then his chest, lingering for a few moments on his nipples. His body arched, longing for her touch.

She came closer and brought her lips to his ears. He could feel her hot breath against his neck. "You've been such a bad boy," she whispered, and he felt her finger trailing down, down, down. Her fingers locked on his throbbing member, warm then hot. He could no longer control himself and he came, exploding in a euphoric frenzy.

∾

I SUDDENLY SAT bolt upright in bed, immediately aware of the wetness that was familiar and known, yet something I had not experienced as an adult.

The dream came back. *Yup, this will definitely complicate things in the future.*

9

INTRODUCTIONS

CONRAD

I WAS UP EARLY that morning. In fact I had a rather troubling night, but that's for another day. For now, I had to focus on how I could convince William that Ellie and I had been dating for a year and that Ellie would soon be my fiancée.

I was a little nervous for today given my...complicated feelings for Ellie, but there was no time to dwell on any of this. I had stopped briefly at the hospital before heading home and all William wanted to know was how my love life was going. I evaded his questions but it was pretty hard given that he was overly enthusiastic at finally meeting the mystery girl. I also wanted to have enough time for Ellie and me to get our stories straight before presenting ourselves as a couple in love to my grandfather.

I knew Ellie probably went to work early—most bakery owners are already at work at daybreak—but I also didn't want to seem too eager if I showed up before they opened. I decided somewhere around 9am would be a reasonable time. I spent the rest of the morning running scenarios in my mind. What possible questions might William ask? What was the most believable storyline for us?

I was still thinking about this when I finally pulled up to

the bakery. There were some customers waiting around but it wasn't as busy as it was the other day. As I walked in I saw the woman I had seen at Aaron's party, Ellie's assistant chef. She was flanked by two other servers who were busy putting pastries and donuts into little pink boxes.

"Hey," she said as she waved to me from across the room over a few customer's shoulders. "You're early. Ellie said you might be coming over."

She was a tall girl with a pleasant and friendly face. I didn't have a chance to really see her at the party and I studied her now. Her orange-red hair was tied in a messy bun and she had striking green eyes. She seemed kind and trustworthy. I immediately took a liking to her.

"Kate, right?" I asked. "Is Ellie already in?" I went on, knowing that she probably was.

"Yes, she's in her office. I'll go get her for you," she said as she stepped out of the counter area and headed to a door at the back of the bakery. I stood around a bit and looked around. This was the first time I'd been inside Ellie's Sweet Haven, and I had to be honest, I was very impressed.

It was a small building but it had a very welcoming ambiance. No stern metal countertops and minimalist décor; everything looked like it had history. From the wide, comfy chairs and cushioned stools, to the wooden counter-tops, it all looked like it came from a loving home. It was a comforting and comfortable place to be in. The décor was very consistent with the name: this place did feel like a sweet haven.

Not ten minutes had passed when I saw the two women emerging from Ellie's office. I didn't really understand how I got to this position but every time I saw Ellie again I felt a lump in my throat. She looked lovely.

She was wearing a simple, flowy cream colored cotton dress with lace accents on the hem and a belt that hinted at, but didn't exactly show off, her figure. It was simple and wholesome and she looked beautiful with her wavy hair down. She looked like the perfect girl to present to William. I couldn't help but smile.

"What?" Ellie asked, looking at me with some suspicion.

"Nothing," I said. "You just look...perfect."

"Okay," she said, still looking at me, disbelieving. "That reminds me, I think we should bring some sweets for William! What do you think he'll like?"

"No, that's okay. He gets all the food he needs at the hospital," I said, not wanting to put her through the trouble.

"Are you seriously comparing my food to hospital food? Are you deliberately trying to ruin this day?" she said.

"I meant no offense. If it really means that much to you, by all means," I said quickly.

"Well, I am your bakery-owner fiancée, the least we can do is bring him some cakes or something. Oh, I remember that your grandpa used to love peach jam. We have a great upside down peach cake I'm sure he'll love, and it's low in fat and sugar too!" she said excitedly, turning to the servers and telling them to get a mini cake from the display. It looked gorgeous, with slices of caramelized peaches at the top and some piped frosting. The server then placed it in a box and started tying a bow around it.

"Now go and pick out stuff he likes," she said. I obediently looked at their display and saw some great looking danish pastries I was sure William would love, including some cinnamon rolls and macarons. Kate took the ones I chose and packed them in a slightly bigger box and handed it to me. Ellie then pulled her to the side.

"The O'Donnel cake is going to be picked up at four and it just needs finishing touches. I made the base and the second tier separately so you can just stack them when they come to pick it up..." she said to Kate. She was writing things down, talking quickly. "The cupcakes for the venue party tomorrow need to be iced and the edible pearls are going to be delivered at lunch, so you need to prioritize those. And please check the orders we made to our suppliers, they said they were going to be a bit delayed but I need to know when exactly."

Kate was nodding her head as she looked over Ellie's shoulder. Ellie seemed as if she was about to say more but Kate snatched up the piece of paper before she could go on.

"I got this Ellie, don't worry about it," Kate said. "We went over it the minute I walked in first thing in the morning and then went over it again when we had coffee. Just go and have fun."

Ellie looked at Kate, smiling. I could tell that Kate was reliable and that Ellie was also a bit of a perfectionist. "Thanks, you are a God-send," she said.

"Don't you forget it," Kate said as she ushered Ellie forward. Kate then turned to me and said, "You take care of her okay?" She said it in such a friendly way and yet I couldn't help but sense a hint of warning in her words. I waved at her and opened the door for Ellie as we stepped out.

I STARTED PULLING out of the parking area while Ellie busied herself putting the pastries away. Her presence in my car, with the idea that she was my fiancée, was driving me to distraction. And she was wearing her perfume again. *God help me.*

"So..." I said, starting a conversation to ease my discomfort. "Have you known Kate long?"

"Yes, we're very close. She's one of the few people I consider a true friend right now," she said, without a hint of sadness. I was glad she was getting over the whole affair with Sarah. If I was in her shoes I'd still be fuming.

"So you tell her everything?" I asked.

"Basically," she replied.

"So does she happen to know about our little...arrangement?"

Ellie smiled a little guiltily. "I was just so alone and Kate was so nice that I told her. She was actually pretty supportive about the whole idea. She told me it wasn't such a bad offer. She's the only person who knows."

"She's a sensible girl. Have you had her with you long? What's it like working with her?" I asked, just trying to fill up the awkward silence.

Ellie didn't answer right away and I noticed her looking at me funny. "Why are you interested? Do you like Kate?" she asked, a hint of annoyance in her voice.

I had to laugh. *Oh Ellie, if you only knew.* "It's not that at all," I said defensively. "You just said she's a good friend of yours and I want to know more about her. And even if I did find her attractive, what's it to you?"

She turned red and looked away. "I don't care if you like her, it's just that she's my employee and we have this arrangement. I don't want this to get even more tangled up."

"I promise, I'm not interested in her in that way. I just want to know more about you. For example, how you came into owning your own baker."

She seemed satisfied with that and settled in again. "Well, as you can probably remember, I was an assistant pastry chef at the Pacific Shores LA. I really thought it was going somewhere, I mean I learned a lot and I was working with a Michelin star chef. But it turned out that they saw me as nothing more than an assistant line cook. I overheard my boss—not the famous one, the one in-charge of our station —saying that I had a long way to go and he didn't see me being in charge for a long, long time. His words," she said, hanging her head a little.

"I told my family and they encouraged me to get the hell out of there. I had an idea that it could be a bit cut-throat in the culinary industry and I realized that I probably would go nowhere in that position. I wasn't getting along with my boss at that time and I felt like he was biased against me. When I found out that a newer, more obedient, fellow assistant pastry chef got the promotion, I quit. Aaron and my parents helped get me a loan and I started my business, and I haven't looked back since."

"It must have been hard, starting your own business," I said, prompting her to tell me more.

"Well, the first thing I felt was freedom. Before I even tried to imagine what it was like to run a bakery I knew I had to come up with good food. I spent a couple of months trying out new recipes, making all sorts of desserts and pastries. When I was finally confident about my menu, I got the loan, rented a space, and started cooking. My artisanal line of croissants and bagels got really popular and more people started coming in and trying more of my food. After around a month I think, we had queues going half a block and I realized I needed help." She smiled.

"Gosh it was work. I would wake up at three in the morning because I was short on help and had to stay at the bakery until past 10pm. I started posting ads and putting up flyers looking for an assistant chef. I went through a few hiring nightmares but luckily, five months ago, Kate walked in with her big smile and her flaming red hair, and I imme-diately felt like she belonged there."

"What do you mean hiring nightmare?"

"Well, there was this one girl who'd just finished pastry school. She would get to the bakery just a few minutes before opening, did the bare minimum, and kept asking me if she could try her new recipes, which was all well and good if she at least helped out with the regular work. Then another girl who'd been a line cook before. In her first week her boyfriend comes bursting through the door on her day-off demanding to see her. I thought it was an abusive relationship and told him off. When she found out, she cussed me out and quit.

"Kate couldn't have walked through that door sooner. When I interviewed her I could see how passionate she was and we found out we got along. She's been such a big help. I'm so glad I got her. That girl saved my life and my business."

"She does seem great," I replied. "But how does she know me again?"

"What do you mean?"

"Well, when we met at the party she looked ready to attack me but when she found out who I was, she smiled and said it was good to finally put a face to the name. I figured she knew about me already."

"Well she's been working at the bakery for almost half a year and Aaron would come up to visit or have coffee. She's probably heard him talk about you, and of course I might have mentioned you a few times."

"So you talk to her about me," I said, teasing her.

"Oh yeah, she knows everything, especially about how big of a pain in the ass you are."

I looked at her through the corner of my eye to see if she was joking but from what I could see, she was dead serious. I know that it was probably my fault she felt that way sometimes but I was determined to change her mind about me. I decided to change the subject.

"So, we should probably get our stories straight, huh?" I said. Ellie just nodded so I went on. "As you know, William is my only parental figure since I lost my parents when I was fifteen. He's been a rock in my life and I don't where I'd be without him. Two weeks ago William collapsed and the doctors can't seem to find out what's wrong with him. Honestly, I'm preparing myself for the worst."

I could see Ellie looking at me with some concern. I just smiled, trying to lighten the situation. "But William is strong and stubborn so I'm still pretty positive he'll pull through. Anyway, with everything that's going on, he's a little obsessed with my personal life. He wants me to have someone and he keeps on worrying about me being lonely and stuff, hence the lie. Last night, he kept asking about you again and I told him we would come meet him today. He doesn't really know who my fiancée is yet and I'm hoping we can come off as natural to him later. I don't want him to get suspicious and start worrying again."

"I was thinking about this," she replied thoughtfully. "You should probably tell me every detail of the lie you told. I don't want to end up telling him details that don't line up with what you've already told him."

"Okay, well I didn't give him a lot of details because, well I didn't have any yet. All I told him was that we've been dating for a year and that I'm planning to propose. That's why I thought you'd be a great fit as a fake fiancée. We already have some history and you already know the basics so we should be all good."

"Well, we should at least get our stories straight about how we ended up dating as well as our first date. I think he might ask a few questions about that." I could tell she'd probably been thinking about this, too.

I drove on, thinking of the most believable way that Ellie and I could have fallen in love. *Well, when it comes to lies, half-truths are always the best option.*

"I think, on my end, I could say that I've always liked you and thought you were attractive, I was just too afraid to ask you out because your brother is my best friend and I didn't know how you'd react since you never really liked me when we were younger," I said, feeling a bit guilty. I was still about to get to the lie part. Ellie stayed quiet so I went on.

"Then we can say we got in touch last year and I've been flying to see you now and then. We can say we went out for dinner to talk because you wanted some advice on how to open a new business and it started from there. I asked you out again and you said yes, and by the date we developed feelings for one another." I noticed that Ellie was smiling.

"Okay, so where did you take me on our first date?"

"Well, I took you for dinner at the Chateau Marmont. You were wearing a sexy silver dress and I just saw you and thought, I want to keep this woman in my life. We had dinner and had a great time."

She laughed. "Please don't remind me of that chrome dress! I want that memory to be buried," she said, but she was smiling. "When did we finally become official?"

"We'd been dating for a while, though technically not really dating. They were just friendly dinners at first but I ended up falling for you. We were walking down Santa Monica Pier on our fifth date and we watched the sunset. I looked at you and couldn't help myself. Your hair was glowing with the sun setting behind you and I came closer, staring into your eyes. I leaned over and kissed you, and the rest is history."

She was so quiet after I spoke that I got worried. Had I offended her somehow? I looked at her and noticed that she was blushing. Not the bright red kind when she was angry, but a soft pink. Her hands were clenched and turning red. I cleared my throat and she seemed to snap out of it.

"That sounds...um...that sounds fine."

We rode in awkward silence for the rest of the trip.

WE GOT to William's VIP room without another word exchanged between us, each carrying a small box of pastries. I didn't know what Ellie was thinking but I was also a little tense at the prospect of being grilled by William in a few minutes.

From across the hallway I could see William pacing across his room. I rushed in, worried.

"What are you doing up? You should be in bed, the doctor said you were still weak!"

"Conrad, my boy! Don't be such a killjoy, I feel great! And you're looking so much better. Now where is she?" William exclaimed the minute he saw me. "There she is," he said. When he finally got a good look at Ellie there was a look of confusion on his face.

"You look familiar," he said as Ellie came closer, looking like a picture in her cream dress.

"William. Grandfather... This is my fiancée, Eleanor Rodriguez," I said, holding a hand out to Ellie. She took my hand and smiled shyly at my grandfather.

"Is this Aaron's sister? I thought I knew you. The last time we met, you were just a teenager, and now here you are!"

"I'm so happy to see you again, Mr. Young. We brought you some pastries from my bakery," Ellie said, smiling beautifully.

"I've heard so much about you and Aaron. You've always been so good to Conrad. Your family has been so good to him over the years," William said as he took the boxes. He opened them and seemed delighted. "These look delicious! No wonder you have your own bakery, these are mouth watering," he said as he took one out and tasted it. "Absolutely delightful, thank you so much my dear."

I was about to ask more questions about his condition when Dr. Monroe suddenly arrived. "Ah, Mr. Young, so glad that you've arrived. There's been some progress in your grandfather's condition." He was followed by a younger doctor holding some papers. Dr. Monroe reached out a hand and the papers were wordlessly passed on to him.

"William's recent tests have been very promising and I can confidently say he's well enough to go home," he said with a smile. "Of course, no stress and strenuous activities, but other than that he's fit as a fiddle."

My brows furrowed from the sudden influx of information, but William was absolutely beaming. "That's great news, Doctor! I feel fit as a fiddle," he said. "I told you there was no reason to worry," he added, turning to me.

Ellie was beaming too, but I was very suspicious. This was all very irregular. Two weeks of not knowing if he was going to survive then suddenly, he was healthy and well again. I was glad my grandfather was coming home but things were not adding up.

"Doctor, can I please speak with you privately?" I said, already heading out. Dr. Monroe followed behind.

"I don't understand how you can think it's safe for my grandfather to be going home when not two days ago you couldn't even figure out what was wrong with him. Hell, you were telling me to prepare for any eventuality. I need you to help me make sense of this," I demanded.

Dr. Monroe, unfazed, simply held up the papers in his hand. "I just received the latest results in William's tests and they look very good. He is perfectly healthy for a man his age. I can assure you, Mr. Young, that your grandfather is safe to go home."

"I find that very hard to believe after our last conversation. You were basically telling me to prepare for goodbyes."

He put an arm on my shoulder in a very condescending

manner. "It must be a miracle," he said, raising his hands to heaven. Before I could protest at how preposterous that was, he was gone, his aide following on his heels.

This was all very suspicious, and knowing my grandfather, there was definitely more to this than was being let on. Was this just a giant joke? Well, there was only one way to find out. I grit my teeth and walked back into William's room.

William was so happy and energetic that I knew what the doctor said was probably true. But I was going to get to the bottom of this whole thing.

"Ah Conrad. Have you finished interrogating my doctor?" he said, practically beaming.

"Can you blame me? I've been worried sick about you."

"Well, no need to worry, I feel great! This is a new lease on life and I think we should celebrate, how does that sound?" I cocked an eyebrow at his suspicious enthusiasm.

"I'm going to throw a party at the manor and invite all my old friends. It'll be a blast!" he said, grinning from ear to ear. He turned toward Ellie and took her hand. "And of course you'll come my dear, won't you?" he said, oozing charm.

Ellie turned to me, unsure. I could only nod. Refusing would only disappoint William and I was sure he would do anything to get his way in the end.

"Of course, how could I not?" Ellie replied. "When is the party?"

"Tonight."

10

INVITATIONS

CONRAD

I COULD SEE Ellie falter at that. Her eyes widened and she looked to me for help. I didn't know what to say. Ellie looked at my grandfather and started to stammer. "Tonight? I'm not so sure about that, it's very short notice..."

"Nonsense," William said, brushing away her hesitation and putting a hand on her shoulder. "It'll be splendid. And you won't have to worry about any of it. I know girls like to take their time choosing outfits and getting ready for big parties, but I'm sure Conrad can get everything ready for you in no time. Isn't that right, Conrad?"

I was dumbfounded. William had suddenly taken the reins on how this day was going to be and was now galloping off at full speed. So much for the sick old gentleman I was expecting to find. All I could do was agree.

"Of course, it won't be a problem, Ellie. I'll take care of it."

"Good," William said, turning to me this time. "Now why don't you go ahead and process my papers so we can get out of here? I'm sick of this place, figuratively speaking."

"Sure, I'll go do that," I said, still reeling from the recent events that were quickly developing before my eyes. "Why don't you join me, Ellie?" I could see the relief in her eyes the moment I said this. She must've been so much more confused than I was. I had to hand it to her, she was holding up like a champ.

William waved at us as we went. The moment we were out of earshot, Ellie let out a small squeak.

"What the hell are we supposed to do? How are we going to plan and host a party for tonight? It took me weeks to get the details for Aaron's party right and we don't even have 12 hours now! And what am I going to wear? I didn't bring anything and I'm not exactly ready to meet the captains of the industry that will undoubtedly be at this party! Conrad," she said urgently, stopping me in my tracks and facing me. I could see a slight hint of panic in her eyes. "How are we supposed to pull off this fake relationship at a big party for your grandfather? This was supposed to be a nice, quick visit to an old man, but now I'm going to be paraded around half of LA's elite and I don't know what I'm going to do!"

I think I must have chuckled at her distress because she rolled her eyes and sighed.

"Just breathe," I said, rubbing her shoulders. "Relax, we'll figure it out. You don't have to worry about getting ready and finding clothes, I've got that covered. I have a stylist on call who'll take care of you. In fact I'll text them right now."

I pulled out my phone and sent out a message as Ellie looked at me skeptically.

"As for guests, we'll probably just invite a few family friends and grandfather's close friends and business partners. It'll be a small party, I promise," I said, even though I knew that, given William's mood, it was likely to get out of hand.

"And don't worry about convincing everyone. Half of those people don't even know what real love looks like. We already have our stories straight, I'm sure we'll pull this off. The best thing you can be for the party is cool, calm and collected," I said, still massaging her shoulders. I was suddenly painfully aware of the shape of her and the warmth of her skin underneath the thin material. I quickly pulled my hand away.

"Just as a warning though," I said, teasing. "We might have to kiss a lot in front of everyone so I recommend a mint or maybe a tic tac?"

"Stop that, you're not helping," she said, obviously stressed.

"I'm joking, we'll just go with our story, okay? We've always fought as kids and when we got back in touch, things were a lot different and we fell in love," I said, trying to placate her.

"But who fell in love first?" she asked, smiling a little.

"Me, of course," I volunteered, knowing it was the most believable way to get around it. I knew for a fact that Ellie wouldn't fall for me if I wasn't at least a bit persistent, presumably.

"Yeah, I think that's a good idea. It should come out like it was your decision. I don't want people to think I was just nice to you because you got so successful." She said it in a very matter-of-fact way but she had no idea how her words stung me. I noticed how she was looking at me funny.

"What is it?" I asked.

She just shook her head. "It's nothing," she replied, so I let it go.

As we were processing the papers, I still couldn't help but think of William's suspicious and very sudden progress. I must have been out of it because I found Ellie looking at me questioningly.

"Hey, what's bothering you? You can tell me," she said,

sincerely concerned. I took a deep breath and just decided to tell her.

"I don't know, it just seems so sudden. I have so many questions. When I left here the other day, that doctor was telling me there seemed to be no hope, and now, all of a sudden William's well enough to go home. It doesn't make any sense."

"What did the doctor say when you talked to him earlier?"

"He said it must be a miracle and I can't bring myself to be satisfied with that answer."

"Yeah, it is a little suspicious. You're right to have your doubts," she said thoughtfully. Then she turned to me. "But it's still good news, you know. No matter what the reason behind it is, you should just be grateful that your grandfather is fine and healthy and well enough to plan a party. Bad things happen so often you should just be glad when good things come your way. You can stand around worrying all day or you can just accept what the doctor said and flow with it. The doctor is the best person to tell you how William is when it comes to his health. We can just see where things lead and worry about the rest later."

I was a bit taken aback by our exchange. Ellie really had grown up. She was a sensible, beautiful, independent, hard-working businesswoman who didn't expect handouts from anyone. She wasn't the same kid I used to tease and fight with in the past. She had bloomed into her own woman.

"Thanks, I needed to hear that," I said to her. We finished up processing William's papers and headed back to the room.

William had already gotten the nurse to help him pack up his things. He had a twinkle in his eye I had never seen before.

"Are the papers done?" he asked me, obviously impatient to get out of there. I just nodded.

"Well let's get the bags and start planning that party, shall we? Time waits for no man," he said, already on his way out. I picked up his bags and Ellie and I had to run to keep up with him. There was no sign of frailty or old age in his steps. I started questioning his diagnosis again but I remembered Ellie's words. I should just be grateful that my grandfather seemed so well, but I couldn't shake the feeling.

When we got to the car, William sat on the front passenger seat so I opened the backseat door for Ellie. We all settled in and I started driving.

William cleared his throat and started to fidget in his seat, trying to turn around and get a clearer view of Ellie.

"Now my dear, it's time we got to know more about each other. We are the only people in Conrad's life after all," he said, talking over his shoulder.

"Of course, what would you like to know?"

"Well, everything really! What are you up to? Tell me more about being a baker."

Ellie smiled. "I'm a pastry chef actually, but I decided I wanted my own business. I own a bakery in the Strip. It's called Ellie's Sweet Haven. We've been quite successful actually."

I could see Ellie smiling to herself. She was always so happy when she talked about her bakery. "I found out that the trick is simply making good food and offering something that customers won't get anywhere else."

"And what is it that makes your bakery unique, my dear?" William asked.

Without missing a beat, Ellie said, "A slice of home, Mr. Young. Anyone can make a good cake but few places will make you feel as comfortable and welcomed as Ellie's Sweet

Haven. Most of our regulars are people who miss home or are new to the city."

"So young and already running your own business, very impressive. And you did it all on your own?" William went on.

"Well, it wasn't easy and I didn't really do it all on my own. My family was behind me all the way, they helped me get a loan from the bank and come up with a business plan," she said humbly. "It took a lot of hard work and squeezing my brain for inspiration, but I did it, and I am so proud of that place."

I could only smile. I loved how unsure Ellie was in her personal life but how confident she was when it came to her professional life. She was very successful and she had a right to be proud. I looked at her through the rearview mirror. When I caught her eye, I couldn't help myself. I gave her a naughty little wink.

I knew she would be annoyed so I avoided looking at the rearview again, chuckling to myself. That was when I noticed William looking at me mischievously. I cleared my throat and kept my eye on the road from then on.

We arrived at Malibu just before lunch time. We had no time to lose. William got out of the car and was already striding into the mansion, calling to our house manager/personal assistant/events coordinator, Devon Jackson. He was a young communications graduate who I had employed 3 years ago to help William with all his needs. He was a reliable young man and got along well with William.

He was also very resourceful and efficient—after all, he was very well-compensated and had a lot of opportunities to network and grow his clientele for the future.

William whispered in his ear and he immediately called Maria and Sandra, our housekeepers, to come and get the bags and help grandfather up the stairs. He headed straight to me.

"What's this about a party, sir?" he asked confidently, walking in place beside me.

"Yes," I said, "William decided on a whim that we should have a celebration for his miraculous recovery."

"Miraculous indeed. I'll call the caterers and organizers then. I'm sure they'll be eager for a party even at such short notice."

We were already headed into the house and I could see Ellie's jaw drop. The grand staircase and the large crystal chandelier were William's choice and really were stunning. Ellie suddenly clutched my hands.

"Conrad, what is this? What have I gotten myself into?" she asked in a panic.

"It'll be fine, Ellie. Just relax and my assistant will take care of everything," I said, motioning for Devon to come closer.

"Devon, Miss Rodriguez needs help getting ready for the party. Can you ask Elaine to help us out?" Elaine was a stylist friend of Devon's. We knew each other from some past...ventures.

"Of course, sir. I'll give her a call," he said, offering a hand to Ellie.

She hesitantly took it and gave me a pleading look. I tried to reassure her with a smile. "Go on, Ellie, everything's taken care of. You'll be fine."

She followed Devon, who was already on the phone and heading to the second floor.

I watched her disappear into the second floor corridor. When they were gone I realized I was alone. Wondering where William was, I headed to his study. was pretty sure that would be the first place he'd go when he got home. And I was right.

I found him rifling through some papers on his desk. He looked up when he saw me but didn't even slow down what he was doing.

"Ah, Conrad, is Ellie all settled?" he said, putting some papers aside as he spoke, not even looking at me.

"She's doing fine. She's being dolled up as we speak," I said. I couldn't stand pretending like nothing was going on. "I've had enough of this nonsense, William. Tell me what's really going on please."

"What are you talking about?" he answered, picking up more paperwork and looking through the pages.

"Well, your diagnosis for one. From what I can remember there wasn't even one and now you're...healthy as a bull? It makes no sense. And this sudden excitement for a party? What is going on?"

He wouldn't even look me in the eye. "It must have been a miracle."

I couldn't stop myself from slamming a fist on his rosewood desk. "William, stop playing games with me and tell me the truth!"

He finally stopped what he was doing and looked at me solemnly. He took the papers in his hand and straightened them before putting them back into the top drawer.

"I would appreciate it if you took a seat and calmed down, Conrad," he said, straightening himself and looking very much like the businessman he used to be.

I sat down, trying desperately to control my temper. William had always played his little games. He was a sharp businessman and had a way of getting exactly what he wanted, but he had never played games with me...until now.

"I know the past few weeks have been difficult for you, I know you've been through a lot of pain. Being in that hospital again must have reopened some painful memories, seeing me there, not knowing if I'd ever get better again and

I'm sorry if I caused you much unnecessary pain," he said, looking at me tenderly.

"It's not like that, I..." I started to say but William raised a hand to silence me.

"Please let me finish. I know you will be angry once everything is said but I only did it because I do worry about you," he said, a slight tremble in his voice. "I thought that if nothing changed, if you weren't jolted back to your senses, then it might be too late. I didn't want you to become this hardened, isolated man, successful yet so alone.

"I came up with a plan. I wanted you to see the fragility of life. I wanted you to appreciate the unstoppable passing of time. And what better way than to put myself on the line? If there were ever any misunderstandings between us, I always knew one thing was true: that you loved me and would do anything for my peace of mind. I called Dr. Monroe and arranged everything. Of course, I had to pretend to fall over so that Devon and the others would not have any suspicions that they could share with you. When I got to the hospital I told Dr. Monroe my plan and he was hesitant but I eventually convinced him."

He wouldn't look at me as he spoke. My anger was starting to boil and my hands were clenched in fists on my lap. "I'm so sorry, Conrad," he went on. "I know the vague diagnosis and the conversations you had with Dr. Monroe confused and hurt you, but I thought that this was the only way to get you back."

"What are you talking about?" I demanded. "I was never gone, I was always going to come back!"

"Physically maybe," he said, sighing as he spoke. "But emotionally, you were getting farther and farther away. I wanted you to come back to the living, to believe in love again and trust people. I'm sorry for deceiving you, but I'm glad of the outcome."

I was about to explode. The fear and worry of the past few days were exhausting and to find out that it was just an elaborate plan to get me out of my shell was too much. Before I could speak, William had gotten up. He walked around his desk and placed a hand on my shoulder. I took a deep breath, counting in my head to calm myself down.

"Why did you have to lie to me about your health?" I asked through gritted teeth. "You could have just told me you were worried."

"But I did, everyday that you called while you were traveling alone, when you came home on your rare visits. I told you all the time. But my words fell on deaf ears. Everything I said about life and how I couldn't leave this world knowing you would be alone, all of that is still true. I wish I didn't have to lie but I'm sure you'll find it in your heart to forgive me," he said, pausing a little before he continued. "After all, I am not the only one who has lied today."

I looked up at him questioningly. I was about to protest but he held up his hand again. "About Eleanor?" was all he said and my entire body tensed.

"What are you talking about, we..."

"Conrad, please. I practically raised you on my own. Don't you think I'd know when you're lying?" he said, smiling as he went back to sit in his chair. "I knew the moment you mentioned a secret fiancée that you were lying. I've been watching you closely ever since the incident with Jessica. I knew it wasn't possible. To be honest I was quite intrigued to know who would possibly go along with your preposterous lie. I even thought you might hire someone, but seeing you and Ellie today..." he trailed off smiling to himself.

He then got up and walked to an old, ornate cabinet behind his desk. He fiddled with some keys before he finally opened the top drawer.

"This," he said, showing me the small velvet box he was holding. "This was your grandmother's. She gave it to your father when he told us he was about to pop the question and your father gave it to your mother. I think now, it is your turn."

He handed me the box and I quickly opened it. It was a 12 karat emerald, white-gold ring. I knew this ring because I'd seen it in countless photographs growing up. It was my mother's engagement ring.

I felt like I'd been floored. So he knew that I lied and that Ellie wasn't really my fiancée. What I couldn't understand was why he would think it was appropriate to give me my mother's engagement ring.

He chuckled after seeing my confusion. "You might think you're pulling the wool over my eyes, that you're the one lying to everyone in the room but I think that you might find out that the only person you're really lying to is yourself."

I was staring at him, unbelieving, but he only looked at me meaningfully. Was he seriously thinking that I was in love with Ellie?

"You have it all wrong," I said, desperate to clarify things. "Ellie is Aaron's sister, I've known her since she was a kid. And we fight all the time. I don't have those kinds of feelings for her, it would never work," I stated matter-of-factly, trying to convince him of this.

"If you say so," he simply said, still smiling. It was infuriating. "Now, go on ahead and get ready before our guests arrive. Go on."

I started to leave but William held me back. I stopped to look at him and saw that he was holding out the velvet box to me. "It's yours now, I'll have no use for it anyway. And it is yours, rightfully."

I put the box in my pocket and just left, knowing that

William would think what he chose to no matter what I said.

~

I GOT READY, changing into a crisp, new suit for the party. People were starting to arrive. It was expected: no matter how short the notice, nobody wanted to pass up a chance for a party at the Young Manor hosted by William Young himself, no doubt to gawk at his reclusive and eccentric billionaire grandson as well.

I was in awe of William. I could see him greeting his guests and cracking jokes with renewed energy. Most of the guests were William's old friends and their close family. I wasn't very close with any of them and I started scanning the crowd for Ellie. I'd been waiting to talk to her for a while.

As I walked around, feeling a little lost and searching for Ellie, I felt a hand on my shoulder. Thinking it was Ellie, I smiled and turned, excited to see what she looked like. I felt my heart turn to ice when I recognized the face. It was Jessica.

My smile was long gone and my brows furrowed in anger. "What are you doing here?" I asked, it took all my strength to control myself. She had the nerve to smile at me.

"Is this how you greet all your guests?" she asked, laying her hand on my chest. I slapped her hand away. Her wince gave me some satisfaction.

"You shouldn't be here," I said under my breath. "You're not invited."

"Really? And here I was thinking someone just lost my invitation in the mail, so I thought I'd drop in," she said, smiling at me and looking me over. "You look good, Conrad."

I was ready to drag her out of my house when I suddenly felt a hand on my arm. Inexplicably, my anger started to fade away. I turned and saw it was Ellie, looking gorgeous. Her hazel eyes were warm and kind. I felt like nothing could be wrong when eyes like hers looked back at me.

"There you are!" she said, smiling up at me warmly. "I've been looking all over for you."

11

A PARTY AND SOME MEMORIES

ELLIE

"DON'T BE SO TENSE, Miss Rodriquez, just enjoy the night. Elaine will take care of you," Devon said after he introduced me to Elaine and her assistant, Justine. They both wore matching shirts and jackets. They brought large container bags, a wheeled suitcase, and several dresses in garment bags.

When we got to the second floor, Devon immediately asked for my measurements and wrote them down before he got on the phone with Elaine. I was then whisked off to a spare bedroom that was bigger than our living room. There was an intricate carpet on the floor, a seating area, a wide screen TV and an ensuite that had a large bathtub. Conrad's spare bedroom was more opulent than any hotel room I'd ever been in. It was definitely better than the most expensive suite in the hotel I used to work for.

The extent of Conrad's wealthiness was starting to dawn on me and I was a bit intimidated. It was one thing to say someone was a billionaire and another thing to actually see it. I guess it just never hit me that way before because Conrad was always just Conrad. At first, we only knew him as the sad kid Aaron kept inviting over, then as Aaron's annoying best friend, not the successful businessman. He never used to flaunt how wealthy his grandfather was and, although he probably tripled their family's net worth himself, he was never showy about his wealth now.

"So we have a few items you can choose from but I think I have the perfect one right here," Elaine said as she started taking beautiful, shimmering dresses out of the garment bags. I could see Justine taking out makeup brushes, palettes, and other products from a container bag and laying them neatly on the ornate vanity by the large bay window.

"What do you think?" Elaine said. She was holding a beautiful, floor-length, gold gown with a sweetheart neckline and off-shoulder sleeves. It was a soft, flowy material with small rhinestone patterns that were delicate and rippled in the light. I couldn't speak.

"Oh, you don't like it? I think it would be perfect on you," Elaine said, looking a bit disappointed as she turned the gown this way and that.

"No, no, I love it. It's just so beautiful I didn't know what to say," I said, still taken aback. This was way more than I'd bargained for and while it wasn't necessarily a bad thing, it did take some getting used to.

"Great! Why don't you put a robe on and we can start doing your makeup!" Elaine said.

I DIDN'T KNOW how long it had been exactly, but it was quite a while before the makeup artist took a step back, smiled, and said, "I think we're done." The makeup Justine had was 10 times the amount I personally owned at home.

I guess that wasn't much of a comparison since Sarah always complained about how little makeup I owned. I looked at the clock and saw that it was already half-past five. 3 hours had passed.

Elaine came forward, smiling. "That is beautiful, Justine, absolutely gorgeous!" she said, holding the champagne gown. They had placed a towel over the vanity mirror and wouldn't let me look. They asked me if it was okay if they filmed a TikTok and posted my reaction once the whole look was revealed. I agreed. I mean I was getting this makeover for free, I might as well help them with their social media.

Elaine went in first and I followed toward the bathroom. The dress fit perfectly and the moment I had it on, Elaine excitedly led me out.

"You're going to love it!" she said as she held my hand and brought me in front of the small vanity. Justine was holding her phone up, filming my reaction as Elaine took the towel off the mirror.

When I saw my reflection, I gasped. That woman in front of me was absolutely gorgeous. Justine had given me a darker color lip and gold glitter eye-shadow that matched the dress. She had done expert contouring that was sensual, yet natural. Justine managed to enhance my features without it all looking too much. I couldn't speak.

"What is it, what's wrong?" Elaine said, sounding worried. "You don't like it?"

But I was near tears. I had never seen myself look like this before. I looked elegant and sophisticated. And I looked sexy, but not in the obvious way. It was nothing like the chrome dress; it was somehow more alluring.

"No, no!" I said. "It's absolutely beautiful!" I exclaimed, and Elaine breathed a sigh of relief.

"Now, for shoes," she said, opening up the rolling bag they had brought with them. I picked simple, beige, strappy heels that gave me an extra four inches. Elaine and Justine looked on appreciatively as I looked at myself in the mirror again.

"Thank you so much!" I said, turning to them. "You've made me feel like a princess today."

"It was a pleasure working with you, Ellie," Elaine said. "After all, an artist is only as good as their canvas."

They started packing up their things and I turned to the mirror again. I had never looked so good in my life and I couldn't help but feel a little bit like a fraud. I was, after all, just pretending to be Conrad's fiancée, pretending that I belonged to his world.

But I knew I had to snap out of it. I stole another look at myself in the mirror, took a deep breath, and said goodbye to Elaine and Justine.

You can do this, you can do this, I repeated to myself as I opened the door.

The second I stepped out of the room I could tell that the party was already starting. There was music playing, the sound of glasses clinking, and the low din of voices on the first floor. Despite my nervousness, I resolutely headed to where the sounds were coming from. I saw Devon and waved to him. He came straight towards me after excusing himself from the people he was speaking with.

"You look beautiful, Miss Rodriguez. Conrad is probably looking for you," he said as he ushered me toward the large double doors and opened one for me.

The party was in full swing and a lot of people had gathered in the large ballroom where it was being held. I could see William talking animatedly to a small group of people that had surrounded him. Conrad was right, he did not look like he'd ever been sick at all.

My eyes scanned the room and found Conrad. He was talking to a tall woman with platinum blonde hair. She was wearing a very revealing, floor-length, black dress with a plunging, halter neckline. Conrad looked angry and hurt as he spoke to her, like he was in pain. On the other hand, the woman was smiling brightly. After a brief exchange, the woman looked triumphant, as if she'd just won an argument. I could probably guess who she was.

Being Aaron's sister, I would often get some word about Conrad's life. I remember the time Conrad left two years ago. The only people he told were his grandfather and my brother. I remember Aaron mentioning it over breakfast, saying that this girl, Jessica, had really done a number on Conrad. I think they might have been really serious about their relationship and she had betrayed him somehow. I hated how she was standing there, as if she was winning while Conrad was visibly in pain.

I don't know what got into me but I found myself walking toward them with purpose in my steps. I was angry for Conrad, and maybe a little bit for myself too. I was so over it. Here was another tall, blonde, insensitive woman who was carelessly hurting someone.

When I got close enough, I held his arm and pulled him to face me. "There you are, I've been looking all over for you," I said. I held his cheek with one hand and pulled him closer, without giving it another thought I gave him a tiny peck on the cheek, looking up at his eyes as if we were really in love. I'd never noticed how strikingly blue his eyes were.

He just looked at me for a while, clearly a little shocked with what I'd just done but then he smiled. "Eleanor," he said, looking very relieved to see me. He'd never said my whole name before and it sounded good coming from his lips. I felt warm inside.

I didn't expect to feel so comfortable playing Conrad's fiancée, but standing here beside him, looking in his eyes, it all seemed to fall into place. Like I belonged here. Before I knew what was happening Conrad had leaned in and kissed my forehead. It was a sweet, chaste kiss, but it still sent my heart racing.

"Ellie, this is Jessica Fuller, an old...business partner of mine," Conrad said. Jessica looked me up and down and gave Conrad a dirty look. "Oh come on, Conrad," she said. "You and I both know we were more than that."

Conrad just ignored her and proceeded with the introductions. "And Jessica, this is Eleanor Rodriguez, my fiancée," he said before turning to me with an adoring smile. I had to admit, Conrad and I were better at pretending to be in love than I thought we would be.

Jessica had her mouth open in disbelief. I could see her eyes scanning my finger. She scoffed. "Fiancée? You seem to be missing some bling. Where's the ring then?" she demanded. It was obvious she was trying to seem cool but she was obviously very surprised at the news, which was very satisfying.

"We're having it resized for now. It was my mother's ring after all and I want to keep to tradition," Conrad answered smoothly. I was impressed at how quick he was with his excuses.

Jessica just nodded, looking very disappointed and out of her element. "Congratulations, I guess," she said hesitantly before adding, "So when's the big day?

I was surprised at my new-found confidence but I found myself answering her. "Unfortunately, we haven't gone through the details yet, but you don't have to worry about it..." I said, smiling sweetly at her. "Seeing as you won't be invited."

I turned to see Conrad smiling at me, looking very impressed.

"Now come on, darling," I said, pulling his hand coyly. "It's time to greet your other guests." I took a look back at Jessica before walking away and I almost laughed to see her expression. Her mouth was gaping and she looked appalled and furious, not a good look to be honest. I couldn't help taking another dig at her.

"It was *such* a pleasure meeting you, Jessica," I said. "Maybe I'll see you around?" She looked dumbfounded as I gracefully walked away, holding Conrad's hand.

As we got clear of her, I pulled Conrad close and whispered in his ear. "So, how was my first performance as your fiancée?" I asked.

He laughed, loud and heartfelt, causing some guests to pause and look at us. "You were absolutely magnificent," he whispered back. His lips brushed my ears briefly and I knew I was blushing, but he didn't seem to notice. I just squeezed his hand as encouragement.

He looked at me funny for a bit but it didn't bother me. If this night was anything, it was definitely a funny night. And the truth was, even if I didn't really appreciate the funny feelings I was starting to feel, I could simply brush them aside.

"Ellie, you look wonderful dear!" It was William walking towards us. I hadn't noticed him and was quite surprised when I heard his voice. "Conrad really stepped up with you my dear, there is no one here more beautiful."

I had a feeling he was saying this not just for my benefit. William must have seen the exchange between Conrad and Jessica. I smiled at the thought. William gave us big hugs, telling Conrad to take good care of me and giving him a wink. Conrad looked embarrassed but I only laughed.

We spent the rest of the night holding hands and smiling at each other as we greeted guests and made small talk with William's friends. Conrad introduced me to a few potential investors who he said could really help get the bakery to a whole new level. I appreciated the thought but I wasn't interested in business ventures and investments at the moment and I discouraged him. He looked confused for a bit but he did stop, and so we had a lovely night that was not mixed with business.

It was surprising, given how I felt about Conrad just a few days ago, but acting like a couple seemed very natural and comfortable. He was such a gentleman and, I guess because I'd known for so long, it all felt safe and familiar.

A few more hours passed before William finally said it was time for him to go to bed. He said goodbye to his guests and walked up the stairs all on his own, with Devon following closely, of course.

"I'll just go and check up on him, okay?" Conrad whispered in my ear. "I'll be right back."

I watched him leave and head up the staircase and felt a sudden wave of loneliness engulf me. I was starting to see Conrad differently, and I didn't know why, but my hand felt empty without his.

I had an uneasy feeling that I was being watched and when I looked up, I could see that it was Jessica, eyeing me maliciously. I just smiled at her and she must have taken this as an invitation as she started walking towards me with an icy smile.

She looked me up and down and said, "Eleanor Rodriguez, Aaron's sister, right?"

"Yes, I am. I didn't know you knew Aaron personally," I replied, genuinely confused. She laughed, which sounded very much like a snort of derision.

"I knew it," she said, as if she had won.

"What's that supposed to mean?" I asked.

"I knew your name sounded familiar. Say hi to Aaron for me when you see him," she said. "I always knew Aaron had other plans. He never really liked me. He's the reason Conrad and I broke up, you know," she said bitterly. "I guess he wanted in on the family fortune."

I turned red, angry at the unfounded accusation against my brother, but I was definitely missing something. Before I could say anything though, a hand caught me at the waist. I whirled around and saw it was Conrad.

"Let's take you home, Ellie," he said. I turned and saw Jessica giving us a withering side eye. "Sorry to interrupt, Jessica, but we'll be heading off now."

Jessica rolled her eyes and walked away in a huff. Conrad just laughed and took me by the hand. I followed him silently.

He led me to his car and opened the door for me. I was still feeling light-headed. Conrad's effect on me was becoming concerning. My skin tingled from his touch and my hands still felt warm. It must be because no one had held me like this in a long while, and certainly no one like Conrad. He was really an impressive specimen of a man even though I never appreciated it before. He had a well-toned body and chiseled features. His bright blue eyes were very striking against his dark blonde hair. And he'd been holding me all night. It was like a dream.

Although I was thoroughly enjoying myself spending time with Conrad and being treated like a princess, I didn't want to complicate things. And things were definitely getting complicated. It was so easy to forget that all this wasn't real. For the first time, I was realizing that it was easy to fall for Conrad and I knew that that would only lead to pain. I'd started to think that this whole pretending-to-be-engaged act wasn't such a good idea after all.

"Penny for your thoughts?" Conrad said, interrupting my reverie. I just smiled and shook my head.

"It's nothing, tonight's just been a whirlwind," I said.

"I saw you talking to Jessica. I know she can be mean-spirited. I'm sorry I had to leave you alone," he said. "What were you talking about?"

I remembered Jessica's words and so many questions came up. How did Aaron fit into all this? Why did she say he caused their breakup? And what did she mean by saying Aaron had other plans? I decided I would risk it and ask Conrad, even though I knew he wasn't comfortable talking about the past.

"She said that Aaron was the reason you broke up. How did he get mixed up in your love life?" I asked. Conrad's brows furrowed and he took a deep breath.

"We already talked about this, Ellie," he said. "No personal histories."

"But this isn't about you," I replied emphatically. "This is about Aaron. She's accusing him of scheming or something, it wasn't quite clear. But I want to know why she would say something like that."

"No personal histories," he repeated. I sighed and gave up. It must still be fresh in his mind if he wouldn't talk about it so I stayed quiet and looked out the window. But it was obvious to Conrad that I was a little upset.

After a few minutes, he finally gave in. "Fine, I'll tell you," he said.

"I met Jessica at a dinner William threw for an old friend. She was Jack Fuller's niece and she was at the party. William introduced us. I think my grandfather was playing at being a matchmaker but I didn't really think much of it. I was still very busy with the company and I wasn't looking for anything serious.

"We saw each other a few more times and it was always very casual. Then, out of the blue, she gives me a call, says she wants to meet me. I said yes, not really thinking it would be anything serious. She told me she had feelings for me and she wanted to know if I was interested too. Jessica is a lot of things, and she's definitely a very attractive woman. Of course she's also a conniving shrew, but I didn't know that at the time."

I just chuckled a little and let him go on.

"So we started dating and it went really well, great actually. She was fun and exciting, very alluring when she wanted to be. We had a lot of great times to be honest."

I was feeling a few pangs of jealousy as he said this, which made me uncomfortable. Who was I to feel jealous of Conrad and his ex? These were dangerous waters and I couldn't afford to be swept away in them. "So what does Aaron have to do with all of that?" I asked, willing him to hurry along.

"Well, I found out later that she had more than a few hidden agendas. At first she never talked about business or money. I gave her gifts but she never asked for any. Then after a few months she would bring up business ideas, saying she wanted my opinion because I was a successful businessman. She kept talking about her big business idea of starting a beauty brand. She already had a big social media following, around a hundred thousand, and she thought her followers would really appreciate it. I remember we had dinner and instead of it becoming the romantic night I intended, it turned into a business pitch meeting.

"She already had a brand name and names for certain products so I got the idea that she'd been thinking about it for a while. So of course, I'm the supportive boyfriend. I give her some input on her business plan and tell her it's a solid idea and she should go for it. A few months went by and I suddenly received papers in the mail. It was a contract for me to be an investor in her company.

"I generally don't like mixing my personal life and business, but I did think it was a solid idea and I didn't want to offend her, so I signed it. It went great at first. She grew her following as she grew her business. She came out with a few solid products, and I'd give her advice every time she ran into any roadblocks. I thought it was going well, she was always going to events, promoting her brand. A year later, she was asking for more money."

I could feel Conrad tense up as he spoke. I knew where the story was going and it made me mad. We all knew Conrad's family was rich, but he never rode his grandfather's coattails. Aaron, Conrad, and some of their other college friends had worked hard to get their business going. As far as I know, they never got an investment from William, they got their investments because of their ideas and work ethic. To find out that this woman had used him left a bitter taste in my mouth.

"It was a pretty large amount of money and just giving her the money didn't sit well with me. I told her that I would consider loaning her the money and that we would talk about the payment details at length. She got mad. She started cussing me out, telling me I was a bad boyfriend, that I had the money to spare but I was holding this over her head to control her. Then she demanded that I cough up the money or else she would break up with me.

"This all happened in my office at YoungTech, and Aaron just happened to be right outside. We were going to a conference on the upper floor and he dropped by to run some things by me. I don't know what came over Aaron but I'm glad he did what he did. He stormed in after hearing our argument and asked Jessica to leave as we were late for the meeting. He then tells me that he's been looking into her financial spending, and since YoungTech was officially investing in her business, he had a right to. He said that she was misappropriating funds, buying expensive designer clothes, bags, trips to Europe, even a car. I was crushed.

"The next day I broke it off with Jessica and shut her out

completely. It was the first time someone had blatantly used me to get to my money and it made me wary of everyone. It was one of the longest relationships I had but she betrayed my trust. I'm glad Aaron's my friend, he's the brother I never thought I needed. If he hadn't done what he did, I'd probably still be wrapped around Jessica's finger."

Although he didn't say as much, I knew that Jessica was the reason Conrad disappeared for those two years. It must have been hard, falling for someone and imagining a life with them and then finding out it wasn't love, just greed. I felt sad for Conrad, but proud of my brother. He was really looking out for Conrad. Now I understood why he said Conrad needed looking after. As for Jessica, I would be glad never to see her again. I might not be able to control my temper if I did.

"You should have told me earlier, before the party," I said, meaning every word. "I would have made sure she didn't even step foot in your house, or at least make her regret ever coming to that party."

Conrad laughed. "It doesn't matter. It's in the past," he said. But I knew it must have stung, seeing her again when he wasn't expecting it.

"When did you finally get over her?" I asked, genuinely curious.

"The moment I received that contract," he replied. I felt glad about that. Jessica didn't deserve Conrad. Conrad deserved someone who would love him, whether he lived in a hovel or a mansion, someone who could hold her own, who had no hidden agendas. Someone like...

No. It was nobody I knew, and I had to remember that.

When we got to the house, Conrad parked. It was time for me to step out and rest but I couldn't bring myself to. My mind knew what I should do but my body refused to cooperate.

Conrad looked at me and I just smiled back. "Thank you for trusting me with your story and I'm sorry it happened to you. Nobody deserves that," I said.

"You don't have to be sorry about anything, it wasn't your fault. In fact, the only good things in my life at the time were you and your brother, and William, too," he said.

I couldn't stop myself, I laid a hand on his arm and said, "I think we'd make great friends."

Conrad turned and looked at me and I was getting lost in those blue eyes when he took a deep breath and sighed, a very sad sigh. He reached out a hand and tucked a loose strand of hair behind my ear. I had stopped breathing.

"I'd really like that," he said, his hand still lingering, grazing my cheek slightly. His touch sent jolts of electricity through me. I felt breathless and dizzy. Time had slowed down and it was just us, in the dim light. Nothing else mattered but the next few seconds...

I was suddenly jolted by the sound of my phone beeping all of a sudden. We both snapped out of it almost immediately. Conrad straightened in his seat and I quickly gathered myself, not entirely sure of what to say. When I got out of the car, I turned and watched him pull out of the driveway. I could only wave my hand lamely.

I checked my phone to see who the unknowing culprit was. I immediately felt a pang of guilt. It was Aaron.

12

A DREADED DINNER
ELLIE

IT WAS JUST a little past 6:00 am when I walked into the bakery. By my standards it was already a bit late, but I had texted Kate the night before telling her to be at the bakery early. It had been a weird night and I needed some extra rest.

I had gone on an early run to clear my head, gone back to the house, and changed before I headed to the bakery. The early morning chill gave me some respite but the indecision and doubts crept back as I walked to the bakery.

By the time I walked in, I was feeling weighed down and more unsure of myself. There was only one light on as I walked in. We generally kept the outside lights off, including the one in the waiting and dining areas when we weren't open yet, and I knew Kate was likely in the kitchen, getting the breakfast menu ready. We served croissants, bagels, and cinnamon rolls with coffee for our early customers and we would usually bake them first thing in the morning so our customers could get the freshest bread.

When I got to the kitchen I could see her folding the dough into half-moon shapes for the next batch to be baked.

The smell of freshly baked bread was already wafting through the place.

I gave Kate a small smile before heading to the coffee maker and getting myself a cup. Kate could probably see my conflicting emotions in my face because she seemed concerned, but she didn't say anything and gave me a funny look.

"Good morning," she said, wiping her hand on her apron as she finished setting up the tray. She walked over and got a cup of coffee and took a seat across from me. "Something bothering you?"

"How do you always know when I'm in trouble?" I asked her, grateful to have this conversation with her.

"Well, you're not really the type of person who hides their emotions or masks their intentions," she said. "That's actually what I love about you. You are who you are, you tell it how it is and you're not manipulative or dishonest. In this day and age, it's refreshing and very rare."

"You're too much," I said, feeling down despite her compliments. "Maybe I'm just naive and simple?"

"So? That's not a bad thing," she said, getting heated. "You know what, I hate how you're always putting yourself down, underestimating yourself, and letting people walk all over you. Look at this," she said, gesturing towards the entire bakery. "You built this, you run this! You have achieved more than most people double your age, and that is impressive! I want you to be impressed with yourself."

"Kate!" I said, giving her a hug. I needed to hear that.

"Now tell me what's bothering you. Sometimes a listening ear can make all the difference," she said, pulling away to look me in the face.

"Okay," I said. We sat back down and sipped our coffees. "It's just the past few days have been such a whirlwind of things I can't understand or even believe sometimes. I don't know where I am right now, and where I'm headed, and it's scary."

Kate, bless her heart, did not interrupt me. She patiently waited until I had gathered my thoughts and was ready to speak.

"Well, as you know, we went to visit Conrad's grandfather, but so much more happened than I ever bargained for. So we got there and his grandfather was apparently well enough to go home and he decided to throw this big party and invited me to be there. Conrad tells me he is suspicious about the whole thing because there was no plausible reason for such a sudden change. And I'm suspicious too but we just went along with it and I had no clothes, I was not ready for a big party..." I turned to Kate, unable to contain my excitement.

"He hired a stylist and makeup artist to come to his house to help me get ready. Look at this," I said to her as I pulled out my phone to show her a selfie I took with Conrad wearing that magnificent dress. I could see Kate's eyes grow wide with surprise.

"Oh my god, Ellie, you look so good! You're like a Greek Goddess," she said, taking the phone from my hand. "You look like a freaking movie star, oh my god!"

"I know, I've never looked like that before. Anyway, I went to the party and it turns out Conrad's ex, Jessica, was there too and I could tell that there was some tension between them. So I walk up and pretend to be his fiancée and tell her off. And we honestly had a great time, talking to people, pretending like we're a couple," I sighed. "We held hands all night, he kissed me on the forehead and had his arms around my waist.

"But the weird thing is that I wasn't uncomfortable at all. It felt natural, familiar even. And I'm not used to feeling that way. I had a boyfriend once upon a time but I was never comfortable with PDA or holding hands."

I sighed, recalling the events in the car. "Then he drove me home and told me about how Jessica used him and hurt him. I found out that Aaron was the catalyst for their break-up. He told Conrad that Jessica was using the money Conrad invested in her business for personal things like clothes, cars, and trips abroad, so Jessica sort of blames Aaron.

"But that's not even the worst part. The worst part was that I knew we were faking it, we were pretending, but I stayed in the car and I waited for a kiss that never came. And now I feel guilty for thinking this way and feeling this way because he is my brother's best friend and we had an agreement. And I know Aaron is going to lose his shit if he finds out that this is happening."

I took a deep breath and looked at Kate, hoping for some understanding. She sat there and sipped her coffee, her brows furrowed, deep in thought.

"So you want to know what I think?" she finally said. I just nodded. "I think you feel that way because it's all new to you. You've never really had a guy go out of his way to make you feel so special. You've been in, what, one relationship in your life? And that didn't last very long, did it? I mean, I get it. He's your brother's best friend and you probably feel guilty because that's all he ever was to you. Conrad's name never comes up if not in relation to Aaron.

"But guess, what? He's just a human being too, and he is honestly a very attractive man. And Aaron might get upset but don't you think in the end he'd just be happy for you? Now, tell me the truth, if Conrad wasn't Aaron's best friend, would you still feel bad about the time you spent with him and how you feel about him?" she said, looking at me expectantly.

What Kate said really jogged my thinking process. What Conrad and I were doing, what I was feeling, it was all normal. It was typical, in fact, of two single people trying to get to know each other. Kate was right, and I told her so.

"Yeah," I finally said. "You're absolutely right, but what should I do?"

Kate laughed. "Well, that's all up to you. You just have to get over feeling guilty about being so happy. Everybody deserves happiness, whether it's with some random guy or your brother's best friend. If it were me, I wouldn't mind getting all that attention from a guy like Conrad."

I blushed and my face turned red. I gave her a playful shove and she just giggled.

"I am telling you," Kate went on. "I know a lot of guys who'd let being a billionaire get to their head, but I don't think Conrad's a player. I mean, look how hard he took it when he broke it off with Jessica. He's a guy that doesn't just let anybody get too close. He's been burned before.

"And I am telling you that man likes you more than you think. I was ready to tear his eyes out at that party when I saw him staring at you. He looked like he wanted to eat you up right on that bar. I only backed off when you introduced us."

This was all news to me. I was out of it at that party and I had no idea about what Kate was saying. I don't remember anything 'loving' about the way Conrad looked at me that night.

I was about to ask her about exactly what happened and what she saw when the shop bell rang. It was Joey coming in to open up the bakery for customers.

Kate and I started to get busy with more preparations for the displays and our conversation went to the back burner. It wasn't long before our early morning regulars started filing in. We were officially open.

I made a mental note to ask Kate about what she meant, but we were so busy and I got so tired I completely forgot, only remembering when it was time for bed.

~

ELLIE'S SWEET Haven only consisted of three other employees aside from myself. There was Kate, my assistant pastry chef and unofficial assistant manager. Joey, our server, had been with me the longest. Joey was my first hire when I opened and he knew nothing about baking when I hired him but he was very industrious, a quick learner, and always followed instructions to a T, which allowed me to let him handle some of the simpler recipes on the menu.

Sonya was my latest hire and she was mostly in charge of taking orders and talking to customers. She was in her early thirties and had a very friendly and warm way about her. She usually got to the bakery an hour after opening, which was when it started to get busy. Sonya was a single mom of two boys who were in elementary school and she needed that extra time to get her kids to school anyway.

It took a while but I finally feel like I had the right team for my bakery. We all got along, did our part, and everything usually went smoothly. And it was a relief, because the bakery was quite popular locally and the orders were always coming in. Before I hired Kate, I had to spend at least 12 to 14 hours in the kitchen everyday just making sure we had enough to meet orders and walk-ins. There was one day when we ran out of display items in the middle of the day; I had to close shop and bake until midnight. That rarely happened anymore, and my team and I had a system that kept shortages like that from happening again.

It was also already Friday, which meant there was an influx of orders for weekend parties and get-togethers. My questions to Kate about Conrad were mostly forgotten as we baked, mixed, and decorated all sorts of cakes, pastries, and cupcakes.

Conrad and I kept it casual after that party. I'm sure he must have been busy with his grandfather at home and taking back the reins of his company so I didn't bother him much. We did text daily, just little updates, nothing serious, but I always felt a little light-headed when his name came up on my phone. I knew I needed to snap out of it so I threw myself into my work.

It was almost closing time when my heart skipped a beat. It was a message from Conrad:

> Hey, Ellie. How's it going? I've been thinking bout U…Anyway, I thot Id give U a heads up, you might get an unexpected visitor today. Text when you find out who it is. Miss you. 😉

I knew it was probably a joke but I could feel my heart fluttering in my chest. I didn't want to be feeling all these things and then find out that he was just being friendly. I was just about to type a reply when the shop bell rang and I heard Kate give a little hiss. I looked up. It was Sarah.

She was wearing an emerald green dress that set off her complexion. She looked like she had just come from a salon. She looked like a million bucks; she always did. I put my phone away before she saw me.

I was squaring myself up for a fight, planning to ask her what she was doing in my bakery, when she gave me an excited smile. She was beaming, looking absolutely ecstatic.

"How did he do it?" she asked very enthusiastically. I had no idea who or what she was talking about and told her so. She looked at me as if she couldn't believe what I was saying. "Oh come on, you don't know?" she asked. I just shook my head.

"Well, remember that really popular restaurant we always wanted to go to?" she explained. "The one downtown that's always fully booked and you have to make a reservation months in advance? We've been trying to get a reservation there for months," she said.

"You mean you've been the one trying to get a reservation there for months," I corrected her. I could even remember how she would chide Tyler for not being able to take us to dinner there.

She dismissed my words with a wave of her hand. "Whatever, Tyler just called me and said Conrad's assistant sent him a message," she said excitedly. "He says we have a private room there for dinner tomorrow. Can you believe it, a private room? At the most sold out restaurant in Los Angeles? How did he do it?"

She was looking at me expectantly so I just shrugged. "That's just Conrad I guess. He probably knows a lot of people," I replied. "He's very successful so he must have a lot of contacts."

"Well whatever it is he did, I'm glad!" she said, almost squealing with glee. "I can't believe we are having dinner in a private room in the Cravate Blanche!" She was a hairbreadth away from skipping around like a little girl. "Oh I'm so glad we got past everything Ellie, I can't wait to have dinner with you! It's going to be so much fun."

It was very awkward for me. I didn't feel an ounce of the excitement she was showing. I just smiled and said, "Okay, I'll see you tomorrow?"

"Of course," she said, giving me a peck on the cheek before leaving. She didn't even ask how I was.

I looked at Kate and saw her rolling her eyes exaggeratedly. I sighed. I had to admit, I no longer saw Sarah as I did before. I wasn't in awe of her or even considered her my friend at this point. She was just an immature, self-centered person and I was tired of having her in my life.

What Conrad said about our dynamic was becoming more obvious to me now. I was always the one bending over backwards to accommodate her in my life, I was the one who always ended up playing second fiddle, I was the one who always followed along with her plans. I never set boundaries, but maybe it's time that I did.

I pulled out my phone and texted Conrad:

> Sarah was just here. U should have told me sooner, i would have gone home early. So dinner tomorrow?

I rewrote the message a few times. There was so much I could have said but I didn't know how. I settled on a text that was playful, friendly, but also a bit aloof. I didn't want him thinking I was too eager.

His reply was even more aloof:

> Sorry, was too busy making reservations to warn you. I'll pick U up tomorow at 8. C U.

This message had a very different tone from Conrad's earlier message. Was my reply too aloof? What if I had offended him? I didn't realize I'd been standing there staring at my phone until Kate cleared her throat.

"It's nothing," I explained. "Just thinking about tomorrow." I smiled lamely at her while I put the phone back in my pocket. I couldn't be analyzing Conrad's texts like a crazy girlfriend. I had to keep it together.

～

It was Saturday night and I was getting ready to go home. Kate was already well aware of my plans for the night and she was going to close up. The truth is Kate was filling in for me a lot lately and I'd never heard her complain, but I didn't want her to exhaust herself. Maybe it was time to hire some extra hands, maybe even another assistant baker who could work with Kate if I wasn't around.

I was walking home when I got a text message from Sarah, asking me if I wanted to get ready together. How she could possibly think that everything was still the same and normal between us was beyond me. I couldn't think of a more unpleasant situation than having Sarah over and getting dressed with her, reminding me of the night of Aaron's party and how Sarah had completely deceived me.

I told her that it wasn't necessary and that I'd see her there. It was a good thing she didn't insist because, although I was angry at her, Sarah tended to bulldoze over other people's arguments when she really wanted something.

When I got home, I took a shower and started getting dressed. I had already chosen a dress I wanted to wear. It wasn't really a new dress but it was something I bought on my own, and Sarah had never seen it. I decided on this dress because it honestly looked really good. The Cravate Blanche was a high-end restaurant and probably had a dress code. This dress was just the right amount of elegant without looking like I was trying too hard.

The dress was a crepe material that was super clingy and embraced my curves. The one shoulder neckline was modest but showed a dash of skin. I honestly wasn't trying too hard to impress Conrad. I knew I would never look as good as I did at his grandfather's party, but I was confident with how I looked, and that was what mattered.

I was just putting on the finishing touches to my makeup when I got a message from Conrad:

My heart skipped a beat and I replied, telling him I would be out in five minutes. I took one last glance in the mirror. I liked how my hair rippled in waves around my face. The makeup was subtle and the dress made me look sophisticated, yet simple.

I headed down and immediately saw Conrad leaning against the passenger side door of his car. The scene was almost funny to me. I could almost imagine us being teenagers on our way to prom.

He looked up when he heard me coming. For a few seconds he just stared at me. I could feel myself getting breathless with his eyes on me, but I managed to smile and walk confidently to the car. Conrad opened the door for me.

He helped me into his car and went around to the driver's seat. I decided I didn't want any awkward silences tonight. There was still a lot about Conrad that I didn't know and I thought this was the perfect opportunity to get to know him a little bit more.

"Can I ask you a question?" I said.

He smiled and said, "Ask away."

"Why don't you have a driver?" I said. "You can definitely afford it, and most billionaires I see on the news have an entourage following them around."

"I did have one a while back but I feel more comfortable driving myself. I can talk on the phone in complete privacy, there's no one listening in on my conversations. Plus driving myself to places gives me time to unwind, get some alone time. I don't get much of it otherwise."

I smiled, thinking of him taking his time watching the sunset as he drove. "Did you always plan to be so wealthy? Was that the goal?" I asked.

"Not really. I always wanted to be independent and to be

able to provide for the people I care about. I always wanted to be in a position where I could really help people. Of course the best way to do that is to have the means. I've donated to charities, I have a few non-profit projects for inner city neighborhoods, and of course, I can help the people I love. Money was never the end goal but it was a great by-product of everything I've worked for."

"Why did you…" I started to say but he interrupted me.

"Where are all these questions coming from?" he asked, smiling.

"Nowhere," I said, blushing a little. "I'm just curious. I want to know more about you, since we are friends after all."

I noticed how he tightened his grip on the steering wheel when I said that. I anxiously looked at his face, not sure if I had said something wrong—but he was smiling, so I went on.

I asked him why he chose the tech industry to get into and if he was comfortable with having his college friends be, technically, his employees.

"We chose the tech industry because we had really good ideas and we had some expertise in that industry. We had a solid business plan before we ever thought about starting a business, so we didn't technically 'choose' which industry to get into. And Aaron and Jordan founded the company with me. I'm the CEO because I got it off the ground, but it wouldn't have happened if it wasn't for them. I don't consider them to be working under me. We're partners."

"Why," I ventured to ask, my heart racing as I said it, "why are you still single?"

He sighed. I almost bit my tongue when I said it. It took a few seconds but he finally spoke up.

"When I was growing up, I knew we were well-off in a sense. William and I were comfortable, but we weren't rich. Money was never a big factor in my life. When I started getting successful, I found that money was becoming a central factor in my relationships. Women tended to expect things from me. They get into the relationship expecting a certain lifestyle to go with it. I'm never sure if they're in it for me or for...other benefits. I find it hard to trust their intentions, especially after Jessica."

He said it in a very matter-of-fact way but I gained so much insight into the kind of person he was. Kate was right, Conrad was no player; in fact he wasn't comfortable with how much his money changed the people around him. He needed people who would care about him the same way even if he had no money, like William and Aaron. *And me,* came the intrusive thought that I desperately tried to shut down.

I decided to ask less intimate questions, like his favorite countries to visit and his favorite part of his job. We talked on and on until we got to the restaurant.

The hotel was on the top floor and we rode the elevator in silence. I felt butterflies in my stomach as Conrad reached for my hand. Our fingers intertwined like they belonged together. When we got to the front desk, Conrad told the maître d' about our reservation. As he led us into that beautiful restaurant, Conrad pulled me close.

"You ready?" he whispered into my ear. I only nodded as the door to the private room was opened for us.

13

TENSIONS RISING

CONRAD

THE PRIVATE ROOM that had been reserved for us was surprisingly roomy. It could comfortably hold 8 to 10 people, but for our particular night there was only a large four-seater dining table made entirely of glass with an intricate bead chandelier just above it. The entire room was off-white, and all the furniture was a soft cream color. There were candles on long console tables and the only pop of color were the bright red roses on both sides of the large bay windows. The view, as expected, was amazing.

The maître d' informed me that Sarah and Tyler were already waiting for us. I gave Ellie's hand a small squeeze, unsure of how she would take this whole affair.

If it was me, the last thing I'd want was to have dinner with the same person who betrayed my trust. I guess that was just Ellie, always trusting and giving people chances. I was glad she was like that because now she was giving me a chance to be a better person and treat her right. But it also meant she was very vulnerable when it came to getting hurt. I didn't know Sarah very well but I knew enough, and she was not the kind of person you allowed yourself to be vulnerable around.

When we walked into the room, Sarah and Tyler both stood up. I stole a glance at Ellie to see how she was holding up. Surprisingly, her smile seemed genuine. I turned to our guests. I immediately recognized the man I had shared the elevator with. So this was the guy Ellie had a crush on. He wasn't too bad looking, but there didn't seem to be anything special about him.

"I don't know if you remember me, Mr. Young, but we've met before!" he said, looking a little starry-eyed as he said this. I had a feeling I knew his type. I'd encountered a great number of them throughout my career and I usually steered clear of them. Sycophants were bad companions and often would nod along and flatter you even as you jumped off a cliff.

"Really?" I asked, pretending to be puzzled. "I don't seem to remember." Tyler looked absolutely dejected.

"We met at Aaron's party," he said hopefully. "In the elevator, you held the elevator for me?"

"Oh yes," I said, acting as if I had just remembered. "Perkins, right? You work under Ellie's brother!" I know it was a bit petty, but I couldn't resist. I wanted to remind him where he stood, and I wanted to test Sarah on how she would deal with this tonight. I had a feeling she had no real feelings toward Tyler and only became interested in him because Ellie liked him. I knew Ellie wouldn't believe me if I just told her that, so I had to gather evidence.

Sarah had gone around the table and she stood on our side now, opening her arms as if to hug me. I was not in the hugging mood, especially with her. I deftly took her hand and shook it. "Good to see you again, Sarah," I said. She looked taken aback but quickly recovered with a sweet smile.

Without missing a beat, she turned to Ellie and caught her in a hug. Ellie wasn't looking too comfortable but she was too polite to say no or be too obvious. "It's so good to see you, Ellie!" Sarah said.

I decided to spare us all any more awkward encounters and asked them to take their seats. I pulled a chair out for Ellie, my hand lingering on her shoulder just a little too long as she sat down. We caught each other's eyes and I couldn't help but hold that look, most likely imagining the tenderness I thought I could see as she looked back at me. I winked at her playfully and instead of a blush or a protest, she just smiled. *Damn, she's gorgeous.*

"Oh Tyler, why can't you ever do something like that? Conrad is such a gentleman but you don't help me take my seat or anything. Chivalry must really be dead!" Sarah protested loudly, smiling widely and making a show of giving Tyler a little pinch. Tyler just looked confused. Poor man, he had no idea what he had gotten himself into.

When we had settled, I called the waiter and ordered some well-aged Bordeaux. I'd dined here before so I gave Ellie some advice on what to order.

"You should try the wagyu steak they have here, it's delicious. It's like nothing you've ever had before," I said and she just nodded.

"I guess that's what I'll have," she said, smiling at me. There was something about that smile that made me want to pull out all the stops, not that I hadn't done that already. I ordered us beef carpaccio as appetizers, then A+ wagyu steak with wild mushroom risotto for the mains. For dessert, I chose something a bit light but exciting, a mango and blood orange sorbet. I wanted to see how Ellie would react as she ate each course.

After I ordered, I did notice that Sarah ordered the exact same items, which was making my suspicions gain more traction.

When we were all done ordering, it grew a little quiet.

Before it could turn into a long awkward pause, Ellie decided to break the ice.

"So, how have you guys been?" she asked, smiling like her life depended on it. Tyler seemed happy to jump at the opportunity to talk. I could see how he was looking straight at me as he spoke.

"It's been great, we're working on developing new Threat Intelligence Platforms that could potentially bring Young-Tech to the forefront of proactive cybersecurity..."

It seemed to me like it was a spiel he'd been practicing for a while but it also told me two things: firstly, that he wanted to get credit for something that he might not deserve to get credit on; and secondly, that he thought I actually had no idea what they were working on in my own company. I decided to throw a wet blanket over that real quick.

"Ah yes," I replied. "Aaron's project. I think he wanted to call it Threat InSight, right? He showed me the algorithms he wanted to test before he showed it to the team."

Tyler's smile grew stiff and waned as he realized that I probably knew more about the company than he first thought. I couldn't really blame him; after two years at the company, this was the first time he'd even seen me.

"Tyler, let's not bore our host with talk about work. Tonight is about having fun and getting to know each other," she said, putting a hand on Tyler's arm. "Please, no shop talk."

Tyler took an impatient breath and slouched back into his seat, clearly defeated. He looked like he was ready to pout. I turned to Ellie, giving her a look with my eyebrows raised. A look that said, *Seriously? You had a crush on this guy?* She just rolled her eyes at me teasingly and smiled.

Sarah probably saw how we were looking at each other, and so she started employing all the weapons in her arsenal of self-love. She talked on and on about what she and Tyler had been doing, the dates they'd gone on too. It was driving me mad.

"You remember Gilbert, don't you Ellie? You used to flirt with him shamelessly," Sarah said. I could see Ellie start to protest but Sarah just went on, not caring how her words landed at all. "Well he's got a new fling. Such a scandalous girl, she's a painter and a part-time actor. We met them when we went to the opening of her gallery. You should have been there, you'd have liked her artwork," she said as Ellie just smiled lamely.

"Oh and you'll never guess who I bumped into on Rodeo Drive," she said, perking up as she grabbed Ellie's hand. "I saw Daniel himself. He was driving a beat up old Buick. I hardly recognized him. I guess you dodged a bullet there, didn't you?" she said, laughing.

I could see Ellie turning beet red. I had no idea why she was blushing but I wanted to shake Sarah. How could she be so crass?

When Ellie didn't say anything she stopped and squinted her eyes at Ellie. "Oh don't tell me you still feel something for him?" she said, feigning disbelief. "Daniel is Ellie's only ex, he cheated on her years ago," she said, addressing me this time.

"I don't have feelings for him at all," Ellie finally said. "I just had no idea he was out here." Sarah laughed like it was the funniest thing in the world. I was losing my patience with this dinner and Ellie's insipid ex-best friend.

My hands were clenched under the table. I closed my eyes and tried to drown out Sarah's voice. I was counting in my head and controlling my breathing. If I had to hear one more mind-numbing story about some stupid dinner with another group of tedious, superficial assholes, I was going to...

My mental breakdown was interrupted by a familiar

hand over my clenched fists. When I opened my eyes I could see that Ellie was looking at me. I relaxed my hands and her fingers entwined in mine. I made a mental note to keep it together until the end of the dinner at least.

She gave me a small smile and I nodded. I understood what she was asking from me. Sarah must have seen us looking at each other. She made a cooing sound and laughed.

"Oh you guys are so cute," she said. "Do you know, Tyler, that these two used to absolutely hate each other? What was it you said just a week ago Ellie? The only thing you felt for Conrad was utter, unbridled hate?"

Sarah was laughing innocently, but I knew every word coming out of her mouth was a calculated attack. I could see Ellie turning red. Thankfully the food arrived before more was said.

The food was delicious, but I found that I'd lost my appetite with such sorry company. It was a shame because I really wanted Ellie to enjoy the meal. I took a few bites of the appetizer but not even the wonderful food could get my appetite back. I looked to Ellie and saw that she was also clearly upset.

Sarah, on the other hand, was oblivious to all this. She exclaimed at the flavor. Tyler was also eating heartily. I felt like the night was already ruined for Ellie and I, but I had to help her out, make it a bit better. I was about to say something to her when she suddenly looked up and spoke.

"So, how did you and Tyler start out?" Ellie asked.

Sarah looked skeptical and asked, "Are you sure you want to know?"

Ellie's face was set. "Yes, I do actually," she said.

"Well, remember when we were introduced to Tyler more than a year ago? It was at a soirée at YoungTech, Aaron had invited us, remember? Well I didn't really think much of

Tyler back then, I honestly even forgot we ever met him. I only started to notice him when he asked us out to dinner and stuff. But even then I wasn't, like, interested in him. At first I thought he liked you actually, and when you said you liked him I was honestly glad for both of you. I thought you'd be great together.

"Then I got a text, I didn't know who it was from but this person was asking me to meet up. Of course I said no, I didn't know who it was," at this point, she turned to Tyler and they looked at each other smiling. "Then he started sending me hints, then I figured out it was him. I said no at first because I obviously didn't want to hurt you. I mean, I know how sensitive you are and how desperate you were to get Tyler to notice you."

I was watching Ellie as Sarah spoke and I could see her turning red and her lips trembling. I wanted to shout at Sarah but remembered that Ellie had asked and I should respect her decision about it. I gave her hand a little squeeze and she smiled at me. Sarah went on.

"Then I finally agreed on one date, fully intending to end everything right away and tell Tyler he should give you a chance. But we had so much fun and before we knew it, we were meeting up without you. By the third date, I felt like I was already falling for him. I couldn't lie to myself and turn my back on my feelings, so I accepted it.

We talked about it and we decided that we had to tell you. I told Tyler that it had to come from me. I wanted to protect you but I just never found the right time, and days went by, then weeks. It just got harder and harder to say anything," Sarah was trying to get Ellie to look at her, but Ellie had her eyes locked on her plate. "We never intended for you to find out that way, but it was all for the best right?" Sarah said. "I mean, here you are with Conrad."

Ellie decided to ignore this and turned to Tyler. "Before

Sarah told you, did you have any idea at all that I liked you?" Tyler looked stunned. He cleared his throat and shook his head.

"It was always Sarah I was interested in," he said. "I always wanted to ask her out but I was a little intimidated by her. I thought taking you both out would be a great way to get closer to her without anybody getting suspicious. I'm sorry if I gave you any mixed signals."

Ellie sat back in her chair and laughed. I could hear a trace of pain as she tried to brush it off. I could only imagine how she was feeling. To be humiliated in that way and then have to sit here in front of them. It was probably best for us to just leave. I was getting ready to make an excuse for our untimely exit but Sarah spoke up.

"But it was all for the best, right? I mean look at you," she said, gesturing at me. "Here you are with Conrad."

Ellie just smiled awkwardly as Sarah went on. "I mean, say what you want but just a few days ago, weren't you dressing up for my man? What's with the total 180? What made you fall for your number one nemesis?"

My hands clenched when I heard her words. I was infuriated. I was about to speak up but Ellie held me back, giving my hand a squeeze. Sarah, oblivious, turned to Tyler.

"Would you believe that these guys had us thinking they hated each other all these years?" she said to him. Tyler just looked at us awkwardly, unsure of what to say. He was probably thinking he didn't want to take part in baiting his own boss.

"Like I said," Ellie finally said, "it happened at Aaron's party. I saw you guys on the balcony so I thought I'd have a drink at the bar. Conrad came over and we started talking, catching up. He was very different and, seeing as Tyler was not interested, I thought it was okay to give it a try. I had a lot of negative feelings about Conrad but I always knew he was a good person, and it was nice getting to know him again."

Sarah gave Ellie a look, indicating that she was not convinced. I decided I had had enough. "Come on Sarah, you of all people know very well the story behind Ellie and I," I said.

Sarah looked uncomfortable. "What are you talking about? I don't know anything about you guys." She averted her eyes and smiled awkwardly. Ellie looked at me, obviously intrigued.

I leaned in and whispered in her ear, "Do you trust me?" I asked her. She nodded so I went on.

"It was my first summer home after college, and Aaron and I decided to spend a few weeks of summer together in their home. I would go around town on errands and I bumped into Sarah. I knew her from school but we never had an interaction before. Remember?" I asked Sarah pointedly. She just shrugged, still refusing to look me in the eye.

"Sarah asked why I was in town and I told her I was spending the summer with Aaron and Ellie's family. That was that, I never thought much of it. To my surprise, the year after that I found Sarah and Ellie were inseparable, suddenly best friends. I didn't really care and I thought it had nothing to do with me."

I looked at Sarah, and she was getting uncomfortable. Good. Ellie was looking at me, probably wondering what this had to do with anything.

"But every time she had a chance, Sarah would try to get my attention and make it very obvious that she was interested in me, trying to get me alone. I didn't want anything to do with that, I just wanted to have fun with Ellie and Aaron.

"And it kept happening, every time I was over, every summer break Sarah would be all over me. I'm surprised no one else guessed her intentions, but I wasn't the type to expose her or anything. I thought she would get the hint and just leave me alone."

I looked at Ellie and noticed that her mouth was a bit open in shock. She was looking at Sarah intently, probably realizing what kind of person her 'friend' really was.

"Then Aaron, Jordan, and I finally launched our company. We had a small party, remember?" I said, turning to Ellie who just nodded slowly. "That was when Sarah confronted me. I think she must have had a little too much to drink at the time. She demanded to know why I wasn't showing interest in her and even asked if I like women.

"I had to laugh and I told her she wasn't my type. She cussed me out and said, 'I'm not your type? So who's your type? Ellie?' I got mad and called her out. It was obvious she was just using Ellie's friendship to get closer to me and I told her so. We stopped bumping into each other after that."

Ellie was looking at Sarah intently. Sarah just averted her eyes and her look of guilt confirmed everything I had said. Ellie took a deep breath and stood up.

"No wonder you always asked about Conrad. I asked you about it but you said you didn't like him, But I guess you lied about that too, just like how you've lied about everything else," she said to Sarah. "You are so conniving and pathetic that you would pretend to be my friend for close to a decade just so you could get a guy's attention? I used to look up to you, but that was my mistake." Sarah looked like she was getting smaller under Ellie's gaze. I was actually glad that Ellie looked ready to end her friendship with Sarah. It was like being friends with a pit viper.

"It's too bad to ruin such a nice dinner, but it's time we left," she said, turning to me. I quickly got up and turned to the couple in front of us.

"Well this was nice," I said sarcastically. I could see Tyler squirming uncomfortably. "You really lucked out Tyler. You should have gone for Ellie," I said, catching Tyler's eye. "Good luck with...that," I said, indicating Sarah. It was very satisfying.

On our way out I told the waiter to send the bill to my secretary. We walked in silence until we got to the car.

~

WE DROVE BACK to Ellie's house in complete silence. I wanted to give her time to process everything that had just happened, but everything I could think of saying rang hollow and insincere.

I parked the car in front of her house and the silence was becoming deafening. I could see Ellie staring straight ahead. I took Ellie's hand in mine. It seemed like the most natural thing to do.

Ellie chuckled as our fingers intertwined. "Hey, what's so funny?" I asked her.

"It's just that things have changed so much in such a short time," she said. "It wasn't too long ago that I was dreading the thought of seeing you while I was getting ready with Sarah. Now I'm holding your hand while wishing I never see her again."

I smiled. Ellie really was made of different stuff. She wasn't feeling sorry for herself. She was still smiling. I gave her hand a squeeze. "Are you sure you're okay?"

"Don't worry about me, Sarah can't get to me anymore," she said. "I'll be fine. I survived you, didn't I?" She gave me a playful shove with our still-intertwined hands. As she tried to pull away, I pulled her back in, forcing her to look straight at me. I started to twirl a loose strand of hair between my fingers. I was letting my impulses take control.

"Was I really that bad?" I asked, feeling a little breathless. I trailed a finger along her cheeks. I could feel her shiver against my touch. Ellie closed her eyes and took a deep, slow breath. "Terrible," she said breathlessly.

I cupped her face in my hand. I could feel her leaning into me. She sighed, as if in surrender. I leaned closer, touching my forehead against hers. "How about now?" I asked.

I felt her hand on my face, pulling me closer. She turned her face slightly until her lips were touching my forehead. "The worst?" she said. I was slowly losing control. I started to pull away but she held me fast, holding my face in front of her. I was inches from her lips.

I watched her eyes look longingly at my lips. I knew she was reading the same expression in my face. I watched her lips part slowly and I couldn't hold back any longer. My lips met hers, soft, warm, wet, and inviting. I fell into a haze as I crushed her lips to mine.

14

TIME-OFF

ELLIE

IT WAS HERE, finally. He was kissing me, his tongue intent and persistent, exploring my mouth. I opened my lips to him, willing him to go deeper, clutching at his hair and pulling him closer. He groaned. *I want this. I want him.*

Before I knew what was happening, he was pulling away from me with a force and urgency that surprised me. I was still breathless and very confused as he disentangled himself from me. He was wiping his face and straightening his suit.

"I'm sorry, Ellie," he said. "I shouldn't have done that."

"What are you talking about?" I asked. "Why are you sorry?" I could feel my face burning. I was getting frustrated and angry. "Why are you sorry?!" I demanded again, letting the anger be obvious in my voice. But Conrad was already out of it. He wouldn't even look at me.

"Conrad, please," I said, trying to calm myself down. "Tell me what's wrong. Say something." I put a hand on his shoulder and tried to make him face me. He just turned away.

"There's nothing to say," he said. I was getting desperate,

but I thought he might need some time. I didn't want this to end badly.

"If you don't have answers now, maybe we can sleep on it and talk about it tomorrow," I said, willing him to help make sense of what had just happened.

"Just go, Ellie. Go," was all he said. I didn't know how to respond. I scoffed at him and opened the car door, becoming increasingly frustrated. I slammed the door behind me.

He sped away, as if running away from something. I watched him drive away, wishing I was back to a time when I didn't really care about the man driving away. I ran back into the house, tears streaming down my face.

I TOSSED AND TURNED, lying awake for most of the night. I couldn't get rid of the feel of him on my lips, or shake off the warmth of his hands from mine. The memory of the kiss kept assaulting my mind. Every time I closed my eyes I could see his blue eyes looking into mine, filled with want and longing. I still couldn't understand why he had acted that way. The night had gone so well. The last few days we'd spent together had been amazing. *Why would he just leave like this?*

After an hour of lying in bed, I finally gave up and headed to the bathroom. Maybe a hot shower would help. I quickly undressed and got under the water, trying to rinse off the dark memories. It was funny, Sarah and Tyler were the dark memories now and Conrad was the only light.

I couldn't stop thinking about him, his strong hands, his fingers grazing my cheek, his tongue in my mouth, warm and hot. I started to feel all tingly and I found myself starting to rub my large breasts, shivering as I pinched my nipples. I could almost feel him, his passion, the pained longing I could see in his eyes. The water trailed down my body and it felt like little kisses. All I could think about were his lips, so soft and hot against mine, his tongue in my mouth, exploring every crevasse. My hand trailed down until I found the little pearl between my legs.

I could almost feel him against my body. His strong arms and muscled chest felt imprinted on me. I could feel him touching me, kissing me, burning for me. I started rubbing myself, little waves of delight running through my body. I remembered how he said my full name. 'Eleanor...' he said, his voice husky. 'Conrad,' I whispered, feeling myself getting closer to the peak. 'Conrad...' remembering the taste of him, the smell of him. My fingers worked faster, rubbing my clit as I felt myself reaching my limits.

'Conrad!' I finally cried as I climaxed, my whole body shaking as I let the sensation run through me. I was breathless as I turned off the water and dried myself.

All I could hope was to be able to finally get some sleep.

KATE WALKED into the bakery just before dawn. She must have expected to be the first person at the bakery that morning but found that I was already in there, which is why she came in looking worried. I had told her the night before that I might come in late because of the dinner. I guess I was a little too optimistic.

Kate looked like she was about to ask a question but stopped herself, looking very concerned. After my little shower, I fell asleep for three hours then woke up at around 2am, unable to fall back to sleep.

The memories of the dinner, with Sarah trying to hurt and humiliate me further at every turn, along with Conrad's reaction when he took me home, overwhelmed me. I had cried in bed for a good hour. I could imagine what I looked like to Kate, with my red, puffy eyes.

"Hey," I said, faking good humor. "Good morning."

"Are you okay?" she asked. "What happened last night? Your eyes are swollen."

"Oh it's nothing," I said, trying to put her concerns to rest. "I couldn't sleep last night. I got a bad allergic reaction to something we ate." I tried to act normally, keeping my hands busy with the tasks in front of me. I was prepping croissants and the muffins were already baking in the oven.

I was expecting her to say something, to ask more questions, but she just looked at me and nodded. I smiled at her and continued to work, clearing my mind and focusing on the tasks set in front of me. And I honestly thought I was managing well.

It was just after the mid-day rush and we were finally getting a bit of a rest. Kate and I were sitting in the office, drinking coffee. It had been an awkward morning and we had hardly spoken. I had done my best to stay busy all morning, but there were moments when my thoughts would wander to the night before, and I let out a sad sigh. Every time I would see Kate looking at me with concern. I knew she had questions but I kept on pretending like nothing was wrong. I couldn't afford to break down at work.

I thought I was doing a pretty good job of making it seem like business as usual, but it seemed that Kate had had enough. She suddenly slammed her mug down on the table and stood in front of me, placing her hands firmly on the table and looking down on me.

"I'm tired of this, Ellie," she said, sighing deeply as she spoke. "I tried to wait for you to tell me the truth but all this sighing and looking into the middle distance is really starting to get me down. Now, why don't you just tell me what happened? You're going to scare away our customers if this keeps up."

I had no words to say. I just looked at her with my eyes tearing up. She quickly walked around the table and held me. I was already bawling my eyes out. "I..I.." I sputtered, trying to get some words out.

"No, no," she said. "Take your time, cry it out, dear," she said, as she rubbed my back. I could hardly breathe, all my emotions were rushing out. Kate, very patiently, held me as I cried.

After a little while, when my cries had subsided, she pulled away from me. She handed me a handkerchief and said, "I'm going to get you a glass of milk and some cookies. Wait right here."

I wiped my eyes then blew my nose on the handkerchief she gave me, almost laughing at myself for breaking down like this. I held back my feelings so much that my later breakdown was worse than it might have been if I had just told Kate outright.

She didn't take long. She was back soon with a glass of milk and a plate of chocolate chip cookies. As I started eating, I realized just how hungry I actually was. I immediately felt my spirits lift and my head clear. I remembered that I had hardly eaten anything all morning. Other than a piece of banana I ate before leaving home, I hadn't had another meal. All I had had was coffee all day.

I had to admit that maybe hunger had intensified my emotions a little. I basically devoured the cookie in half a second. "Feel better?" Kate asked. I gulped down the milk and nodded.

"Kate, I'm sorry about breaking down like this, it's just that last night was so weird and complicated," I said. "It's just a bit too much to process."

"Tell me everything," Kate said as she got comfortable

on the couch and patted the seat next to her. I obliged and went to sit next to her. "It was such a weird night," I said as I plopped down.

"I wouldn't have expected otherwise," she said. "What were you thinking, agreeing to go on a double date with that snake?" she said vehemently. I was a bit surprised to find that Kate had such strong feelings against Sarah.

"Kate!" I said, giving her a playful push.

"Oh come one, I've seen that girl with you. Every time she comes into this bakery she acts all condescending," she said, rolling her eyes at a hypothetical Sarah. "Remember after we changed the decorations and everything? She came in here, looked around with a raised eyebrow and said 'Oh, this is cute,' like a smug little bitch," she said with some venom. "Every chance she got, she talked down to you. It made me so mad!"

I felt a little stupid, just now realizing that everyone around me probably noticed how badly Sarah treated me, and I was the last one to see it.

"Well, she was at it again last night," I said. "She took every opportunity to put me down and humiliate me. She kept holding my crush on Tyler over my head, reminding me every time she could. She even asked me how I could fall for Conrad so quickly when just a few days ago I was dressing up for her man."

Kate scoffed and shook her head. "That bitch has a lot of nerve," she muttered, sipping more coffee.

"I honestly expected that from her and that's not even the worst part about it. Conrad starts telling me the story behind him and Sarah, how she was trying to get his attention all throughout the length of our friendship. I found out that Sarah only befriended me because of Conrad, because she wanted to get close to him. One of the most important relationships I thought I had turned out to be a lie based off of her own selfish motives."

I took a deep breath. I was still really pissed at Sarah but I was also over it. I had made up my mind the night before: I was gonna cut Sarah out of my life and find people who actually truly cared and valued me as a person.

"I almost didn't survive if it wasn't for Conrad. He was so sweet and supportive the entire night. He even defended me against Sarah and it felt really good to be with someone who seemed to care about me so much. But then he took me home..." I paused and breathed deeply. I was still perplexed about how the night had ended and I could feel tears welling up again.

"Then what happened? Why are you crying if he was so nice all night?" Kate asked with some urgency. I took a steadying breath before continuing my story.

"We... Oh my god, we kissed and it was...it was so much more than anything I ever imagined. It was perfect. But he pulled away and said he was sorry. Then he just left like something was after him. I don't understand it!" I cried, laying my head in my hands.

"What? He pulled away before you finished the kiss?" Kate asked, clearly confused as well. "Why would he do that?"

"I have no idea," I said, sitting back on the couch. "I was hoping you could tell me."

Kate seemed to think about this for a little bit. Then she leaned in, looking me dead in the eye. "But more importantly, how do you feel about it? Do you have feelings for him?" she asked.

I was a little uncomfortable with her question but I also knew that it needed to be asked. This was the first time someone was asking me point blank, and I decided I needed to give a straightforward answer, more for myself than Kate.

I thought about it for a little while but I honestly didn't have a clear cut answer. "I don't know," I answered somberly.

"What do you mean you don't know? Surely you've been in love before?" she asked, unbelieving.

"I'm really not sure. The only men I've had feelings for were my ex, Daniel, and maybe Tyler. With Daniel it was never like passionate love. I weighed all my options, looked at the pros and cons, and I rationally decided that it was time to be in a relationship," I said.

"And with Tyler," I continued, "I feel like it was puppy love, like a crush that I watered and that grew into gigantic proportions. It was never based on anything real. I didn't even know him but I thought I was in love because I had this dream scenario in my head that was based purely on fantasies."

"And how do you feel about Conrad?" she said.

I thought of him, how he was so protective and supportive throughout my ordeal, how he would listen to me and showed that he paid more attention to my life than I ever thought he did. I remembered how his hands felt in mine, and how I felt safe with him. I remembered his kiss, his hot breath on my neck, his fingers against my bare skin.

"You don't have to say anything," Kate said, smiling at me. "I can read it all on your face. Is this honestly the first time you've fallen in love?"

As she said the words, I knew in my heart that it was true. *Yes, I've fallen in love with Conrad Young.*

$\sim$

AFTER I ADMITTED TO KATE, and to myself, that I had fallen for Conrad, it all seemed easier to bear. Kate told me that he probably needed some time to process his feelings too.

"I'm sure that he really likes you too, Ellie," Kate had said when I expressed some doubts about his feelings for me. "Have you seen how that man looks at you? I knew it the first time I met him. He had hearts in his eyes when he looked at you, and so far everything you've told me about him points to the same conclusion."

I had taken her advice and given it a few days. But a few days had passed and I had heard nothing from Conrad. I was getting worried. Of course, the minute Kate saw me she knew something was bothering me.

"So he still hasn't called?" she asked. I shook my head and took my phone out just to be sure. Nope, still nothing.

"Have you tried to contact him?"

"Yes," I said, my frustration clear in my voice. "I've texted and called him but he just ignores me."

"Don't you know where he lives?" she asked again. "Why don't you pay him a visit?"

"Are you crazy? What if he completely blows me off? I can't do that," I said, turning red. I was never the type to go chasing after a guy. I mean, it took me a whole year of working myself up to even start talking to Tyler, and look how that turned out.

"Ellie, do you still feel the same about Conrad?" Kate asked, putting a hand on my arm. I just nodded, unsure of what to say. "Honey, if you love him then you have to take risks. It'll be worse if you sit at home and wait for him to come to his senses. You'll regret it for the rest of your life, asking yourself, 'What if I did this or that?' without ever getting an answer. If you care about him, go over there and tell him."

"What if he ignores me?" I asked, unsure.

"He can't ignore you forever, especially if you're standing at his front door," she said. "You should go ask him. In fact, I think you should do it now. Go over there and get your answers. God knows you deserve it, Ellie."

I was speechless. My heart was racing at the prospect of going to see Conrad. "I can't do that, can I? It's going to get busy soon, I can't leave the bakery..." I said, struggling to find any kind of excuse.

"Oh come on, we can handle things here," she replied. "Don't make the bakery an excuse not to do what you have to. I can manage the bakery while you're gone and Sonya is coming in soon. Joey and I can handle things in the meantime."

She's right. I knew what I had to do. I hugged Kate. "Thank you," I whispered in her ear, "for everything."

"Don't mention it," she said to me. "Now go!"

My heart was racing as the taxi weaved through traffic on the way to Conrad's apartment. I was on the edge of my seat and unsure of what I'd do when I got there. When he wasn't in their Malibu Mansion, Conrad lived in a penthouse apartment in Downtown LA. I already knew he wasn't staying in Malibu with William because I'd called the house and William said Conrad hadn't been home since the party.

Conrad lived in a doorman building and I had no idea how I was going to get inside, especially if he chose to ignore me or not let me in. As I was getting closer to the building, my mind was struggling to form a plan. I wasn't even looking at where I was going, which explained why I bumped head on into another pedestrian.

Our heads bumped and I reeled. I almost fell but the stranger shot a hand out to hold me steady. I was rubbing the sore spot on my head when I saw who I had bumped into. It was Daniel, a little scruffier than I remembered him.

"Ellie?" he asked, recognizing me right away. "What are you doing here? Wow, you look really good!"

"Daniel? What are *you* doing here?" I asked. I did not expect to see him again, and especially not like this.

"Me? I live here, in that building. I got a job at an accounting firm here," he said, pointing to Conrad's building. "I moved to town a few months ago. How have you been?"

"I'm really good," I said, an idea forming in my head. "Hey, can I ask you a favor?"

Daniel escorted me into his building without any complaints or questions. I had just told him it was important that I talk to someone in his building but that they weren't expecting me and he had readily agreed.

"I'm really glad I got to see you again, Ellie," he had said before we parted ways. He was on his way to work. He paused and made a double-take. "You know I really messed up back then," he said, smiling shyly.

"Yeah," I agreed. "You really did."

He seemed taken aback by my answer but he just scratched his head. "I'm sorry about everything, I wish I could take it back," he said.

"Well you can't," I said. He just nodded and said goodbye.

I watched him go. I headed inside and pushed the penthouse button on the elevator.

Conrad's door was right at the elevator doors. His apartment took up the whole floor, so I wasn't afraid about running into anyone. I knocked on the door then rang the doorbell. No response.

"Conrad!" I called, banging on the door with all my might. "Open the door and talk to me!"

I alternated knocking and ringing the doorbell for a good five minutes, but he still didn't open the door. I was slamming my hand against the door so hard it was hurting.

"Conrad! I am not leaving!" I yelled. "So unless you plan on hiding in there for the rest of your life or calling the police and getting me arrested, you might as well open the door, you coward!"

I guess my words finally had the desired effect. I heard the lock click on the other side. The door swung open and without another word, I stepped inside.

15

CONFRONTATIONS
CONRAD

Days had passed since I kissed Ellie, but it felt like yesterday. The past few days had been torture. Every waking moment was filled with her. Ellie's skin, Ellie's lips, Ellie's scent, all swimming around in my head. There was no relief for me. I'd been holed up in my apartment, completely unproductive and useless for the past few days. I couldn't focus, I had no interest in work, I couldn't do anything.

Jordan had called a few times but I either let it go to voicemail or made some lame excuse about how I had to deal with family matters. When William and then Devon called, I made some lame excuse about being needed at work. William's one call that I had answered was already too much.

"Conrad, where have you been? It's been nearly a week and you haven't come to visit me at all," he said, "Are you mad about my lie after all, even though you said you forgive me? Is that it?"

"No, that has nothing to do with it," I replied. "I've just been busy at work. I've fallen behind on some paperwork and I need to clear it up right now."

"Oh? Alright then," There was silence on the other line

and I could practically hear the gears turning in his brain. "And how about Ellie? How is she?"

"I honestly don't know. You'll have to ask her."

"Conrad, you didn't." I could hear him sigh on the other end. "Conrad..."

"Please, whatever you thought there was between us," I said, cutting him off, "it was all a mistake. You misunderstood. Like I said, there's nothing going on between us."

I started evading any more calls from William after that. I had no desire to hear how worried he was or him trying to convince me to talk to Ellie or come home and talk about it with him.

I was in limbo, all I wanted was to see Ellie, talk to her, and explain myself, but I knew it couldn't be. I had to stay away, or else I was sure I was going to fall off the deep end and there would be no going back from that.

But the days were brutal and the nights were unbearable.

The deal we made was all based on a lie and I never thought that it would get so complicated or be so significant. I couldn't close my eyes without thinking of Ellie, but with that came the knowledge that there was nothing I could do. Ellie and I had made a deal and I couldn't stick to it. I couldn't be her fake boyfriend anymore, because it would drive me insane.

I felt pretty pathetic. I didn't know what she must think of me. She's been calling and texting but I didn't know what to say. I knew she had questions but I had no answers, so I chose to ignore them, until finally, I just turned off my phone. I need time to figure things out, to get myself under control and back on track. I'm just not sure when that was going to be.

I'd been rolling around in bed all day, just as I had been for the past few days. My days had alternated between lying in bed and being utterly useless and working out in my home gym until my entire body ached. I was lying in bed after a very cold shower when I heard banging on my door, then the doorbell ringing. I was not expecting anyone so I got up and looked at the video intercom in my living room. My mouth fell open. It was Ellie, banging on my door like I owed her rent.

I stared at the screen in complete shock for a good minute before I finally snapped myself out of it. I thought for a second that I was imagining it, but no dream of mine could have seen such passion contained in such a cute, sexy package.

She was banging on my door and shouting with a vengeance. A small part of me was happy that I had no neighbors who would be scandalized with what was happening, but another part was a little worried that there would be no one to see or wonder about this, no witnesses.

"Unless you plan on hiding in there for the rest of your life or calling the police and getting me arrested, you might as well open the door, you coward!" she cried, cursing at me through the door. She was pacing back and forth in front of my door like a hungry tigress.

Her words jogged me back to reality. What was I thinking, that we wouldn't eventually have a confrontation about it? I guessed I could get away with it, but not without causing irreparable damage to our relationship, and also possibly my relationship with Aaron and their whole family.

I took a deep breath and tried to gather my courage before finally opening the door.

Ellie flew into my apartment like a hurricane, and she stood in front of me, breathing hard. I don't know if I imagined it or if she really did have smoke billowing out of her nostrils and ears. We stared at each other for a minute and I noticed her eyes go wide and her cheeks turn red. She looked flustered. That's when I realized I was wearing nothing but some boxer briefs.

I cleared my throat and slowly closed the door. "Hello, Ellie," I said, "what are you doing here?"

It took Ellie a little while to get herself together. She looked like she didn't know where to look. Finally, she just closed her eyes and took a deep breath.

"I need... We need to talk," she said, opening her eyes and looking straight into mine. I was drowning in hers.

I regained my composure and continued., "There's nothing to talk about," I said. "Is that all?" I added, as she seemed too stunned to speak.

She just looked at me, hurt in her eyes. I knew that I couldn't let this go on. Having Ellie in my apartment was a dangerous and risky situation for me. I needed to get her out of here. I opened my front door and gestured for her to just leave. I breathed a sigh of relief as she started to go.

To my surprise, instead of leaving my apartment, she grabbed the doorknob and firmly closed the door, still looking me in the eye. I should have known that she would make this as hard for me as she could. "If you think it's gonna be easy to get rid of me," she said, and I could feel the frustration in her voice, "then you have it all wrong! I'm not leaving unless I get some answers."

I couldn't look at her for long. I turned around and walked away, saying as I went, "That's too bad, because I don't have any answers."

"That's not good enough!" she shouted after me. Before I could get far, I felt her hand on my arm. "At least fucking look at me," she cried out. I could hear the hurt in her voice.

I turned and looked at her. She was crying silently and I could see all the questions she had in her eyes. I wanted to make it better, but I couldn't. I didn't know where to start.

"How do you think a girl is supposed to feel," she asked,

her voice shaking, "when a guy practically runs away and ghosts her after they kiss?"

I couldn't answer her question and I couldn't keep looking her in the eye either. "I'm sorry," was all I could say. She scoffed and turned from me, wiping away the tears.

"I don't understand," she said. Her voice was pleading, soft, on the verge of giving up. "It was going so well, you were so nice. I actually thought we could finally be friends."

I felt a bitter lump in my throat after what she said. I groaned, determined to get out of here. "That's too bad, because I don't want to be your friend." She whirled around and turned on me. Her anger and frustration were clear to see, but she seemed determined to get some sort of answer from me.

"How could you say that? You had a whole speech about wanting to be my friend," she said, almost crying. "You said you wanted us to get along and that you'd do everything to make it right. Was that all a lie?"

I sighed. "No, I wasn't lying," I said slowly, "but I changed my mind."

I heard her gasp, as if she was in pain. "Why?" she asked.

"I don't think I have to give a reason," I said. It hurt me to see her crying, and to know that I was the one causing her this pain was too much. But I also knew that this was better than going on with it, for both of us.

"Yes, you do!" she shouted, "You're the one who roped me into this, who made me change the way I saw you. You're the one who came up with this fucking arrangement! I think I deserve an explanation and you have to give me one."

"I don't have to do anything," I said, steeling myself for whatever reaction she might have. "The arrangement is over. You don't have to convince Sarah anymore and I don't need a fake fiancée. William already knew we were lying. He knew the minute I told him."

She blinked and looked like I had slapped her. "William knew? Why didn't you tell me?" she demanded.

"I don't know. He wanted me to keep it up, he liked seeing me with you," I admitted. "But it's no use now. You don't need me, I don't need you. The arrangement is over."

"So you're done? You're done playing with my emotions?" she said. "You have no use for me so you throw me aside like a dirty rag?" Her words stung me more than she could have known. *Oh, Ellie, you couldn't be further from the truth.*

"It's not like that!" I said, my hands raised in exasperation. "You know it's not like that!"

"I don't know anything," she replied with an equal amount of exasperation. "I won't know unless you tell me and help me understand. That's all I want. Can't you at least give me that?"

There was so much I should have said, so much I wanted to say, but the words caught in my throat. I couldn't find the words to make this better. I wasn't prepared to tell her the truth.

"It doesn't matter. It's done, a clean break. Isn't that what you wanted?" I asked, feigning indifference. "To have nothing to do with me? I'm giving you your wish."

"You immature, selfish, spoiled little brat!" she cried. "Every time you run into trouble, you run away. You ran away when Jessica hurt you, and now you're running away and hurting people who care for you!"

This floored me and I had to take a seat with my face in my hands. I was slowly realizing that there was no clean break from this. And yes, I did owe her an explanation, but I wasn't ready to say what I should be saying.

I felt a hand on my knee. I looked up and froze. Ellie was kneeling down in front of me, her eyes soft, tender, and vulnerable. "Please, just talk to me," she said, coming closer.

My whole body was tingling. I couldn't imagine how it had come to this.

"Tell me I'm not crazy," she said, her hand taking mine. "Tell me I wasn't imagining things. Tell me the truth."

"Ellie, please," I said, closing my eyes, desperately trying to keep my composure. "Please, I can't do this. Just leave...please."

"No," she said resolutely. "I'm not going anywhere, I'm not leaving. You're not getting rid of me that easy. You can't run away anymore, you can't hide behind your money and your trips to Asia. I deserve to be heard and I deserve an explanation."

I took a deep breath. She was right, there didn't seem to be any other way out of this. I lay back on the chair. She was still holding my hand, and I pulled it away. She was sitting on the floor beside my chair.

"I can't be your fake boyfriend anymore, it's not healthy and Aaron might take it the wrong way. I don't want your family to end up hating me. What I did in the car the other day was out of line and I'm sorry." I said it all in one breath, afraid of losing my nerve, midway.

"Why?" was all she said.

"Because I shouldn't have taken advantage of you. You were hurting and I shouldn't have crossed that line. We don't have to keep pretending we're together and it's just... it's just going to get messy," I said lamely. I was running out of things to say. I knew that I would probably end up just telling her the truth in the end.

"How? Why do you want to cut me out of your life all of a sudden? Why can't we even be friends?"

I laughed sardonically and got up, pacing the room. I was searching for the right words. *How can I tell her the truth? How can I admit any of this when I promised her that it would be simple, easy?*

"I...I can't fall in love with you Ellie," I finally said. "I can't let that happen, and if we spend any more time together then it'll start to get impossible."

I was expecting a reaction from her. Maybe a laugh, maybe more angry shouting. But I was never expecting to feel her arms around my waist.

"Why would falling in love with me be so bad?" she asked. "Do you really hate me that much?"

Her head rested against my back and her arms locked together around my waist. I was frozen. I knew that if I moved, there was a big chance I would not be able to control myself.

"Ellie, let go of me, please," I said. My throat was dry as a desert and I was suddenly feeling woozy. My heart was pounding in my chest.

"Tell me you'll be my friend," she whispered and I almost lost it. I jumped away from her hold abruptly and took two strides away from her before she could protest. I held a hand out, trying to keep her away.

"I can't be your friend! It doesn't work like that!"

She just stood there, her eyes filled with confusion. She was crying again and it took all of my self-control not to run to her and hold her, comfort her, kiss her.

"Why? After you helped me out with Sarah, made me feel special, and told me over and over how beautiful I was. Why don't you want anything to do with me now?" She wasn't looking at me as she said it, wiping the tears that were falling from her eyes. I had no idea that her next words would be so devastating.

"I'm not Jessica, Conrad. And I'm not like Sarah either. I want to be your friend for you, because you showed me what kind of person you really are," she said, smiling up at me like an angel. "I don't care that you're rich or successful. I like you because you're kind, and you just want to provide for everyone. I want you to trust me because you know what kind of person I am. I just want you to let me in."

"I can't do that," I said, turning toward her. "If I do, I'll never recover. I can't stand it Ellie. I'm falling in love with you and I can't stop myself!"

"Why do you have to stop yourself?" she asked, slowly coming closer. "Why do you think this is so wrong? Why are you so scared?"

"We had a deal, and I can't keep it. Please, Ellie, let's just pretend it never happened."

"I can't do that," she said, reaching for me. "That's the last thing I want to do."

I finally snapped. I couldn't take it anymore. "Why are you being so difficult?" I groaned. "Why do you have to be so contrary about everything? Why can't you just leave well enough alone?"

Instead of getting intimidated or turning away from me, she just came closer. I could smell her now. Instead of an angry retort, I could see that she was smiling at me.

"It wouldn't be consistent of me if I suddenly just followed your instructions, would it?" she said. "You're the one who's complicating this, you know. You're the one being difficult."

"What the hell are you talking about?" I said, frozen in place. The proximity of her was holding me down, and I had a feeling she was well aware of her effect on me.

"Because we're both adults, Conrad. And you're talking to me as if I'm a child with no say in this," she said, taking another step toward me. "You don't have to be so guilty about your feelings for me, you don't have to run. I want you in my life, I want you to stand with me... Conrad, I've fallen in love with you, too."

Her words hardly registered in my head. I felt like it couldn't be true. But Ellie didn't give me time to think, she just came closer and held my head with both hands. Before I knew what was happening, she pulled me to her and kissed me. It was no more than a soft peck on the lips but it bowled me over. Before I knew what I was doing, I had grabbed her and pulled her to me, crushing her against my body. She gasped.

"You love me?" I asked, my voice hoarse. My face was buried in her thick, fragrant hair. I was painfully aware of her breasts against my chest.

"Yes, Conrad, you stupid idiot, I'm in love with you," she whispered breathlessly. Her hands clutched at my hair as she made me look at her. "Now, what do you have to say for yourself?" she asked.

I said nothing. Instead I laid my lips to hers and breathed her in, savoring her taste, her warmth, still thinking this was all a dream. But she was so real, so solid next to me. My heart was pounding and she shivered a little. I kissed her neck and ran my tongue across her cheek. I felt her teeth nip my earlobes and it drove me wild.

I groaned and held her closer. The shirt she was wearing was light and thin and I could feel her curves underneath. I could hardly move, my entire body felt stiff and electric. My hand held her neck and kept her head in place as I laid my lips on hers again. I felt her open her mouth to me and I groaned again, my tongue exploring the depths of her mouth.

I felt her responding, rubbing against me as she squirmed and clutched at my hair, pulling me in, deepening the kiss. I felt her tongue against mine and the soft pressure as she sucked. I growled and lifted her up.

16

PASSIONS RELEASED

ELLIE

He held me fast and I let him in. It was urgent, almost frantic. I could feel his strong arms enfold me, I could hardly breathe. I kissed his neck and ears and then his lips were on mine. His tongue explored my mouth and I sucked on it, urging him to go deeper, to dive into the depths of me, with me.

I felt him lift me up and I held on, or lips still locked. He carried me as if I weighed nothing and all that mattered was the kiss. I massaged his tongue with mine, and all I knew was this was what I wanted, this was what I came for. He sat down and I was on his lap. I could feel his hardness through his flimsy boxers and I ached for it. He pushed me down, and I lay there, looking up at him.

It suddenly hit me that we were in his bedroom and I panicked. I sat bolt upright, suddenly nervous.

He seemed worried by my reaction. I could see the haze of passion dissipate from his eyes. "What's wrong?" he asked, his voice husky and low.

I couldn't look him in the eye. I turned away from him a little, but I knew I had to tell him even though I was a little embarrassed to admit it. *I'm 26 years old, after all, and still a virgin.* It was almost ridiculous.

"This...would be my first time," I said, still not looking at him. He didn't move for a few seconds but then he came over and kneeled beside me, looking into my eyes.

"I understand, we don't have to rush," he said, rubbing my knee. "I can wait until you're ready."

The minute he said these words I knew that waiting was the last thing I wanted to do. He looked out of breath and his lips were red from our frenzied kissing, and I could feel an ache deep inside me, longing for him to touch me again. I had waited long enough.

"No," I said, touching his cheek. "I want to do this. I've been waiting to do this. With you."

He leaned into my hand, caught it in his, and kissed it. "Are you sure?" he asked.

"Absolutely."

He stepped back and helped me up. He kissed me lightly on the forehead and began undressing me. He unbuttoned my pants and pulled them down, then pulled my shirt off over my head. This was the first time I'd ever been half naked in front of a man, and my hands went over my intimate areas, trying to cover up my body.

Conrad pulled my hands away. "Don't do that," he said. "I want to look at you." I could see his eyes glaze over as he looked at my body. I had to fight the urge to shield myself from his gaze.

"You look absolutely beautiful, Ellie," he said. He caught me and kissed me again and I could feel his fingers working on my bra. It came off and I heard him groan. His hands caught my breasts and started caressing them until his fingers found my nipples. He rubbed my nipples gently and I felt a whole new sensation. I started to arch my back and undulate my body against his touch. His lips left mine and his kisses trailed down my neck, sending ripples of pleasure down my spine, trailing down to my breasts.

He started kissing my voluptuous mounds, circling round until his hot mouth caught an erect nipple while his hand fondled my other breast, softly pinching my other nipple in his fingers. I gasped and clutched at his hair. The pleasure was making me rock my body back and forth. I could feel him pushing me down gently until I was sitting on the bed again and he was kneeling down in front of him. I could feel his tongue flicking back and forth against my nipple. I was moaning from the pleasure, the sweet heat from his mouth.

He started sucking on my nipples and I felt his other hand trailing down, stroking my thighs and making me shiver. I could already feel the wetness between my legs and I was a little embarrassed. I resisted as he tried to push my knees apart, but I had no strength left. I could feel his hand over my underwear, rubbing at my clit through the black lace. He groaned and pushed me down so that I was laying back in bed, but my feet still touched the floor.

A sudden fit of modesty hit me. I knew that as he kneeled in front of the bed, he was staring directly at my sex, and I'd never even looked at it myself. It felt too vulnerable, too exposed. I struggled to get up but I was weak with sensation. All I could muster was a faint, "Please."

Conrad heard and paused. "What's wrong?" he asked.

I had to struggle to speak up. "No one's ever seen me down there before," I managed to say.

"I want to see you, Ellie, all of you," he said. "Do you trust me?"

All I could do was give a little nod and I could see him smiling down at me. "If it gets uncomfortable or if you have second-thoughts, all you have to do is say so, okay?" he said.

I nodded again and watched in nervous anticipation as he knelt down again.

I felt his hands slowly pulling down my underwear. "You look absolutely beautiful," he said. He laid his hands on my thigh, and then I felt a finger touch my labia. The tingling sensation made me squirm. He rubbed a finger over my clit and I cried out, his other hand stroking my belly. To my horror I suddenly felt his hot lips on my pussy, then a tongue shooting out, licking my clit. I wanted to cry out, to beg him to stop but I couldn't speak. My body heaved to the rhythm of his tongue.

His kisses made the pleasure well up between my legs, ready to explode. My hands clutched the sheets and I wanted to beg him to stop, but all I could do was moan. My hand was on his head, wanting both to push him deeper into my slit and pull him away from me at the same time.

He started sucking on my clit and I felt him slide a finger inside me, gently exploring my sex. I couldn't hold it anymore. The sensations exploded in my belly and reverberated throughout my body. I cried out, deep and loud as my climax shook me to my core.

"Please, please, enough," I whimpered. Mercifully, he stopped and got up. I was still shivering in bed, shaken from the devastating orgasm that I had never experienced before. He must have stepped into the bathroom because he came back with a towel.

He had wiped his face, and I could see there were rivulets of water on his chest and his hair was wet. I got on my elbows and looked at him. That was when I saw his bulging erection, straining against his thin boxers.

I had never done anything like this before, but at that moment, I wanted a taste of him too. I sat up and ran my fingers over his chiseled abs. I slipped a finger under his waistband and started pulling it down. He held my hand to stop me.

"What are you doing?" he asked, his voice hoarse.

"I want to taste you, too," I said, pulling my hand from his grasp abruptly and freeing his throbbing member from his underwear.

It was big, bigger than I expected, and it made me a little scared of what I might experience later. But I also felt a ravenous desire. I laid a hand over his rock-hard cock and I could feel him shiver under my touch. I ran my hand up and down his shaft and it was gratifying to see him close his eyes and gasp as I did.

I kissed his stomach and I could feel his hand caressing my cheek. His cock was pulsing in my hand and I trailed my kisses down and kissed the tip, lightly at first, unsure of what it might taste like. He groaned and I could feel his body tense as my lips touched his member. I started running my tongue on the tip while stroking his shaft gently.

He was clutching at my shoulders as I did this, and it encouraged me to take the length of his shaft into my mouth. It tasted like nothing, but his gasps and growls excited me. I started sucking on his cock, running my mouth over it. In and out, slowly, then faster. I knew that if I took it all in, I would probably choke, but I wanted to try. I brought it as deep as it would go and slowly sucked as I pulled my head back.

He groaned and I felt him squeeze my shoulders as his body tensed. I reached down and had his balls in my hands. Although I was a virgin, I'd read enough to know what might excite a man, and I wanted to try it now.

He shivered as I cradled his balls with one hand, stroked his shaft with another, all the while sucking on his dick with great enthusiasm. I soon felt his hand on my face, but then he stepped back.

"That's quite enough, Ellie," he said. I looked up and saw his face was red and there was sweat on his brow. "I want to make love to you," he said.

I nodded and laid back. He placed a towel underneath us and asked me again if I was ready.

"I'm 26 years old, Conrad. I know what I want," I said. "I want this."

"If I hurt you in any way at all," he said. "Tell me immediately and I'll stop, okay?"

I nodded and he laid beside me, kissing my neck, then my lips. He shifted his weight and slowly got on top of me. I could feel his cock on my belly and I reached down to stroke it, kissing him back all the while.

"Tell me if I hurt you, okay?" he whispered in my ear. I just nodded. He knelt up on the bed and held his cock in his hand, getting in position. My heart was racing. I knew this was going to hurt and I was a little nervous. I could feel his hard member against my wet pussy.

"Ready?" he asked, his eyes half-closed.

"Yes, I want you inside me," I whispered back and he groaned. I could feel the pressure as he slowly slid the tip inside me. I cried out from the pain, but also the excitement. I wanted to feel it inside me. I wanted to feel his cock in my pussy.

He paused when I cried out and started kissing me again. The pain subsided and I raised my thighs, meeting his cock and driving it deeper. The pain was sharp, but the pleasure loomed over me: it felt like it was just around the corner. I started to rock back and forth, finding my rhythm. He groaned as I undulated my body underneath him. He laid a hand under my ass and I could feel him squeeze the flesh.

I became bolder with my movement and wrapped my thighs over his waist. He started moving too, his cock going deeper with every thrust. The pain was being replaced by a need for satisfaction. Conrad grew frantic as I continued to meet his thrusts and he grabbed my ass and pulled me closer, placing one of my legs over his shoulder, kissing my thighs as he drove his hard cock deeper into me. There was no resistance anymore.

I felt his hand reach for a breast and pinch my nipple. The little prick of pain was overshadowed by the excitement and the pleasure welling up inside me. I was punching up against every thrust and I could feel my orgasm coming closer and closer. I couldn't take it anymore. I pulled him down to meet me, my hand reaching for his ass and I pulled him against me as I gyrated my hips against him. He groaned, still thrusting in rhythm.

"I'm coming," he said, his voice raspy. I quickened my movements.

"Yes," I cried as my body tensed. I felt him shiver as he thrust deeper, then I gave a final cry, arching my body as I was rocked by another, shattering orgasm. He tensed up and I could feel his cock pulsing inside me.

As the pleasure subsided, Conrad fell in a heap beside me, utterly spent. I was still breathing heavily, exhausted, when an intrusive thought suddenly popped into my head.

"Oh my god, did you use a condom?" I blurted out, suddenly sitting bolt upright. He didn't respond immediately and I could feel the panic rising up in my throat. "This is not happening!" I cried, getting up to go to the bathroom to try and "wash it off" but Conrad stopped me.

"Of course I did, Ellie," he said. "What do you take me for?" and he proceeded to show me the used condom in his hand. I breathed a sigh of relief and hit him on the shoulder.

"That was scary! I can't get pregnant on my first time!" He was chuckling beside me and put a hand over my shoulder. He pulled me down until I was lying down next to him.

"Was it good? Did you enjoy it?" he asked, twirling a finger over my breasts.

"Yes, I did," I replied. "And I plan to enjoy it even more later on. But for now, I think I need a shower." He laughed and held me closer.

"Yeah, I think I'll join you later," he said, his eyes closed.

"But I really need a shower right now," I said, taking his arm off me and getting up. I went into his bathroom. It was the typical bachelor's shower, with the gold-plated faucets and shower head against black and white marble tiles.

I got the hot water going and felt the relief of it on my skin, lathering soap on myself leisurely. I wasn't paying attention to my surroundings, completely content with my hot shower, when I heard Conrad clear his throat.

I whirled around and found him looking at me with a huge erection. I was no expert but didn't men usually need recovery time?

My mouth dropped open as I stared at his dick, which he was stroking ever so slightly. "Can I join you?" he just asked.

I laughed. "It's your shower, Mister Young," I said, stepping aside to let him in.

When he got inside, he kissed me again, his rock hard cock poking my belly. I looked at it and raised an eyebrow. "Really?" I asked, smiling mischievously.

"I can't help it," he said guiltily. "You're not the only one who's been waiting, and you excite me, Ellie. If anything, this is all your fault." I smiled at this, getting excited too.

"Can I wash your hair?" he asked and I nodded. He took some shampoo from the shower caddy on his bathroom wall, lathered it up and massaged it into my head. I breathed out a little sigh and leaned against him as he worked it all over my hair. It didn't take long before his hands started to stray.

I slapped his hand away playfully as he started caressing one of my breasts. "That's not part of the deal you know," I said as he chuckled.

"I'd like to remind you, Miss Rodriguez, that this is my shower," he said, his hands wandering over my shoulders and giving me a massage. I moaned.

"And I'd like to remind you that these are my breasts," I said, smiling, "I have to admit, that does feel good though."

"Do you want me to make you feel even better?" he whispered in my ear. I laughed. "What do you have in mind, Mr. Young?"

He didn't respond. Instead he just put some liquid soap into his hands and started massaging it into my body, starting from the neck then working downwards. There was no more funny business from him. He seemed intent on just cleaning me up. I, on the other hand, was getting excited by his touch.

I turned to face him as he lathered on the soap into my legs and feet. When he got up, I reached for him and we started kissing, the hot water raining over us and leaving my skin tingling. His hands sought out my breast and he knelt down to kiss them, licking and sucking until I thought I'd lose my mind.

I pulled him up to face me so I could kiss him again. My hand traveled down and caressed his cock, and I could feel his muscles tense up at my attention. His fingers sought my pussy which was soaking wet now. He started rubbing my clit and I moaned. Before I knew what was happening, he held my leg up with one arm, put another under my ass and lifted me up.

My back hit the tile wall, which was warm from the hot

steam. I still had his tongue in my mouth and started sucking on it gently. He groaned and shifted his body a little and before I knew it, he had slipped his huge, hard cock inside me. It went easier this time, and there was not as much pain anymore. But, the pleasure was even more intense. I moaned into his mouth, sucking on his lower lip and holding on for dear life as he thrust his member deep into me.

I was amazed at his strength. I no longer had trouble when it came to controlling my weight, but by no means was I skinny. Yet here he was, holding me up like I weighed nothing. He started thrusting faster and faster, and I was just about to cum when he stopped. I groaned and opened my eyes as he set me down again.

"Let's take this back to the bed," he said, his voice husky. He turned off the water and led me out of the shower. He took a towel from the closet and dried himself first before turning to me and drying me with the fluffy towel.

"Come here," he said, and took my hand, leading me back to the bed. I got on the bed and laid down on my back. He came up and knelt on the bed in front of me. I had raised my knees and was giggling as he tried to pry them apart. We wrestled a little, laughing and tickling each other until we were in each other's arms again. He pushed me down on the bed and got back on his knees. Conrad sure seemed to like being in control.

He pushed my knees apart and I felt his fingers in my slit again. I gasped as he slipped his finger inside of me and bent down. He kissed my pussy and started licking my clit again, moving his fingers in unison. I cried out from the pleasure. But I was hungry too.

I reached over and started stroking his shaft as he worked on my pussy. I was moaning and gasping, but he didn't let up. I pulled on his cock and shifted in the bed, maneuvering myself until I was directly underneath him, the tip of his erection right in front of me.

I started sucking on his dick, working my hand back and forth. I could feel him tense up and groan, sticking his finger deeper into me. I took his cock deeper into my mouth, sucking and licking until I felt him start to thrust his hips.

He started sucking on my clit and cried out, his dick still in my mouth. I couldn't take it anymore. I got myself from under him and told him to lie back. He got up and ran to a drawer, pulling out a condom and sliding his cock into it before he obeyed and laid on his back in front of me.

I got on top of him and straddled him, gasping as his hard cock slid deep into my pussy. I felt him grab my round ass before giving it a resounding slap. I gasped then giggled as he squeezed my butt cheeks and groaned. I started to undulate my body against him, feeling new sensations.

I gyrated against him, hot flashes of pleasure running through my body. I felt myself getting closer and closer to another climax as I quickened my pace. He raised himself up against me and caught my breast in his mouth, sucking on my nipples. The pleasure and sensations were becoming too much and I cried out.

"Conrad, yes!" I cried, pushing myself up against him and undulating my body against his. "I'm cumming," I cried out again, my pleasure bubbling up and overflowing. I held him close as I felt him tense up and shiver against me.

I was totally spent. I rolled down next to him and laid a head on his shoulder. He tucked a strand of hair behind my ear, looking at me tenderly.

"I love you, Ellie," I heard him say before I fell into a deep, exhausted sleep.

17

A BROTHER'S LOVE

CONRAD

I WOKE up to my stomach growling. I was famished. I don't know how long we'd slept but I could guess that it was probably late afternoon already.

It all seemed like a dream to me, but here was Ellie, breathing softly with her head on my shoulder. I kissed her forehead and she just sighed, still deep in slumber. I gently took my arm from under her head and got up. I picked up my phone and ordered food.

I washed up in the bathroom and put on some clothes. I picked up the clothes strewn across the floor and put them in the washing machine in my bathroom.

It wasn't long before the doorbell rang. I went to get our food and tipped the delivery man generously.

His eyes widened when he saw the fifty I was offering. "Wow, that's a lot, man," he said, taking the money hesitantly. "It wasn't that far you know."

"Take it," I said, smiling. "I had a good day." He thanked me and went on his way. I placed the food on the table and was surprised to see Ellie standing in the doorway, a blanket thrown over her shoulders.

"Is that food?" she asked enthusiastically. "I'm starving."

I laughed and nodded, gesturing for her to come and eat. Her hair was disheveled and she wore no makeup, but she still looked divine. I went back into my room and got her a shirt to put on.

She was already holding a spoonful of Chinese food when I got back. "Here," I said as I handed her the shirt, "you're too distracting when you're strutting around naked."

She laughed as she took the shirt from me. She let the blanket fall to the floor and put on the shirt while I stared, wide-eyed, at her beautiful naked form. I could feel my cock getting hard again and I shifted in my seat involuntarily. Thank God she didn't notice. I was starting to feel like a schoolboy with Ellie.

My stomach growled loudly again. Ellie and I looked at each other and laughed. We ate with gusto, hardly saying a word.

"Oh god, I don't remember ever being this hungry," she said, forking chow mein into her mouth. "It really is a work-out, isn't it?"

"Oh," I said, raising an eyebrow. "Why do you say that?"

"Well, I always used to ask Sarah why she was so skinny," she replied. "Maintaining her weight seemed easy. She always said it was because sex was such a workout."

I snorted, rolling my eyes at the mention of Sarah. "If anything," I said, "I have a feeling Sarah's the type to lie completely still during sex. Most women who think they're 'too good' tend to."

She raised an eyebrow at me. "How many of these women have you slept with?" she asked. "You seem to know so much about it."

I laughed, swallowing a mouthful of Kung Pao chicken. "Not that many to be honest, and I'm not speaking from experience, just analysis."

"You've got to be kidding me," she said. "Of course you

fucked around. You're a big successful billionaire. Women must've been falling at your feet."

"Believe it or not, Ellie," I replied, "I didn't fuck around too much. I never really enjoyed casual sex. Once I got YoungTech off the ground, I was focused on the business. I had to be more responsible with my personal choices. After that? I guess it just got to be too much trouble."

I ended up saying more than I had intended to. I guess I was just comfortable talking to Ellie. She always listened and seemed to think about what you said instead of jumping to conclusions or judging you.

She was quiet for a moment, then turned to me. "Was it because of Jessica?" she asked.

"Kind of," I replied. "But I've never been a trusting person and what happened with Jessica just sort of aggravated that. I mean, lot's of people get fucked over by people they trust. Look at you for example. The level of betrayal you got from Sarah is arguably worse than what I went through with Jessica, but you're still the same sweet, trusting person. It takes a different sort of person to go MIA for two years because his ex-girlfriend turned out to be a gold digger."

She sighed and sat up. "You should never blame yourself for how you react when someone hurts you," she said, looking at me tenderly. "You had a different experience. You lost your parents really young and you had to be guarded. Jessica was the one who messed up."

I looked at her with wonder. Her kindness and understanding always amazed me. I couldn't help but feel how lucky I was to have her in my life. Her sexuality was also surprising. I knew she had no experience but honestly, I had had the time of my life.

"Ellie, you really are something else aren't you? What did I do to deserve someone like you?" I said. And it was true: I could hardly believe she would fall for me, especially after I found out about how my words had affected her in the past.

"After we got past the bullying, I kind of discovered what a nice, gentlemanly man you were," she said, smiling at me and munching on some fried dumplings. She licked her fingers and cocked her head thoughtfully. "I never imagined you'd be a romantic interest in my life, you know," she admitted. "You were always just Aaron's friend and you intimidated me a little when we were younger, even more so when you got your career."

"Really?" I asked, surprised. "How did I intimidate you?"

She laughed and shook her head. "I don't know, I think it had a lot to do with my self-esteem," she said. "You're the kind of guy a girl like Sarah would have her eyes on. I never thought I'd even be in the running. I didn't think a guy like you would ever be interested in a girl like me, especially with your little 'jokes' about my appearance."

I felt a stab of guilt with what she said. "Ellie!" I said, "You really have no idea?"

"What are you talking about?" she asked, looking a little suspicious. I knew I had to confess.

"You know what they say about a 12 year old boy when he likes a girl?" I asked. She just looked at me with her eyebrows furrowed so I explained. "There's this thing that they say when a boy likes a girl, that he'll pull her hair, or throw rocks at her, but it's just a way to get her attention."

"Okay?" she said, still looking puzzled.

"Well that was me, okay? I was that kid, even though I was probably sixteen or seventeen at the time," I said, a little ashamed to admit it. "I had a crush on my best friend's little sister and I didn't know what to do with that or express it in a healthy way. So...I teased you."

I was surprised to hear her snort, her eyes wide in

surprise. "You liked me? Even then? I always thought you saw me as an annoying kid sister," she said, laughing at the realization.

"Well at first I did," I joked, "Until you grew out your boobs, and by then I had other ideas."

"Conrad!" she cried, acting all scandalized. "You had a dirty mind for a sixteen year old! All those summers ago I was too scared to wear a bathing suit around you, and to think that you probably would have liked it if I did."

"I think I might have liked it a little too much," I said, chuckling. It was true, too. If I had gone home on one of those summers and found Ellie in a bikini, I would have been driven to distraction. "How about you," I said, changing the subject. "What changed your mind about me?"

She paused to think about this before answering. "Well," she finally said, "it never would have happened if we hadn't made that arrangement, which probably wouldn't have happened if Sarah hadn't blindsided me with Tyler, so I think you have Sarah and Tyler to thank for it."

I groaned loudly, running my hand over my face. She just laughed. "No, seriously," I protested. "I want a serious answer."

"Okay, okay," she said, laughing. "I think I just needed to get to know you a little better. I had a lot of prejudice against you and I almost didn't consider ever pretending to be your fiancée..."

"What changed your mind?" I asked.

She shifted in the chair and laughed. "Kate did, actually. She told me it wasn't such a bad idea and that I should give it a try."

"Remind me to thank Kate, then," I said. I still couldn't believe that this was all real. "Now that our relationship has...changed," I added, "how do you feel about pet-names knowing that I am absolutely enamored with you and your figure?"

She smiled and rolled her eyes. "I can accept Ellie-belly, but note that it should be used sparingly and never during arguments or times when I feel down. Ellie-phant, on the other hand, is a resounding no."

I laughed and took her hand, "My Ellie-belly," I said, and she just rolled her eyes again.

"How about you, what were you up to?" she asked. "What did you do in those two years you were gone?"

I thought about how I would describe it. I had gone to a lot of places, tourist attractions, and hidden gems, I ate at the finest restaurants and at street corners. I told her about all the countries I went to, where I went, what I ate, but she didn't seem satisfied with what I said.

"You're technically telling me everything you did but you're not telling me anything important," she finally said after some moments of silence.

"Important? Like what?" I asked.

"Like why you did it, what you were thinking?" she replied. "If you missed us? And if those two years helped you at all..."

I thought about it for a minute. "Why? I guess it would be easy to say that it was all about Jessica, but that wouldn't be entirely true," I admitted. "Part of it was the humiliation of being played for a fool, the other part was that I wasn't ready to face the future, I guess, knowing that my wealth would have a negative impact on my relationships. After what Jessica did, I realized that I couldn't trust people right away, no matter how I felt about them. Then I figured it wasn't a priority and I just decided to take a step back.

"I wasn't really thinking about it in terms of what I wanted to achieve or where I wanted to be. It was just a place where I wasn't, I was in an 'anywhere-but-here' mindset and I just kept going."

Ellie seemed to take her time to process my words. "What finally made you come back?" she asked after mulling it over.

"William. I guess he got more and more worried as time went on and he finally gave me an ultimatum. He said I had to come home or else he would disown me. He was quite frantic on that phone call. That's why it hit me a little differently when he lost consciousness on my visit. I was blaming myself for not listening and possibly having too little time left with him."

Ellie smiled before she got up and brought the empty takeout containers to the sink. I got up and cleaned up the table, smiling at the concept of us acting like an old married couple already.

It didn't take long before I got impatient, watching her bent over the sink. She was all kinds of sexy, with my shirt barely long enough to cover her beautiful ass. I started to make my way toward her. She hardly noticed me, she was so intent on what she was doing.

I pressed up against her from behind and reached down, finding my way between her legs. But Ellie slapped my hands away and splashed water on me. We laughed but I continued to hold her, my face buried in her luxurious locks as she finished washing up.

"Are you done?" I asked impatiently.

She laughed and nodded. I carried her in my arms and brought her to the bed, frantically pulling the t-shirt off as I tumbled in with her. I kissed her luscious lips, drinking in her taste and inhaling her scent. There was something about Ellie that seemed so real, so wholesome to me. I couldn't get enough of her.

My hands traveled to her breasts, then her shapely waist,

finally landing on the round, voluptuous curves of her ass. She wasn't wearing any underwear, and my fingers quickly found their way to her hot, soft, and moist sex. The feel of her, how ready she always seemed for me, drove me wild. I gave her lips a little love bite as I slipped a finger inside her. She gasped in my arms. I loved that, I wanted to make up for any pain I may have caused her. From now on, I would always give her pleasure, and *only* pleasure, if I could help it.

Her finger pulled on my boxers but I wanted us to slow down a little. "Not yet," I whispered, pulling her hands away from me. I started kissing her neck and ears, running my tongue over the sensitive skin, delighting in her little gasps. Her hands were in my hair now, pulling lightly.

My fingers went soft and slow over her nether lips, my thumb gently rubbing her clitoris. She was moaning and shivering against me. God, she was delicious. My lips traveled down to her ample breasts, licking and sucking on her aroused nipples while my fingers continued working her.

She was pulling my hair with a bit more force before crying out. "Conrad! Please darling," she said. "Please fuck me!" I lost myself and groaned. I slipped on a condom that was ready on my nightstand and pushed her down onto the bed. Before I knew what she was doing, she had turned around and had her back to me. She looked over her shoulder and said, "I want to try it from behind."

I almost couldn't believe my ears so I sat there, dumbfounded, for a good minute or two. She turned to look at me and laughed. "What's wrong? Come on," she said, before getting on her knees. The view was glorious. I ran my tongue down her ass and gave it a little smack. She giggled and wiggled her butt at me.

I straddled her and pushed my cock inside her. Her gasps and moans excited me. I slammed against her ass, a little harder than I had first intended, but she seemed to enjoy it, moaning loudly. I slowed it down, determined to be gentler, but then she started moving against me, backing her ass up and swallowing my cock with her juicy vagina.

I lost all thought. All I could do was ram my cock inside her with increasing urgency. I slipped a finger between her legs and found her jewel, flicking at it until she shook in my arms. "Conrad, Conrad," she cried out frantically. "I'm coming!"

She started moving faster, gyrating against me. I slammed into her, faster, harder, everything she asked for until I couldn't delay it any longer. "Conrad, I'm coming," she cried again, and I let myself go, losing myself in sweet release.

～

I woke up to my alarm at exactly 6:30. I was a bit dazed. I had had the best night's sleep I'd had in a long time and I had Ellie to thank for it. She really was something else.

Last night, we made love again, but it was much slower and less frantic this time. Ellie was very expressive when it came to sex and I loved how in tune she was with her sexuality and her satisfaction.

She lay next to me with her head on my arm, her hair tumbling all around her. I touched her cheek and caressed one exposed breast, but she just grunted and shifted in her sleep. I decided to let her rest, gave her a kiss on the forehead and quietly got up. I wanted to make breakfast for Ellie.

I got to the kitchen and started the coffee. I was already taking eggs and bacon out of the refrigerator when I heard the doorbell ring. I wasn't expecting anyone at this time of the morning so this puzzled me.

I headed to the video intercom and almost dropped the

eggs. It was Aaron and he was pacing angrily in front of my door. I took a deep breath and tried to gather my thoughts. I watched as he slammed his fists against the door impatiently and rang the doorbell again.

I decided taking too long would just make it worse, so I opened the door and Aaron came storming in. He didn't pause to greet me or even look at me. His eyes were directly scanning the apartment as soon as he got inside.

"Have you seen, Ellie? She didn't come home last night," he finally asked, still looking around the room before looking at me.

I didn't answer him right away. I was at a loss as to how to explain things to him so I knew I better stall. "What are you doing back in town?" I asked instead. "I wasn't expecting you to be back so soon."

He finally stood still and looked me dead in the face. "I need you to tell me where Ellie is right now!" He had raised his voice and was getting agitated.

"Aaron, would you please calm down? I don't understand what is going on with you."

"I'll calm the fuck down when I see Ellie, okay?" he said, walking into the kitchen and then back again, unable to stay still.

"What's going on, can you calm down and explain this to me please?" I said, trying to sound calm myself. "Why are you back?"

"Here," he said, handing me his phone which already had an email displayed on the screen. I took it from him and read the contents of the email:

From: Perkins.Ty.99@YoungTechUSA

To: Rodriguez.Aaron.94@YoungTechUSA

Subject: Immediate Resignation

Aaron,

I am sending this letter as a notice of my resignation from my Systems Developer position at YoungTech effective immediately. I thank you for the opportunity, mentorship, and great work environment I have had in the past two years while working for and with you.

It deeply saddens me to have to leave YoungTech but I feel it is impossible to continue working there. I won't go into the details but I am afraid my relationship with our CEO may have been irreparably damaged after an unfortunate dinner I had with him and a few friends. Thank you very much for understanding.

Tyler Perkins

So Tyler had quit. What a pansy! At least he didn't get into detail about why, but an employee with a good record and good trajectory suddenly quitting would definitely raise a few eyebrows. I couldn't believe he had even roped me into it. I could understand Aaron's surprise though, considering I'd never exchanged more than two words with Tyler Perkins.

"Don't worry about it, I'll handle it," I said, handing him back the phone. Aaron just shook his head. I tried to give him my signature smile but he wasn't buying it.

"No, I'll handle it," he said, pointing at his own chest. "I need to know what happened at that dinner and why one of my developers decided to quit out of the blue."

"Well I don't have to tell you anything," I said stubbornly, "And you're not in a position to ask me about what happens outside company hours!"

"I have a right to know, he was on my team and I was his direct supervisor!"

"You're his supervisor?" I retaliated. "I'm the fucking CEO!"

"Oh are you? I almost forgot, you're the fucking CEO," Aaron said sarcastically before rifling through his phone again and handing it to me. It was a text message from Sarah:

> Aaron, just want you to know that Ellie and Conrad R dating. Didnt think they told u and i think its ur right as her bro to know this. Im concerned about Ellie, she changed a lot n I worry bout her. Tell her I said hi. XOXO

I wanted to curse out Sarah and Tyler for ruining everything as soon as they got a chance. I couldn't understand how they could both decide to give Aaron a reason to come back, then tell him that Ellie and I were dating. As I thought about it, I realized that there was only one answer. *Sarah, that conniving little...*

"So you're the CEO huh?" Aaron said, interrupting my thoughts, "I'm her brother! Tell me where my sister is right now."

I just turned away from him, realizing that this was going to be a difficult conversation, if there was going to be a conversation at all. I was starting to get the picture. Aaron must have cut his trip short when he got these messages, then he went home and couldn't find Ellie anywhere, before heading here, already worked up and seeing red.

"So what was your plan?" he asked derisively. "Did you just wait till I got to Singapore so you could make a pass on my sister? Were you even planning on telling me? Or were you hoping I'd stay in Singapore forever so you could just do whatever the hell you wanted? Maybe this was the whole point of the trip in the first place!"

I couldn't bear to hear Aaron talk that way. I couldn't believe he actually thought that about me. Taking advantage of Ellie was the last thing on my mind.

"You have to be kidding," I said, looking him in the eye and keeping my rage in check. "You know that's not how this went. There was never a devious plan, it just happened."

He lost some steam when I spoke up, but then we heard the bedroom door open and the sounds of someone moving around. I looked over to Aaron and could see he looked ready to explode, but he said nothing. I knew what was coming so I took a seat and waited.

"Conrad?" Ellie called. "Where are you? Is there someone with you?"

Aaron was shaking his head and giving me the evil eye, but then I saw him turn red. He turned white first and was slowly turning very, very red. When I turned my head to the doorway, I understood why.

Ellie was standing there, looking at us both in shock. She wore nothing but an old T-shirt of mine.

18

THE TRUTH THIS TIME

ELLIE

I woke up feeling a little confused, knowing I was lying in someone else's bed. I rubbed my eyes and suddenly remembered I was in Conrad's bed after spending a magical night with him. I had read about how awkward and uncomfortable it usually was during your first time, but I couldn't have wanted anything more for my first.

I had made love to the man I loved—several times actually—and it was everything I wanted and more. I smiled to myself, recalling all the events of the day before. The past two weeks had been magical and I couldn't be happier that this was the outcome of it all.

I was actually glad that I waited if it meant it was Conrad I would end up with. I wasn't naive though; I knew relationships took work. But I also felt that Conrad and I were mature enough to ride the waves together. I knew in my heart that he loved me, and I knew I loved him, no strings, no hidden agendas.

I got up and looked for something to wear. I grabbed the shirt Conrad lent me yesterday, not bothering with any underwear. I wasn't sure where they were anyway. I went into the bathroom and splashed some water on my face. I gargled with some mouthwash I found by the sink and combed through my hair with my hand. I could hear the faint sound of voices. Did Conrad have company?

I opened the door to the bedroom and the voices abruptly stopped.

"Conrad? Where are you? Is there someone with you?" I called. When there was no answer, I figured he might be on the phone or something, so I headed out. My footsteps were silent against the marble tile and I was smiling when I saw him in the kitchen. But something was off. When I got closer, I stopped dead in my tracks. It was Aaron staring at me, wide-eyed and furious.

I looked at Conrad, but he seemed as lost as I felt. He just scratched his head and sighed deeply. I quickly tried to pacify Aaron's wrath. He looked about ready to go to war.

"Aaron, I need you to calm down," I said, holding up a hand towards him. "This is not what it looks like."

My words, instead of calming him down, set him off. Aaron came toward me in two strides and was on me with his eyes on fire.

"Really, it's not what it looks like?" he shouted, his face all red. "Please, please give me a fucking explanation as to why I found you both in his apartment, half-fucking-naked at 7 am! Please! What else could it be? Coz to me it looks like my best friend is banging my little sister!"

I was about to say something, anything, to get Aaron to stop freaking out, but Conrad had gotten up and laid a hand on my shoulder. Aaron looked like he was gonna go off on another tirade, but Conrad cut him off by saying, "You should go and get dressed. We can settle this later."

Aaron bit his lip and stood between us. I could only look over Aaron's shoulder at Conrad, but I knew that Aaron was probably glaring at him so he couldn't even look at me. Without saying another word, I headed back into Conrad's room and looked for my clothes. I finally found them in the dryer but I couldn't find my underwear. I decided to give up and just put my pants on, keeping my ears open for any arguments breaking out while I was out of the room. But I heard nothing.

I put my clothes back on, racking my brain for the right words to say to Aaron to make it better. I could tell he was on the warpath. He was in his protective-big-brother-beast-mode right now and it was going to be hard to get him to see reason.

I had prepared a little speech about love, acceptance, and the importance of family when I walked out of the room. I had planned to stand next to Conrad as I explained everything.

When I walked into Conrad's living room I saw that neither of them had moved an inch since I went into the bedroom. I headed in Conrad's direction, but Aaron pounced on me. He grabbed my arm and pulled me back.

"Don't even fucking think about it!" he growled under his breath. I was about to speak up but I saw Conrad shake his head, looking at me tenderly.

My gaze shifted to Aaron and I could see there was no use talking to him now. He was absolutely livid. I knew my brother well enough to know he would be deaf to anything I had to say at this point.

I tried to pull away from him but his grip was firm and he practically dragged me out of there. He walked fast and I had to jog to keep up with him. I looked back to see Conrad slowly closing the door behind us.

"Aaron please, let's be adults about this," I said, hoping he would slow down or at least let me go. But he just grunted and held my arm in a vice-like grip. I was a little scared of Aaron when he was like this. I decided I'd talk to him when we got home and he'd had time to cool off.

When we got outside, I saw that his car was parked right in front of the building. There was already a parking ticket on his windshield. He took it and put it in his pocket without a word.

He only let me go after he had firmly closed the car door on my side.

I tried to talk to him several times on the ride, but he didn't respond. I finally gave up and we sat in silence. Not telling Aaron had been the right decision when Conrad and I had talked about our fake relationship, but the situation had changed.

We'd developed feelings for each other and Aaron would have had to know eventually. I just wished we had some time to break it to him properly. I didn't like the fact that he had to find out this way; it made it seem as if we were hiding it from him somehow.

To my surprise I realized halfway that we were not headed home. Aaron was taking me to the bakery.

"Aaron, why don't we just go home and talk about this?" I said, putting a hand on his shoulder. "This is ridiculous. I'm an adult and you're being absolutely unreasonable about this."

Instead of softening even a little bit, he just pulled away from my touch and grunted, his brows furrowing even more. I knew he must have been tired and extra-grumpy. Time would be an ally in this situation so I decided to let it go.

He parked the car in front of the bakery and I wordlessly went in. Kate's face lit up when she saw me but the moment she saw my expression, she paused. Aaron came in next, looking like he had thunderclouds over his head. Kate gave me a questioning look but all I could do was shrug.

I didn't know what I was expecting from Aaron at that point but I definitely did not expect him to sit around the bakery all day, looking out the window like he was expecting an invasion. He watched me like a hawk and even followed me into the kitchen, sitting on the stool by the kitchen island and sipping coffee all afternoon.

"Aaron get some sleep," I suggested when I noticed how red his eyes were. "You can have a nap in my office."

He had scoffed at the suggestion. "So you can sneak off to your boyfriend?" he said bitterly. "No thanks." And that had been that.

Kate tried to get my attention several times that day. I knew she must have been itching for some updates, but with Aaron's ears perked up, I didn't think it would be a good idea. I just shook my head at Kate whenever she tried to engage in conversation. She raised her eyebrows at me then motioned to Aaron. I turned my eyes to heaven and shrugged. She seemed to understand.

We just concentrated on baking for the rest of the day and any conversations we had were about inventories, supplies, and deliveries.

It was 8 o'clock when we started closing up. Kate and I cleared away the display cases, with Aaron looming over us. "Uhm, did you get the sugar you were looking for yester-day," Kate said nonchalantly. I was quiet for a minute, not knowing what she was talking about. "You know, you said you were gonna taste some of that organic sugar from the deli for our new recipe. Did you get to try it?" Of course there was no organic sugar or deli, so I could guess that she meant my trip to confront Conrad.

"Uhh, yeah I got some sugar," I said, trying to hide a smile.

"Was it good?" Kate followed up, looking absolutely serious. I had to take a breath.

"It was absolutely delicious," I said. Looking over my shoulder to make sure Aaron was out of earshot. "I couldn't get enough," I said, and we both fell into a fit of giggles.

"What are you talking about?" Aaron asked, coming over to us.

"Nothing, just some new recipes we wanted to try," Kate replied, as we both struggled to keep from laughing out loud. We cleared up the displays, put all the sweets and pastries into the refrigerator, and wiped down the tables. Despite his foul mood, Aaron helped us out, clearing the stools and tables, and washing some dishes.

I felt a pang of love for my brother. I remembered all the nights he used to do this; it was when I was incredibly busy and the bakery was still short-handed. No matter how late it was when he left his office, he would come by and help me close up. When he got to leave the office early, he would wait around and even help me with some of the prep work for the next day.

I'd never introduced Aaron to any boyfriends in the past because there was never anyone worth introducing to him. Although I had some idea about how protective he could be, I had never really experienced it before. And of course, the fact that Conrad was his closest friend must have had a big effect on how he was taking my first serious relationship.

It was almost 9 pm when Aaron and I finally got home and, just as I expected, we had a big sit down talk. It started when I told him, for the umpteenth time that day, that he was overreacting and being unreasonable.

"What do you think is going to happen here? That you can forbid me from seeing who I choose to see? That's impossible!" I said, feeling exhausted already.

"I'm going to tell you what's going to happen," he said, with his hands crossed over his chest. "I'm going to walk you to the bakery everyday and I'll watch you work. When the day is over, I'll walk you back and make sure you don't go anywhere without me. When I asked you to watch out for Conrad this isn't what I meant!"

"That's ridiculous Aaron!" I cried in exasperation, "You have a job and I'm an adult! You can't chaperone me every single day."

"You don't think so?" he said with a sneer. "Watch me, Ellie. And you know what, I really want to congratulate you for your amazing acting skills. You even convinced me that you didn't like him. I didn't expect this level of deception from either of you, but you had me fooled!

"It's either you're really great actors or maybe I'm just a gullible idiot," he said, his voice raised in anger. "But either way, I'm gonna make this as difficult for the both of you as I humanly can!"

"You're being crazy! I am a 26 year old woman," I said, desperate to get him to see reason. "Conrad and I are consenting adults. You can't stop us from seeing each other."

"You're my little sister and I'm responsible for you," he said stubbornly. "I always will be."

My fists were clenched in frustration but it wasn't worth it anymore. I cursed under my breath and turned around, heading straight to my room and slamming the door behind me.

I immediately took my phone out of my bag and saw that I had several messages and missed calls from Conrad. I dialed his number right away, knowing how worried he must be. He picked up at the first ring.

"Ellie? Are you okay? What's happened with the two of you?"

It was so good to hear his voice. It had only been a day but I missed him so much.

"Oh Conrad, I can't get through to Aaron. He has this ridiculous plan of watching me 24/7 to make sure we don't get a chance to meet up," I explained. "He has this idea that we've been making a fool out of him and deceived him all this time. I tried to tell him the truth but he's not listening."

Conrad sighed. When he spoke, there was a hint of resignation in his voice. "It might take Aaron a while to come around, especially because he found out about us through Sarah and Tyler. He showed me one text from Sarah but who knows what else she's been telling him."

I gasped. I had no idea Sarah and Tyler had anything to do with Aaron coming home out of the blue. "God that bitch!" I blurted out. Conrad laughed on the other end.

"Hey, I finally heard you say it!" he said, still chuckling. "I'm so happy for you Ellie."

"Happy for me? What are you talking about?" I demanded, "How can you be happy for me when my brother has gone bat-shit crazy over us dating?"

"Not about that," he said, his laughter subsiding. "I'm happy that you finally have a clear idea on what type of person that Sarah really is. After everything she's done, this is the first time you've called her a bitch. And I agree, she absolutely is."

"I just can't believe she'd stoop so low, you know?" I said, finally getting a clear picture of Sarah. She was the type who could never be truly happy because she was always after the next big thing. She was also the type who would sabotage someone else's relationship out of jealousy. I even got the idea that that might be the reason she even started going out with Tyler in the first place.

"Well, you better believe it," Conrad said. Then his voice shifted to an almost tender tone, saying, "We should cut Aaron some slack. I think he feels blindsided and he can't believe that this all happened all of a sudden. It is a little hard to believe to be honest. Even I think I'm still dreaming sometimes."

"Yeah. I get it," I replied. "Just a week ago I would have said this was impossible. And it was just at his going away party that I told him I couldn't stand you. He had to convince me to go when I found out you were coming."

"Exactly," Conrad agreed. "Given how close he is to the both of us, it's understandable that he'd think we were playing him or actively being deceptive about our 'real' relationship, even though the truth is that there really was nothing to hide. I'm sure he'll get over it, though I don't know when."

"God, I hope it's soon," I said, longing in my voice. "I already miss you." I didn't do it on purpose, but my voice was becoming all breathless. I did miss him, I wanted nothing more than to curl up next to him, even if Aaron did decide to loom over us with his crazy stare.

"I miss you too, Ellie," he said, then I noticed a naughty tone in his voice. "Which reminds me, you forgot something here."

I wondered what he meant when I suddenly remembered. I had left my thong in his apartment. I had tried looking for it, but I couldn't find it and had just given up.

"Shit, I forgot about that," I said, my cheeks starting to burn. I knew I was blushing. "I looked for it but I couldn't find it. Then Aaron brought me to the bakery and I just couldn't bring it up. I think he would have freaked out even more if I said something. Where was it?"

I could hear Conrad chuckling on the line. "Do you mean to tell me that you went commando at the bakery all day?" his mirth was clearly audible, and it was very annoying. "I'm not an expert but I'm pretty sure that's a health code violation. The State of California might have to shut that down."

"Conrad, would you please stop that?" I said, losing patience with his childishness, and also a bit mortified by the whole thing. "We have serious problems that we have to get through and you're acting like a child. Where did you find it?"

"It was in the dryer, but it snuck its way to the very back which is probably why you couldn't find it," he said. "I wish I knew that this was going to happen. I wouldn't have washed it and kept it as a souvenir."

I was scandalized by the idea and was sputtering into the phone, "What? I...no! What the hell are you saying, you pervert?" I cried out, then lowered my voice to a whisper. It would be a fine mess if Aaron found out I was talking to Conrad.

But Conrad sounded perfectly happy over the phone, teasing me. "Just something to hold on to to remember our night," he said, sighing. "Oh Ellie, the things I want to do to you right now. You have no idea."

I felt myself getting aroused with his words. "Really? Why don't you tell me?" I asked, a little surprised at my own forwardness.

He took a deep breath. "I'll tell you," he said, his voice raspy. "But you have to do what I say, okay?"

I was starting to feel a little hot and bothered. "Yes," I breathed into the phone.

"Are you in your room?"

"Yes."

"Take your clothes off," he said, his voice sounding hoarse.

"Okay," I said, pulling my pants and shirt off. I was wearing nothing but a bra. "What are you gonna do to me?" I said into the phone, feeling myself getting wet already.

"I want you to touch yourself, get that pussy wet. Remember when I was licking you down there, just like that..."

"Yeah?" I said, obeying his words. My fingers found my

clit and I started rubbing myself, thinking of Conrad's hot lips the whole time.

"Squeeze your tits for me, babe, squeeze those beautiful tits," he whispered, breathless too.

"I am, my boobs are so big," I said, playing into it. I could hear him grinding his teeth on the line. "Are you hard, baby?"

"Fuck," he said. "I'm hard for you Ellie."

"Conrad, call me Eleanor please," I said, breathing hard against the phone as my hands went from my pussy to my breasts and then back again. "Are you hard for me now, Conrad?"

"Damn it, Eleanor, I feel like I'm gonna burst..."

"I want you to put it in me, baby," I said, sticking my fingers deep into my wet pussy. "Stick it in me deep, I'm so wet for your big hard dick."

He didn't reply right away but I could hear his heavy breathing. "Eleanor, if you were here I'd have you face down on my bed and you'd be begging me to keep going."

"But I am," I said, working my fingers, getting even more breathless. "I'm face down right now, and I want you to keep going, Conrad. Don't stop, don't ever stop..." I was getting nearer and nearer to the climax and I had to put the phone down as I bent over on the bed, fingering myself until I lost all control.

I was breathless when I took the phone again, a thin layer of sweat covering my skin. "I came," I whispered into the phone. "It was so good."

"Yeah, I bet it was," he said, still sounding hoarse.

"Didn't you come?" I asked, genuinely curious.

"No, I think I'll wait for the real thing. It's definitely worth it," he said. I had to laugh.

"You sure? It might be a while you know. Aaron seems pretty mad."

"I know," he said, sighing. "I'm sure he'll come around to it, he just needs time."

"Yeah," I said, unable to suppress a yawn.

"Go to bed, Ellie. We can talk again tomorrow," he said. "I love you, Ell."

"I love you too."

IN THE FOLLOWING DAYS, Aaron became a constant pain in the neck. My neck in particular. He hung around the bakery all day, marinating in his own anger and vindictiveness. He followed me everywhere I went, whether it was to the supermarket or the gym. I even went on a hike, which Aaron hates, just to see the lengths he'd be willing to go just to make sure that Conrad and I had no contact. He was really serious.

To make up for it, Conrad and I called each other almost everyday, either really early in the morning before I went to work, or in the evening when I came home from the bakery. Since the first night of phone sex, he'd seemed a bit distracted and we would usually just update each other with how things were going. Conrad always asked me how Aaron was, or if he seemed more inclined to listen to us now, but I honestly didn't think he had softened at all.

Since he had come back from Singapore, Aaron and I hadn't had a proper heart-to-heart. Although a week had already passed, he never even engaged in conversation with me. When I asked him about how his trip went and what places he had visited, he just glared at me.

"How dare you talk to me as if things were normal," his eyes seemed to say and I never did find the right words to bring him around. It hurt me that our relationship was like this, and I was already wondering how long Aaron was going to keep this up.

I couldn't let things continue as they were though, and this was reinforced when Kate came to my office after lunch. I was surprised to hear the soft knock on the door. "Come in," I called, knowing full well it was going to be Kate.

She popped her head in and took a seat on the chair opposite my desk. She looked rather uncomfortable.

"What is it?" I asked her.

It took her a second to gather her thoughts. "It's about Aaron," she finally said, looking me in the eye. "It's bad enough he's always in a bad mood when he's here, but the problem is he's *always* here. Me, Joey, and Sonya have talked about it, and he's really getting in the way of our work.

"I can't concentrate with him always glaring at everyone and I can't even talk to you freely in your own bakery. Sonya says she's scared of him and Joey's been going outside if he doesn't have anything to do. Joey would literally rather dehydrate in the California sun than be in a room with your brother."

Kate was getting worked up as she spoke. "And that's not even the worst part. He's starting to bother the customers. Earl asked about him the other day."

Earl was one of our earliest regulars. He was a retired mechanic who always had his morning coffee at our bakery along with a breakfast bagel. He was a sweet old man who never found trouble with anybody.

"What did he say?" I asked.

"He asked me if Aaron was an employee or if we owed him money," Kate said, clearly frustrated. "It wouldn't bother me so much if he didn't act so intimidating. He hardly ever says a word and he *never* smiles. This can't go on Ellie, I know he's your family and everything, but this is a business and you have to remember that."

Kate was right. Aaron might be angry at me on a personal level, but his behavior was now affecting my business and the people I worked with, not to mention the quality of my work as well. It was time to have a talk with him.

"I'll go talk to him now," I said. I walked out of the room looking for Aaron. I found him in our waiting area, sitting around doing nothing but looking as intimidating as Kate had said. I could understand now how our customers might be uncomfortable with him around.

"Aaron, I need to talk to you," I said. I motioned for him to follow me and led him into my office. Kate quickly got up and left when she saw Aaron following behind me.

"We need to talk," I said when we were alone. Aaron just hung his head, refusing to look at me. "Why are you here all day? Don't you have work? They're probably looking for you at YoungTech. You have responsibilities there, and you can't just not show up all of a sudden."

"I'm on indefinite leave," he said coldly. I hated seeing him like this. He seemed so far away and I just couldn't reach him.

"This is getting out of hand, Aaron," I said, trying to soften my voice. "You're having a negative effect on my business. Ellie's Sweet Haven is supposed to be a home away from home, but you're making everyone uncomfortable, including my customers."

"Oh so you want me gone?" he scoffed, "What? So you can meet your boyfriend again? I am not moving an inch until I'm sure you and Conrad are through. I'll be right here until our parents come home, and maybe then they can talk some sense into you."

He was so resolved I knew I had to let it go. But I also knew this had to end. I got up and left him in my office without a word. Kate was in the kitchen making some cake orders. I walked up to her.

"I'm really sorry about this," I said. "I know this isn't an ideal work environment but I promise you, this will be the last day Aaron spends in my bakery."

~

THE MINUTE WE GOT HOME, I decided to talk to Aaron again, hoping against hope that he might listen to me.

"Aaron, I'm serious this time, this can't go on," I said when we were both in the kitchen. He was still giving me the cold shoulder but that wasn't going to change anytime soon. I just needed him out of the bakery.

"I'm sick and tired of you trying to sneak away like this, Ellie," he snapped at me. "I already told you, I'm not going anywhere unless I'm sure you're not going off to meet Conrad."

"I'm an adult, Aaron," I said, getting very impatient with his line of thinking. "I'm a business owner for God's sake. I can make decisions for myself, including who I decide to go out with. You have no say in that!"

"That's where you're wrong," he said stubbornly. "You're my little sister and, until Mom and Dad get here, you're my responsibility. Mom and Dad told me to look after you while they're gone! And what do you know about relationships anyway? A big fat nothing. You don't know what you're doing."

"Stop bringing Mom and Dad into this," I said. I was hurt that he would imply I was an innocent child when it came to relationships. "Even if they were here, they would be telling you the same thing I'm telling you now! You are acting CRAZY!"

He sneered at me. "Well it's too bad for you that they're

not here then," he said derisively. I was just about to give him another piece of my mind when the front doors opened.

"What are you two fighting about this time?"

We couldn't believe it. It was our mother.

"What are you standing around for?" she asked. "Go help your dad with the luggage."

We were both stunned. This was the last thing we expected. We had no idea how it happened, but Aaron and I both knew we were in trouble.

19

AN UNEXPECTED HOMECOMING
ELLIE

AFTER THE SHOCK of suddenly finding our parents, who were supposed to be vacationing in Europe, at our front door, Aaron and I quickly helped them into the house. I went into the kitchen and poured them both some lemonade and came back into the living room. Aaron had brought their bags into their room and was coming back as I handed them their drinks.

"Thank you so much, dear," my mom said, taking the glass from my hand. My mom had the same hair color as I did, but unlike me, she was tall and lean. I got my curves from my father's side of the family. He had a stockier build and had sisters with the same figure as mine.

I think my unrealistic beauty standards and insecurities later on most likely stemmed from watching this beautiful woman raise us. Rosa Rodriguez was now 52 years old, but you wouldn't know it looking at her. She looked like she was in her late thirties, and was still very elegant.

My father, Matteo, on the other hand, was a stocky, well-built man in his mid-fifties. He still looked useful, but you could tell he was a working man. He had been a builder almost all his life. He loved working with his hands and seemed at a complete loss when he retired. Mom had thought it was a good idea for them to start traveling, just to help Dad get his mind off things.

Dad was a quiet but firm man. I had always been his princess and he tended to dote on me. Throughout my life, I had never heard him raise his voice, and I think my mom had a lot to do with that too. They always talked to each other in a loving way, and during disagreements, they were always respectful. The worst argument they had was about our education.

Despite the changing times, my father was still very conservative and religious. He wanted Aaron and I to go to Catholic School but it was too expensive, and he and mom had argued about it. We heard them, but it never seemed like a big argument until, years later, when mom admitted that they had taken time off. We had been told that Dad was just going on a trip to Miami to see some cousins. We were completely oblivious to their struggles.

I guess my point was, my parents always put my brother and I before everything and we had a fun and healthy family life, which was probably why Conrad gravitated towards our family so strongly.

For me, having them at home was a great relief. I knew they would be more reasonable than Aaron was right now, which honestly wasn't very hard to be, seeing as he'd completely gone crazy.

Aaron sat down on a chair opposite the couch while I sat across from him.

"So what are you two doing here? Isn't it a little early for you to be home?" he asked, crossing his legs as he spoke and refusing to even look at me.

"Well I could say the same about you," Mom replied, smiling at him teasingly. "Aren't you supposed to be in Singapore right now, dazzling some businessmen?"

Aaron looked away guiltily, a fact which did not escape my parents. Dad cleared his throat, and said, "I think it's about time you told us what is happening here."

I was just about to speak and tell him how insane Aaron had been acting when he beat me to it.

"Ellie and Conrad are dating!" he blurted out. "I found her half-naked in Conrad's apartment and who knows how long this has been going on?"

"Nothing's been going on!" I cried out. "And if anyone should be telling Mom and Dad about my relationships then it should be me!"

"So now you're all honest because they found out," he said bitterly, "but I had to find out from someone else?"

I tried to explain myself but Aaron was talking over me, and before I knew it we were yelling at each other from across the room.

"That is enough!"

It was my dad and it was the first time he had ever shouted at us. But when I looked at his face, he didn't seem angry at all. In fact, I caught a hint of amusement in his expression.

"I think," Mom said, "it would be best if we talked to each of you separately. We won't get anywhere if you keep shouting over each other."

I turned to Aaron and he wasn't moving. I knew he wanted to talk to them first so I would be on the defensive. However, it was very clear to me that I had done nothing wrong, which is why I let him have this one. I got up and went upstairs, slamming the door behind me.

I laid in bed, my heart racing. I could hear some faint mumbling from downstairs and the occasional raised voice, probably Aaron's. The whole situation seemed so unreal.

I took my phone out of my pocket and called Conrad.

His phone rang but there was no answer so I decided to text him.

> Hey, u'll never believe this but mom and dad came home 2day. They're talking 2 aaron ryt now. I hope you can come over and see them, I mis u.

I waited a few minutes but he didn't reply. Come to think of it, Conrad's texts and calls had been few and far between in the last few days, and when I did manage to get a hold of him, he always seemed very distracted and didn't have enough time.

I was starting to worry about our relationship. Although I had no doubt that what we felt for each other was real and deep, I was doubting whether Conrad would really choose me over his friendship with Aaron, his best friend of nearly 15 years and an important partner in his company. I knew it was unfair to think these things when Conrad had no way of defending himself, but I couldn't help it. I didn't want Aaron to be the reason why I lost a relationship that had barely even started.

I was still lying on my back when I heard footsteps coming up the stairs. It wasn't long before I heard Aaron's voice.

"Ellie?" he called.

"What?"

"They want to talk to you," he said. "It's your turn."

I took a deep breath and got up. When I got to the hall-way, Aaron had disappeared. I headed down stairs and went to my parents. To my surprise, Aaron was already there.

They were still sitting in the same position as when I had left, sipping their drinks casually. When they saw me in the doorway, Mom got up and held her hands out to me. I felt a cry catch in my throat as I went to her, holding my hands out for a hug.

We held each other for a while when I heard my dad say, "Hey, it's my turn." I laughed a little and turned to him, giving him a warm hug. There were tears welling up in my eyes. *God, I missed them so much.*

We were always a very expressive family. Hugs and kisses were freely given and gratefully and lovingly received. These hugs made me feel like everything would be alright no matter what.

After the hugs, Mom asked me to sit down again. "Now Ellie, for everyone's benefit," she said, giving Aaron a look, "would you please tell us exactly what happened while we were all away?"

There was so much to say, so much that had happened, but I didn't know where to start. I took a little while to think about the best way to tell them, deciding which details were important and which weren't. I decided to start with Tyler and Sarah.

"Well, it started with Aaron's party actually," I said, getting my thoughts in order. "I don't know if Aaron knows this but I've had a pretty big crush on someone who works for him, Tyler Perkins." I could see Aaron squint his eyes a little at this information.

"I've been working up the courage to ask him out and Sarah was with me all the way. Long story short, they were already dating and I had no idea," I continued. I could see my mother's eyes widen a little and Aaron shaking his head. My father remained perfectly stoic.

"I found out they've been dating for a while and that Sarah just betrayed me and let me think I had a chance with Tyler all that time. Conrad and I ran into them on our way back from the airport and that's when I, probably just to spare myself the humiliation...I pretended that Conrad and

I were dating, and Conrad played along. I just hated to see how Sarah was acting like she pitied me and everything. I couldn't take it, so I made Conrad pretend to be my fake boyfriend.

"Fake?" Aaron said sarcastically, but Dad cleared his throat and gave Aaron a look. "Sorry," Aaron muttered. Encouraged, I went on.

"What I didn't know was that Conrad had also just lied to his grandfather about having a fake fiancée because his grandfather was supposedly very sick at the time and was worried about Conrad's personal life. He told me that he was looking for someone to pretend to be his fiancée to put his grandfather at ease. He told me that the lie I told Sarah and Tyler had given him an idea. He proposed that we have an arrangement and agree to be in a fake relationship, him as my fake boyfriend and me as his fake fiancée.

"It was the same night that Sarah invited Conrad and I to go on a double-date with her and Tyler. So pretending to be dating was becoming a win-win for both of us. We made an agreement and everything, we wrote everything down. My feelings for Conrad at the time were less than favorable, so I was a bit cautious about the whole thing. Then we did it. We pretended to be in a relationship. He introduced me to his grandfather who then threw us a party because he's not sick after all and I enjoyed myself. I honestly thought I wouldn't but I did," I admitted, talking faster now.

"Then we went on that dinner with Sarah and Tyler, which opened up a whole new can of worms. My friendship with Sarah has been fake this whole time, I was feeling very lousy about my personal life, and I was alone here. But Conrad was so kind and understanding. He defended me, he made me feel special and not alone, and protected. I developed feelings for him.

"Of course we knew that Aaron was gonna have a reaction. We didn't know how extreme it was going to be, but we knew there would be one. Conrad honestly tried to stay away from me. He didn't want to complicate things or hurt you and he was willing to just bury his feelings, but I wasn't. I confronted him and told him how I felt and he told me that he's always had feelings for me. It wasn't anything planned, we didn't sneak around trying to hide from Aaron, or intentionally try to deceive him, it just happened that way.

"The reason why Sarah told you about my 'relationship' with Conrad before I could was because, at the time, we technically didn't even have a relationship yet. At least not a real one. I don't know what else Sarah may have told you, but I can honestly say that we never tried to deceive you. When you saw me at Conrad's apartment that morning, it was literally the first time I had been there as anything more than a friend."

Aaron was looking down when I finished. "So to be clear," my mother said, "your alleged relationship with Conrad has been fake up until the day before Aaron discovered you in Conrad's apartment?"

"Yes," I said firmly.

"Now, Aaron," Mom said, turning to Aaron and putting an arm on his shoulder. "Why do you think you are so upset? Is it because of the way you found out? Or is it simply because Ellie is your sister and no man can possibly be good enough for her?"

Aaron squirmed and refused to answer. "What do you think your reaction would be if it had been any other girl?" Mom continued. "Wouldn't you say that that girl was lucky to have Conrad? Wouldn't you say that he is a good and kind man who is worthy of any girl?"

Dad was smiling by this time, not really looking at anything. It was as if he was remembering something.

Aaron finally looked up at Mom and shook his head, rubbing his forehead. Mom took it as an admittance of guilt.

"Now, your father and I are going to bed and we're going to rest," Mom said, getting up and touching Dad's shoulder. "You two have a lot to talk about in the meantime, right Aaron?"

Aaron just nodded and the two of them left, heading to their room. There were a few moments of awkward silence when Aaron and I were finally left alone together. I started to say something, but Aaron got up and took a seat next to me.

"I have to admit…" he said slowly, "I may have gotten carried away."

I knew it was a serious moment but I couldn't help bursting out laughing. "You think?" I said, before breaking into a fit of laughter. There were tears in my eyes by the time I had recovered my composure, and seeing Aaron's grumpy face made me laugh again.

"Are you done?" he demanded impatiently, looking at me with much annoyance. I took a deep breath and straightened up.

"Yes," I said, my voice a little shaky from mirth. "Yes, I think I'm done."

"Can you please not laugh when I'm trying to explain myself?" he said, rather petulantly.

"Of course. I won't laugh, I promise," I said, fighting the urge to smile.

"Okay," he said as he took a deep breath. "I was surprised to say the least. I thought I knew how you felt about him, and vice versa. I left thinking that you hated each other, I was even a little worried that you might end up fighting while I was gone. You couldn't even believe it when I asked you to look out for Conrad, remember?"

He was looking to me for answers, so I nodded.

"Well, imagine my surprise when I got a text from Sarah saying you and Conrad were dating. And that's not all, she said you'd changed and that she was worried about you. I couldn't believe it, it didn't seem possible, but then she sent me pictures…"

"What?" I exclaimed. I couldn't believe what I was hearing.

"Here," he said, handing me his phone. It was a picture of me and Conrad holding hands and smiling at each other. The next picture was us walking away, with Conrad holding me close. The pictures were all from our dinner with Sarah and Tyler. So she had sneaked pictures of us. She really was out to get me.

"She said that you were only with Conrad because of his money."

I gasped. How could she say that?

"I didn't believe it," he went on, " not at first anyway. But the more I thought about it the more it seemed plausible. I mean, you practically hated him before I left and all of a sudden…"

Before I knew what I was doing, my hand shot out and slapped Aaron. He looked stunned and a big, red welt was slowly forming on his cheek. I didn't realize that tears were already forming in my eyes from the anger. How could he think that about me?

Aaron was too stunned to speak.

"How can you say that?" I said, wiping the tears from my eyes. "How can you possibly think that about me? How can you believe what Sarah said?"

"I'm sorry," he said, taking my hands in his. "When Sarah said it, I wanted to shout at her. I hated to think that about you or hear other people say things like that. I didn't want to believe it, Ellie, I swear."

"But you did," I said, crying. "You are supposed to know

me better than anyone. How can you think I'm that type of person? How?"

Aaron came closer and hugged me. "I'm sorry. It was Sarah, she planted doubts in my head. She was your best friend for years, I assumed she knew more about you than I did.

"Honestly, I didn't believe it right away. After she sent me the pictures, I texted you, waiting for you to tell me. I couldn't think of a reason why you wouldn't tell me since it was obviously true judging from the picture. But then you never mentioned it, and neither did Conrad. I thought maybe I was just reading too much into it. I got William's number and I called their house asking for him. The guy who answered said he was out and asked if he could take a message. I told him it was Aaron Rodriguez. He asked if I was Miss Ellie's brother. I asked him how he knew you, and he said you came to the party and was introduced as Conrad's fiancée.

"I started seeing red after that. It seemed as if I was the only one who didn't know that you two had a relationship. To me, this meant that it was something you were both keeping from me on purpose. I was so angry. I was mad at you because of the implication on your character, and I was mad at Conrad for not telling me about his relationship with my sister."

I was still crying, but I also sensed the pain in Aaron's voice.

"I was so stupid, Ellie," he said, pulling away from me and wiping my eyes himself. "I shouldn't have thought that about you. The truth is, I knew in my heart it wasn't true, but I let my doubts and suspicions get the better of me. And the fact that there were people who were thinking that about you made me even madder. I overreacted, I didn't even want to hear your side.

"I made some excuses to my hosts in Singapore and high-tailed it back here. When I got home and you weren't here, I just lost it. Then I found you at Conrad's and...I lost my mind, okay?"

It took me a while to get my tears and emotions under control, but when I did, my heart felt a lot lighter. I was glad that Aaron and I had cleared the air. It was almost unbelievable to me that Sarah would say things like that about me to my own brother. I really was better off without her in my life.

"When Conrad and I talked about our fake relationship, we agreed not to tell you because I was afraid you'd freak out and get all protective of me. But I never thought that Sarah would say such horrible things about me to you," I said, pulling away from him. "But now that everything's cleared up and out in the open, I want you to trust me. I'm well aware of how I used to feel about Conrad, but I really did develop feelings for him. It had nothing to do with his money or his success. I got to know him really well while you were gone and I see him for who he is. I love him. You have to trust us."

He just nodded and patted my hand. "It was my fault, Ellie. I should have talked to you like an adult. I guess I just got overprotective. You're still my little sister you know," he said with a smile.

"Of course, and you'll always be my big brother. But you have to let Conrad and I work things out for ourselves. When I need you, I'll let you know, okay?" I said. He nodded.

"And I'm sorry you had to find out that way," I added. "I was going to tell you, but Sarah and Tyler had to ruin everything."

"Yeah, I never really liked Sarah," he said thoughtfully. "You're not still friends, are you?"

I just rolled my eyes and he chuckled.

"I'm really sorry for my behavior, Ell," he said again.

"I'm not the only person you should be apologizing to, you know," I said. "There's someone else's story you should hear."

"Well, I'm listening," he replied.

I shook my head. "It's not my story to tell."

He just smiled and said, "Don't worry about it. I'll talk to him tomorrow."

I WOKE up the next morning to the smell of breakfast wafting through the house. I headed to the kitchen and found my parents drinking coffee while my mom was cooking breakfast.

"Did Aaron leave already?" I asked, pouring myself a cup of coffee.

"Yes," Mom replied. "He said he had to apologize to Conrad. He didn't even eat any breakfast."

Dad chuckled, turning the page of the newspaper he was reading. "Those too can never really fight for long. They were practically joined at the hip when they were kids."

The two of them laughed and Mom started handing out plates. I was glad they were home. For one thing, it had been months since I'd seen either of them. It was also a huge plus that they turned out to be the voices of reason.

We were contentedly sipping our coffee when I suddenly remembered something.

"Hey, why are you guys back so soon again?" I asked. "What happened to your trip? You still had a few weeks to go, didn't you?"

They gave each other a knowing look. I saw Dad nod at

Mom, who then took a deep breath. She turned to me and smiled.

"The truth is, Conrad told us about your relationship and Aaron's...concerns," she said, "and we decided we had better get home before things got out of hand."

I was speechless. Conrad had talked to my parents already?

"But...how? It takes days for us to get a hold of you, and even then, the connection is so bad we hardly understand each other."

"Not over the phone, dear," Mom said nonchalantly. "He came in person. It was very sweet and a very welcome visit. We just heard a knock one day and there he was at our front door."

"He was very straightforward and talked to us about your relationship frankly," Dad chimed in. "He told us everything, including about the fake relationship you two had, and asked for our blessing. He said we were the closest people he had to parents and he didn't want us to think he was taking advantage of you. And for the record, we never even considered that. It was quite surprising to find out that Aaron was being a complete ass, but we figured he was just being a big brother."

My heart was filled with love and gratitude for Conrad. He went all the way to Europe to clear things up. He was three steps ahead of me the whole time.

"Well, why did you make me explain everything if you already knew?" I asked.

They both laughed. "That was mostly for Aaron's benefit," Mom said. "And we had already heard Conrad's side of the story, so we thought it would be nice to hear yours. And darling, we heartily approve."

"Mom!" I exclaimed. They just laughed as Mom went back to cooking while Dad went on reading his newspaper.

20

REUNITED

CONRAD

I'D BEEN UP since 4 am and getting back to sleep seemed impossible. Instead of tossing and turning in bed, I decided to get up and do some workouts.

The past week has been hell for me. It felt like I'd finally found the right girl, and she'd been right under my nose the whole time. I'd always liked Ellie, but I never thought anything would come out of it. She was just my best friend's hot younger sister. She caught my attention early actually, and it seemed that Sarah had noticed it, but Ellie and Aaron certainly didn't.

Remembering Aaron's reaction brought me dread. I'd never seen him so angry or unhinged. I could hardly wrap my head around it. He wouldn't take my calls or text back, he didn't even show up to work. I was starting to be afraid of the fact that Aaron seemed willing to throw everything away just to stop Ellie and me from continuing our relationship.

I knew there was no way that we could fix things on our own, which is why I decided to get some help.

I always knew where Rosa and Matteo Rodriguez were staying because Aaron had asked me to help them with an itinerary. I had gotten Devon to make them a calendar for the best places to visit and the best hotels and Airbnbs to stay at. Once they approved the calendar, I asked Devon to make reservations and bookings for them.

At first, I tried to contact them, but it was close to impossible. They were in a secluded beach in the Balearic Islands in Spain with no cellular signal. According to their itinerary, they were supposed to spend 2 more weeks in the region and I just couldn't wait that long.

I rented a private jet and flew over. Getting to Spain was no problem, it was the island that was the hassle. You could only get there by boat and so I rented one in the middle of the night from a very drunk-looking captain. It was surprisingly smooth sailing even though he seemed inebriated to me, and by dawn, we were on the island.

When I showed up at their rented villa they were stunned to see me, but quickly invited me in. They asked about my grandfather and about Aaron and Ellie of course. I decided to tell them everything right away.

"I want to start at the beginning and be honest about how this all happened on my end," I said, weighing the words that needed to be said. "A few weeks ago, I thought my grandfather fell ill. He seemed very weak and the doctors had no idea what was wrong. He started getting very concerned about me and my personal life. He said he wanted to make sure I had someone in case he got sicker and didn't make it."

Rosa and Matteo looked at each other with concern in their eyes. "And how is your grandfather now?" Matteo asked.

"That's the thing, it was all a ruse to get me to find a girl," I said, shaking my head as I recalled my grandfather's antics. "He got the doctors to go along with his plan and everything. It was very elaborate and very foolish."

Rosa chuckled when she heard this. "William does have

a flair for theatrics," she said, smiling. "Now what does this have to do with us?"

I swallowed a little, unsure of how to explain it to them. I decided to just go with head-on.

"Given William's condition, I wanted to put his mind at ease and lied to him about having a fiancée. That's where Ellie comes in," I said hesitantly. I could see Matteo's brows furrow, but he did not interrupt me once. I went on.

"When I was taking Ellie home we bumped into Sarah Miller. You know her right?" I asked and they just nodded. "It turns out that Sarah has been dating a guy that Ellie's had a crush on. She played Ellie for a fool. I don't know how it happened but Ellie introduced me to them and told them we were dating, I think to save face. I played along."

"I never liked Sarah's influence on Ellie," Rosa said. "I could see how she made Ellie insecure and was very flippant about it."

"Yes, well, she showed her true colors later on. Anyway, it got me thinking that maybe Ellie would agree to be my fake fiancée for my grandfather's sake at least. To my surprise she did. It all started so innocently. We played at being engaged in front of William and his friends, then in front of Sarah and Tyler but..."

"But it started getting serious?" Rosa interjected. I nodded.

"I never meant for it to happen but the more time we spent together, the more I realized how great she was. I tried to stop it and stayed away, but I was miserable without her. I really have developed strong feelings for her and I've come to ask for your blessing," I confessed to them. To my surprise, they voiced no objections and asked me why I felt the need to come all the way to Spain just to tell them.

Then I told them about how Aaron had reacted. Matteo shook his head.

"Aaron always doted on Eleanor," he said reflectively. "But he is also very protective. He wants to know everything and to help with the decisions. He takes his responsibilities a little too seriously when it comes to his sister. He is more old-fashioned than me in that sense."

"From what Ellie tells me, he's been watching her every move," I explained further. "He stays in the bakery all day and won't leave. He hasn't come to work or reported about his trip to Singapore. Ellie's been saying that he's causing some negative effects on her workplace and his team members at YoungTech are starting to ask questions. I've had Jordan, our other partner, step in but I can't hold off the questions for much longer. I don't know how to get through to him."

"Aaron gets stubborn sometimes," Rosa said. "It doesn't happen often but when it does, he can't think straight and he'll stand by it. I think it's time we intervened."

That very afternoon, we all got into the private jet and traveled back to LA. When I got home, I was so exhausted from almost 48 hours of no sleep that I conked out. I only read Ellie's message when I woke up at 4am, but I knew she was sleeping so I let it be.

I was already in my kitchen making breakfast when I heard the doorbell ring. I looked at the video intercom and saw Aaron standing at my doorway, significantly more humble than the last time he was here.

I opened the door. He was standing there with a sheepish grin. "Can I come in?" he asked.

"I thought you'd never ask," I replied with a smile, standing back to let him inside.

I motioned for him to join me in the kitchen. It was funny to think that the last time we were in good humor with each other, the last meal we had shared was also breakfast. It seemed fitting that we fix our friendship over breakfast too.

I handed him a cup of coffee and added another egg and bacon to the pan.

Aaron took a sip of his coffee as I cooked. "So," he said, rather tentatively. "You and Ellie, huh?"

I didn't turn around. "Yup," I just said.

"I know about your fake relationship, your grandfather, Sarah and Tyler...everything," he said.

I smiled. "You know, I never even considered it at first, she was your sister after all. But with what happened with Tyler and Sarah at the café...I wanted to protect her. It just turned out to be perfect for my situation too."

"Of course," Aaron said sarcastically. "If it were me and you had a little sister, I would definitely do the same thing."

I grimaced. "That's not even remotely the same!" I said with a grimace.

"See," Aaron said triumphantly. "That's me right there! Now do you get how uncomfortable this is for me?"

I had to sigh. It was kind of weird. "Yeah, I get it. And I don't even have a sister," I admitted. "But I really do care about her Aaron. I would never hurt her."

He chuckled and walked over to me. The stove was off and I was taking plates out of the cupboard. He tapped my shoulder and when I turned he was facing me with a stern expression. He placed both hands on my shoulders and said, "You know I love you like a brother and we've been friends for as long as I can remember," he was smiling but there was a hint of a threat in his tone. "But she is my little sister. I watched her grow up. She is sweet and innocent, kind and forgiving, she's an amazing person..."

I knew this was going to take a turn but I was still surprised when he squeezed my shoulder hard and pulled me a little closer. "If you do anything to hurt her, if you cause her any pain, if you disappoint her in any way, or make her cry, I swear to God..."

"Calm down!" I said, eager to get this part of the conversation over with. I patted his hands which still had an uncomfortable grip on my shoulders. "I love Ellie. I was insensitive in the past, I teased her. I was a douche. When I found out how that affected her, I swore I would change. I will never do anything like that again. I care for Ellie, more than you know. I love her."

This seemed to satisfy him. He nodded and stepped back, returning to his seat and taking a sip of coffee. "Seriously man," he said again. "You're my best friend and technically my boss, but if anything happens I'll always be on Ellie's side. Okay?"

I nodded, handing him a plate of eggs and bacon. "That seems fair and I respect that."

"And do me a favor," he said. "Don't ever talk to me about your relationship with my sister unless you have problems and I can help. If you just want to talk about how well everything is going then I don't need the details. Okay? Just problems or favors you can ask. And even then, just the appropriate ones. In fact, only talk to me about your relationship when you're about to break up. Okay?"

"Of course," I said, trying to hide a smile. "You're being perfectly reasonable, Aaron. Or at least more reasonable than you have been so far."

"Give me a break, will you?" he said, forking bacon into his mouth. He swallowed and continued, "This is new and very awkward for me. Do you realize how weird it's gonna be when I see you during the holidays, all lovey-dovey?"

"I get your point," I said. "But you will have to get over it eventually. I love Ellie, and I really see us making it in the long-run. I promise you, you're going to be seeing a lot of the lovey-dovey stuff for years to come."

He groaned, shaking his head as if trying to will the images away. I just laughed at him.

"I swear to you, Aaron," I said frankly, "I will treat Ellie like a princess and I will never do anything to hurt her."

"I would expect nothing less," he said. "Now, about Singapore. Things were really going great, they said there was a real market for YoungTech there and..." And he went on, telling me about the trip and the projects that were approved and the ones still in discussion.

A great sense of relief washed over me. *My best friend is back.*

MY HEART WAS RACING as I drove to the bakery. After our talk, Aaron and I parted ways in good spirits. He was headed back to YoungTech to clear things up with his team and coordinate with Jordan about how Singapore went. I knew it wouldn't be long before we had him back on a plane to Asia.

I was on my way to Ellie's Sweet Haven with a bunch of flowers I picked up on the way. It had been more than a week and I was desperate to finally see her again. We'd been talking almost every day but it just wasn't the same. Being away from her made me realize how much I needed her presence in my life. She had texted me a few times but I decided to hold off on replying. Soon, we would be together.

I pulled up in front of the bakery and quickly got out. I was almost running when I got to the door. I immediately saw Kate at the counter. They had just opened but they already had a line forming at the cash register.

She smiled at me brightly and motioned for me to follow her into the kitchen.

"She's in her office right now, talking to some of our suppliers," she said. "She told me everything. I'm so happy for you guys! Ellie deserves to be happy and I think you're the man for the job."

I smiled back. "Thanks for that," I said. "I actually just found out I have a lot to thank you for."

"What do you mean?" she asked.

"That you encouraged her and vouched for my character," I said. "I didn't expect that."

"I pride myself in being a good judge of character," she said. "By the way, thanks for getting Aaron out of our hair, he was really starting to cramp our style."

I laughed. "What was he doing while he was here?"

"Nothing. Just standing around and giving everyone the evil eye, including our customers," she explained. "He was starting to be a liability. I'm glad it didn't last any longer. We would have started losing our regulars if you hadn't done what you did."

"Well, he's gone to be an asset of YoungTech again," I said. "I'm glad everything is cleared up."

Kate smiled and then checked her watch. "She should be done in a few minutes. Here," she said, handing me a small tray with a cup of coffee and some cinnamon rolls. "You can take these to her office. She'll be so happy to see you.

I obediently took the tray from her hands and headed to Ellie's office. The door was unlocked and I listened before going inside.

"Yes," I heard her say, "that would be fine. We really need those deliveries the day after tomorrow so if you could ship them today, it would be a great help. Okay, thanks."

I heard the phone click as she hung up. I knocked softly before opening the door. "Hey, good news," she said without looking up. She was holding a pen and writing on a piece of paper in front of her. "They said they can ship them today so we should be..." she trailed off as she looked up and realized who it was.

"Conrad?" she said, before suddenly slapping her face. I stared at her, surprised by her reaction. "Okay, I'm not dreaming," she said. "You talked to Aaron?"

"He came early this morning," I said. "We cleared things up. I've missed you Ellie-belly," I said, looking into her eyes.

"I missed you too, Conrad," she replied, her eyes full of love.

I placed the tray on the table and took two long strides toward her. She had gotten up and I handed her the flowers. She took them and smiled. "These are beautiful, we'll put them in a vase and have these by the register."

It seemed almost unreal. Here she was in front of me and all I could do was look at her.

She put the flowers down and looked up at me. She held out her hands and I melted inside.

I took her hand and caught her in a fierce embrace. I bent down and kissed her, savoring her taste and scent. She opened her lips to me and I felt my passions rise with every second. I was home.

EPILOGUE: EVER AFTER
ELLIE

The crisp, early-morning air was invigorating. I'd always loved walking to the bakery in the mornings. All the lights were still off when I got there, meaning I'd beaten Kate to work.

We'd made it into a little game and she even had a scoreboard written up in the kitchen. The winner was going to get an iPad, courtesy of Conrad. She was up by two points, but I wasn't going to let her win that easily.

Six months had passed since Aaron came storming into Conrad's apartment and it was all going really well so far. Conrad and I spent most of our free time together and had really started getting to know each other. He was such a thoughtful boyfriend, always so romantic and spoiling me every chance he got.

But the best thing about Conrad, in my opinion, was how truly supportive he was. He was always so patient when I got too busy and had no time for our weekend dates. He never made me feel guilty about how much time and energy I spent on my business, something that was quite hard to find according to Kate.

"Most men I know, heck, most men I've been with,

would get all mopey when I was too busy at work," she said. "They're not interested in a woman's career. Some men even get threatened if you're successful. I'm amazed at your billionaire boyfriend honestly. Most wealthy men out there just want their partners to be their wives, the mothers of their children, and housekeepers full-time."

"Conrad's not like that," I said, smiling. "He's never even brought it up. He knows how much I love Ellie's and he's never said a bad thing about me being a business owner. He knows this bakery is my life."

Kate nodded, saying I had found myself a unicorn. And I really think she's right.

Kate and I have become even closer and I consider her my best friend. It really was surprising to experience real friendship after I cut all ties with Sarah. It was only later that I realized that all of Sarah's bluntness and critical comments about me were undeniably toxic and wore me down. There was a point in our friendship when I was only confident because she was around because I thought that if someone like her was my friend, that must mean I was fun and worth having around.

Kate showed me what it really was to have a friend. There were never any double meanings or snide remarks, just understanding and compassion. I didn't have my guard up and I found that I could just be myself and still be appreciated and validated.

I walked into the kitchen and started taking out various batters from the fridge. I heated up the oven and did some prep work in the meantime. It wasn't long before I heard the shop bell ringing. I peeked around the kitchen door and saw that it was Conrad. He was wearing a light jacket and his hair was still a bit tousled.

"Hey!" I called. "You're early."

He came into the kitchen, hugged me, and gave me a soft

kiss. Everything was great in our relationship, but things had been a little off lately. He seemed distracted, was constantly forgetful, and he seemed to be busier than usual. It might have been because of work, but he seemed wary of telling me whatever was bothering him.

Conrad was on his way to the airport to pick up Aaron. After his sudden return six months ago, he reported on the results of his trip and they sent him right back after a few weeks. I didn't know much about what happened but I was under the impression that it was an unrivaled success.

"Don't forget about our dinner tonight," he said, giving me another kiss.

I turned to face him and put my arms over his shoulders. "Of course, I remember," I said, smiling. "You've been reminding me every day for a week, you know."

He chuckled and gave me a deep kiss and I immediately responded. With him being so busy lately, I'd missed getting to spend more time with him.

"I have?" he said. "I gotta go, Aaron's plane should be arriving soon."

"Ok," I said, reluctantly pulling away. "Drive safe, okay?"

"Okay," he said, hedging for the door. "I'll see you tonight babe."

I walked him to the door and watched him drive away. I was feeling a little giddy about tonight. It must be a special night for Conrad because he'd been planning tonight for a while now.

I walked in and got back to work putting muffins in the oven and prepping our breakfast croissants. A few minutes later, Kate came in.

"Ugh," she exclaimed. "You beat me to work," she said, as she was adding a point to my side of the scoreboard.

I laughed. Kate was really making work a joy. She put on

her apron and started pouring cupcake batter into our cupcake liners.

"So, do you have any plans for tonight?" Kate asked, her hands still busy with her work.

"Yes actually," I replied. "Conrad and I are having dinner at his apartment."

"A romantic evening? Good for you. Things aren't still weird with Conrad, are they?"

I had been telling Kate just the other day about how Conrad was acting a little odd lately.

"Not really," I said. "It might have been about work. With Aaron's trip being a success, I think they're expanding a bit, but he hasn't really told me about it."

"I'm sure it's nothing," Kate said reassuringly. "Our new pastry chef is coming in later by the way. I think you should talk to him before she starts work."

I smiled. Ellie's Sweet Haven was doing really well and we had decided to hire another pastry chef. Kate was going to be the head pastry chef while I would be more focused on the business end of things. Conrad had advised me to start thinking about expansion, even if it was just a new branch on the other side of town. I was a little reluctant at first, but Kate was very enthusiastic when I told her about it and Conrad said he would help me along the way.

It was a very exciting new chapter and I was learning more about market strategies and brand development. Kate was in charge of interviews and hiring, but I knew I had to get to know the new hire at least.

I nodded and said I'd talk to him when he came in later. The shop bell rang again. It was Joey, opening up. It was time for another busy day.

$\sim$

It was early when I left the bakery. As usual, I left the care of the bakery to Kate, with fewer instructions than I had in the past. I was very confident in her abilities and I knew that I was leaving the bakery in capable hands.

I had talked with the assistant pastry chef earlier and I had to admit, he seemed like a really good fit. Kate always did say she was a good judge of character and I totally believed her.

As I walked home, I got a message from my mother.

We are taking your brother out to dinner tonight and will be home late. He says he misses you but we wanted tonight to have him for ourselves. Don't wait up for us.

That's fine. I'll be staying at Conrad's tonight. Tell Aaron I miss him.

Alright, dear. Take care of yourself.

After Mom and Dad got back from their trip, which was about a month after they took a detour home, they spent a lot of time with Conrad and me. Whenever they had a chance, they would invite him over for dinner and it all seemed so natural to have him there with the family. They'd always loved him but they'd certainly gotten closer since we started dating.

As expected, the house was empty when I got there and only the porch lights were left on. I immediately got into the shower, eager to get ready. Conrad had asked me to dress up even though we were just having dinner at his apartment. He had hired a private chef and he said he wanted to have memorable pictures of the night.

I had gone dress shopping with Kate and we bought a lovely dress on Rodeo Drive. It was a nice lilac color with a sweetheart neckline and some beading. I really liked it and it was the first time I was wearing this color, which was exciting.

I was already doing my makeup when I got a message from Conrad saying he was running late and asking me to wait for him to pick me up.

Although I was about to protest and tell him it was much easier if I just went to his apartment directly, I thought better of it. I texted him saying I'd be waiting. It was actually a relief knowing I could take my time getting ready.

I got up to get the dress out of my closet when my eyes landed on the sexy chrome dress I had only ever worn once more than six months ago. I couldn't help but think of Sarah and how glad I was that she was finally out of my life.

After the whole Aaron situation, she still had the nerve to message me, asking me if we could talk. I firmly said no multiple times before she gave up, but not before sending me long messages about how she was only looking out for me. In the end, she sent me a message that was two paragraphs long. She told me I was a selfish brat who was willing to throw away years of friendship over a guy. She said I was a cold-hearted bitch among other things. I blocked her number after that.

I still wondered what might've happened if we not run into each other that day, but I couldn't really care less at this point. From what I'd heard, she was still living in LA but she and Tyler were history. Apparently, the relationship hadn't lasted long.

I did, however, bump into Daniel constantly, once with Conrad. We had just smiled awkwardly and I introduced them. I said Daniel was "an old friend" and Conrad was my boyfriend, and I did notice Daniel's eyes widened a little when I said that. It was ironic because I was probably the one person in LA with just one ex and he happened to be living in my current boyfriend's building.

It was half an hour later when Conrad finally arrived. I went downstairs to meet him and found him leaning against his car, waiting for me. He was trying to act calm and cool, but I knew him well enough to see that he was nervous.

"Hey, I've been waiting for you," I said teasingly. He smiled nervously at me. "What's wrong?" I asked. "Are you okay?"

"Nothing," he replied. "It's just work. It was a bit hectic today."

He opened the car door for me and helped me get in before getting into the driver seat himself. I could tell he was a bit tense so I started talking about work, Kate, and Allen, our new assistant pastry chef.

"Oh, that reminds me," he suddenly said. "After my talk with Aaron, it seems we have Asia in the bag. We're thinking of expanding to Europe and opening a new division in London. Since it was Aaron who went to Asia, and with Jordan basically running things here, I thought it should be my turn and oversee it myself."

My heart sank when he said that. Was this the reason why he'd been acting all weird lately?

"How long will you be gone?" I asked. I knew that as his girlfriend I should be more supportive. This was an exciting chapter in his life, but I couldn't help but feel anxious about how long we would have to spend away from each other.

"I'm not really sure," he said after some thought. "Probably around the same as Aaron spent in Asia."

I took a deep breath, feeling lonely all of a sudden. "Let's talk about it at dinner," I finally said. Conrad just nodded and we drove on in silence.

When we got to his building, Conrad parked his car and we went into the elevator holding hands. I didn't want to ruin our special dinner because of my concerns about

Conrad's trip, and I willed myself to keep things light-hearted throughout dinner.

The elevator door opened and Conrad led me to his door. He took his keys out then suddenly stopped, slapping himself in the forehead.

"I forgot my suitcase in the car!" he said frantically. "I have to go get it. Here, you go in first and make yourself comfortable. I have to go back down."

He handed me the keys and was gone before I could say anything. Conrad really was getting forgetful. It definitely had something to do with the expansion of their company and I had to help lighten the load. I decided I wouldn't bring up the London thing unless it was to congratulate him. I didn't want to worry about my reaction when he already worried about so much.

I opened the door to his apartment and found that it was in total darkness. I turned on the living room light and was greeted by a beautifully arranged table for two. There was a gorgeous bouquet of flowers by the table and string lights on the walls. I could see that Conrad had redecorated his apartment just for the night. There was already champagne on a bucket of ice.

I wondered where the chef might be or if he would come later. I went over to the table and saw a card on the bouquet of flowers. It only had a short phrase on it:

It's in the kitchen.

I turned the card over and saw that it was blank on the other side. I headed to the kitchen, wondering what Conrad had up his sleeve.

I went into the kitchen expecting a feast but it was completely empty. Then I noticed a small velvet box on the kitchen island. My heart was racing as I picked it up. I opened it and...it was empty.

"Ellie?" It was Conrad. I wheeled around and saw him

by the door on his knees. "These past few months, you've made me the happiest man on Earth and I want to spend the rest of my life with you. Will you marry me?" he asked, holding up a ring with a large emerald on it.

My jaw dropped and I could feel the tears welling up in my eyes. Joy flooded my heart as I nodded. "Yes."

There was suddenly an eruption of applause and the light to the hallway was turned on. I could see my whole family there, laughing and cheering. William was there too, beaming. So was Kate, Jordan, even Devon.

I was full-on crying as Conrad took my hand and put the ring on my finger. He got up and looked me in the eye.

"This is it," he said, "it's you and me." He laid a hand on my cheek and gave me a deep, passionate kiss.

THE END

ALSO BY ANNIE PAIGE

For more books by Annie Paige visit

https://readerlinks.com/mybooks/5445

Or scan the QR code below: